CARMEL CLAY

S0-BBS-382

ANOTHER PART
OF THE CITY

Also available in Large Print
by Ed McBain:

Give the Boys a Great Big Hand
Killer's Payoff
Poison
Cop Hater

ANOTHER PART OF THE CITY

Ed McBain

G.K. HALL & CO.
Boston, Massachusetts
1989

Copyright © 1986 by Hui Corporation.

All rights reserved.

Published in Large Print by arrangement with
Warner/Mysterious Press
666 Fifth Avenue, New York, New York 10103.

G.K. Hall Large Print Book Series.

Set in 18 pt Plantin.

Library of Congress Cataloging in Publication Data

McBain, Ed, 1926–
   Another part of the city.

   (G.K. Hall large print book series)
   1. Large type books.   I. Title.
[PS3515.U585A84   1989]   813'.54   88-34818
ISBN 0-8161-4520-2 (lg. print)

This is for ALAN LANDSBURG

GOING to be a cold one tonight, Sadie thought.

She didn't know what the exact date was, never kept track of such things no more, but she knew it was December, and she knew it had to be getting close to Christmastime because of all the holiday trimmings in the store windows and all up and down the street.

They put up trimmings in the fall, too, down here, same kind of trimmings, hanging colored lights on metal arches that crossed over the streets from building to building. That was when they were celebrating some kind of Italian feast, they did that in October down here. Had to move out of her doorway when they celebrated that feast down here, whatever it was, 'cause there were stands all up and down the street selling food and running games of chance, like wheels of fortune and such, and there were people from all over the city down here. It wasn't *her* feast, so she didn't much care about it except that she couldn't use her regular doorway when all the stands were up and all the streets were crowded with people.

The decorations were the same when it got to be Christmastime, except for the lamp-posts twined with ropes of spruce or something, and the wreaths hanging everywhere, still it was almost the same, one feast was pretty much like another. Christmas wasn't her feast, neither, not no more it wasn't. Christmas was you bought things for people and people bought things for you. Sadie didn't have nobody to buy for no more, and nobody to buy her nothing.

The doorway she used all the time, winter and summer except when there was a feast down here, was a doorway used to be the front door of an olive oil company, but the man went out of business, oh, this must've been two, three years ago, and nobody took over the store, and now it was all boarded up, and nobody used it but her. She came back to the doorway every night along about this time, finished with her rounds by then, had her shopping bags full of scraps to eat and things to pick over, see if they was worth anything. Used to take the subway uptown before the fares went up so high, but now she mostly made her rounds along Canal Street before it got to be Chinatown; the Chinks never threw out *nothing*, cheap bastards. And sometimes she wandered over to Centre Street where all the big buildings were with the courthouses in them and all. You could sometimes find some good things in the garbage cans down there, lawyers threw away a lot of good stuff.

She was glad she'd picked up a lot of newspapers today, because tonight was going to be a real cold one, she could tell, and newspapers were good for wrapping around you, better than blankets, in fact, especially the *New York Times*. She never *read* the newspapers, didn't give a damn about what was happening here in New York or anyplace else for that matter, just picked up the papers to wrap around her later if it got cold, like it was going to be tonight.

She made her nest with care, laying down the corrugated cardboard first, and then spreading the scraps of rags over that, and then putting her newspapers aside in a neat pile for when she'd use them later to wrap herself in. She put the heaviest of the shopping bags down on the pile of newspapers, case a wind blew up or something, she didn't want to lose what she was going to wrap herself in, have the papers blowing all over the street. She dug into the other shopping bag for something to eat, and then made herself comfortable in the doorway, knees pulled up against her chest, long cotton skirt and black coat tucked between her legs, going to be a cold one tonight, she thought, and shivered in anticipation. Her gray woolen gloves were cut off at the fingers. In her right hand, she held a stale crust of bread she had found in a garbage can on Lafayette Street. Nibbling toothlessly at the bread, she sat huddled in her doorway, peering out at the street, at the lights, at the decorations for a holiday she never celebrated anymore.

Sure hope it don't snow, she thought.

Snow was dangerous.

Made you feel warm, but actually you could *freeze* to death you got covered with snow in your sleep.

She kept nibbling at the hard crust of bread.

The automobile came cruising slowly up the street, big brown car, nosing into the curb some dozen feet from where Sadie sat with her back against the boarded door to the old olive oil company. She watched the car. Mercedes, she thought. Years ago in Vegas, when she was young and beautiful,

4

she had ridden in a Mercedes convertible, her long blonde hair blowing in the desert wind. This one wasn't no convertible. Big sedan, it was, brown and sleek, the three-pointed star sticking up on the hood, nice car, Mercedes, blonde hair blowing in the wind, Paul's hand under her skirt.

Two men got out of the car, one on each side of it.

A third man sat behind the wheel, his face obscured in shadow.

The car doors slammed, one on each side of it.

The two men who'd got out of the car were wearing ski masks over their faces.

They know it's gonna be cold tonight, Sadie thought.

Nibbling at her bread, she watched them.

The two men walked diagonally across the street to the Italian restaurant there. One of them kept checking the street over his shoulder, his head moving back and forth. At the door to the restaurant, both men reached inside their coats.

Sadie saw guns.

The mandolin is too loud, he's playing too loud, Ralph thought. He always plays too loud when they're here. Trying to im-

5

press them, maybe they'll invite him to one of their big gangster weddings, ask him to play for them. I wish they wouldn't come in here, he thought. I don't need them in here.

At seven P.M. the restaurant was full and Ralph was worried that the loud mandolin playing might upset some of his customers. But everyone seemed oblivious to the steady plinking coming from the corner of the room where Ralph's son had set up a small Christmas tree on a table covered with a white cloth. Ralph shrugged; maybe everybody here tonight was deaf. Everybody but the *mafiosi*, who sat at a table in the corner of the room, facing the entrance door, backs to the wall, they always sat where they could see the front door. One of the two goons with Fortunato was snapping his fingers in time to the mandolin music. The mandolin player gave him a smile of acknowledgment. Near the door to the kitchen, one of Ralph's waiters was nodding his head in time to the music, his attention on the mandolin player instead of on the customer who was trying to catch his eye. Ralph went to him at once. In Italian, he said, "See what they want at table three."

He walked briskly through the restaurant then, stopping at one table or another, asking in English whether everything was all right, beaming as he approached the bar just inside the entrance door, where his son was busy mixing drinks, and his wife sat at the cash register, tallying a check. He was about to ask her if she didn't think the mandolin was too loud, when the front door opened.

Two men holding guns were standing in the doorframe.

Mandolin music spilled out into the street.

Both of the men had ski masks pulled over their faces. One of them closed the door behind him.

At the cash register, Ralph's wife whispered, *"Madonna mia!"*

The entryway was small and tight and cramped. Overcoats hung on a rack to the left of the doorway, where the two men stood with the guns in their hands.

The one standing closest to the bar said, "Be quiet, no one gets hurt."

He spoke with an accent. Ralph couldn't place the accent. Spanish? No, it didn't sound . . .

"No!" the second man said.

He had whirled toward Ralph's son, who was reaching under the bar. Ralph knew there was a gun under the bar.

"Hands up!" the man said, and then, louder, "Hands *up!*"

His voice registered. Until now, the customers in the dining room were unaware of what was happening near the front door. But the gunman's voice cut through the steady hum of polite conversation, the click of silverware against plates, the tinkle of ice in cocktail glasses. Everything stopped. Even the mandolin stopped.

The first man moved toward the dining room, his gun extended.

"Everybody stay where you are," he said. "No noise."

The same peculiar accent again. Not Spanish, but something else, something Ralph still couldn't identify. The second man turned from the bar, where Ralph's son now stood with his hands over his head, backed up against the mirror and the whiskey bottles.

There was a moment of hesitation, of seeming uncertainty.

At the rear of the restaurant, the three men who sat at a corner table with their backs to the wall watched silently. One of the men reached into his jacket. The man sitting on his right gently placed his hand on

8

his arm and shook his head almost impercep-
tibly.

In the small archway that led from the
dining room to the front entry, one of the
gunmen still stood with the pistol in his hand.
The other gunman looked from Ralph to
his son. "You," he said. "Who are you?
Your name?"

"Mark. Mark D'Annunzio."

The man turned to where Ralph stood
with his hands over his head.

"And you?" he said.

"Ralph D'Annunzio."

"Go there," he said, gesturing with the
gun.

Ralph turned toward the bar.

The gunman standing in the arch turned
at precisely the same moment.

Sadie winced when she heard the shots.

Four of them.

Four quick explosions shattering the brit-
tle night.

She blinked and looked across the street at
the restaurant.

The front door flew open, and the two
men wearing the ski masks came running
out onto the sidewalk and then across the
street to where the Mercedes was parked,

its engine idling. From inside the restaurant, Sadie heard someone scream. The car doors slammed. There were loud voices from inside the restaurant now. The Mercedes pulled away from the curb, tires squealing. People were running out of the restaurant now, shouting.

Sadie picked up both her shopping bags. She left her stacked newspapers, and her rags, and her corrugated cardboard bed where they were.

She did not even glance at the restaurant across the street as she moved swiftly out of her doorway.

The moment she turned the corner, she began running.

In Chinatown, not two blocks from the restaurant, Santa Claus was coming out of a souvenir shop on Mott Street. The front window of the shop displayed fans and sculpted figurines and little brass ornaments and beads and abacuses and a large poster of a Chinese girl standing beside a willow tree. Santa Claus's sack was brimming. He carried the sack over his shoulder, and he carried a bell in his left hand, and the moment he came out of the shop, he began shaking the bell and singing. The street outside was ablaze with neon and thronged with tourists and shoppers on this Monday night, ten days before Christmas. Santa Claus was fat and jolly-looking, dressed in the traditional red suit and hat, the black belt and boots, the white mustache and beard. Santa Claus was singing merrily.

"Jingle bells," he sang, "jingle bells, jingle all the way. Oh what fun it is to ride . . ."

"Hold it right there, Santa."

The voice came from behind and slightly to the left of Santa. He turned at once to see a man holding a pistol in his right hand. The man was perhaps thirty-seven, thirty-eight years old, and he was wearing dark corduroy slacks and a black leather jacket and a seaman's woolen watch cap. The man had red hair and blue eyes, and he was holding a police detective's shield in his left hand. Santa turned to run, and came smack up against an other man holding a gun.

"What's your hurry, Santa?" the other man said.

He was maybe fifty years old, wearing blue jeans, a blue plaid mackinaw and a peaked baseball cap. His hair was gray, and his eyes were the darkest brown Santa had ever seen. Santa stood between the two

11

men, wondering which of them would be more reasonable.

"Hey . . . uh . . . what is it?" he asked. "What's the beef?"

"Your reindeer's overparked," the man with the gray hair said. "Let's see what you got in the sack."

"The sack?" Santa said, as if discovering it in his hand for the first time. He grinned a sickly grin. "What's with you guys?" he said. "I'm with the Salvation Army."

"Put the sack down, Santa," the one with the red hair said. Santa put the sack on the sidewalk.

"Now open it for us," the redhead said pleasantly.

Santa opened the sack. The redhead holstered his gun, and put the leather fob containing his shield back into his pocket. He took his time doing this. The gray-haired one watched him as if this was something of enormous interest. Then the redheaded one reached into the sack. The first thing he pulled out of the sack was a radio.

"Well, hello," he said.

Santa smiled.

The redhead reached into the sack again and pulled out a toaster.

"Nice," the one with the gray hair said.

A crowd was gathering on the sidewalk.

The redhead reached into the sack again and pulled out a pair of Chinese fans, and a camera, and a woman's sequined cocktail jacket, and a wristwatch, and a fountain pen, and a silver tray and a silver sugar bowl and a silver creamer.

"Little early to be flying over the rooftops, ain't it, Santa?" the gray-haired one said. "This is still only the fifteenth."

"Hey, come on," Santa said, "what's *with* you guys? I was doing my Christmas shopping."

"You hear that, Bry?" the gray-haired one said. "He was doing his Christmas shopping."

"I heard it, Chick," the redhead said, and reached for the handcuffs at his belt. "Mister," he said, "you were shopping for a Class-E felony."

"They're busting *Santa* Claus!" an eight-year-old kid said.

A radio voice said, "Five P.D., auto Four-Oh-Three," and Santa turned to where an unmarked car was parked at the curb, the door open.

"Hands," the redhead said, and Santa automatically put his hands behind his back.

13

"Five P.D., auto Four-Oh-Three," the radio voice said again.

"I'll get it," the gray-haired one said, and walked toward the car.

"You guys are making a terrible mistake," Santa said.

The redhead was already leading him toward the car. The gray-haired one was picking up the walkie-talkie on the front seat.

"Four-Oh-Three," he said.

"Hoffman," the radio voice said, "you've got a Ten-Twenty on Mulberry and Hester, the Luna Mare restaurant. Gunshot victim. D.O.A."

"A *terrible* mistake," Santa said again.

The auction at Sotheby's on Seventy-second Street and York Avenue was scheduled to start at seven-fifteen P.M. The movable walls of the main salesroom on the second floor had been rolled back to accommodate what was expected to be a larger than usual crowd, but even so there were hundreds of people standing in what normally served as a sort of reception area. A television crew had finally set up its equipment at the top of the stairs leading from the main entrance below, and Julio Garcia—the station's roving reporter—was waiting impatiently to do an interview with a man who, at the moment, was surrounded by newspaper reporters. Garcia thought of himself as an investigative journalist, and he was miffed first that he was covering an *art* auction, and second that the newspaper reporters had managed to collar Robert Sargent Kidd before he had. There wasn't any pressing deadline or anything, that wasn't the point, this wasn't a hot newsbreak, and the interview would be taped. It was just that he considered television newsmen superior in every way to newspaper reporters, and it irked him that they were maybe getting stuff from Kidd that would later sound rehearsed instead of spontaneous and on-the-spot.

He looked over to the knot of reporters around Kidd, and noticed that his a.d. had finally managed to grab hold of Kidd's elbow, and was gently urging him toward the steps where the camera crew was waiting. Kidd was perhaps six feet two inches tall, Garcia guessed, weighing in at about two and a quarter, a huge, burly man in his early thirties, wearing Western gear and a white Stetson hat. The a.d. was practically shoving reporters aside now as he led Kidd toward Garcia.

"Roll it," Garcia said to his cameraman,

and began his lead-in. As the a.d. brought Kidd within camera range, Garcia was saying, ". . . perhaps the finest and most extensive collection of Impressionist art in the world. The owner, Robert Sargent Kidd, is here with us at Sotheby's . . ."

He nodded to his cameraman who panned slightly to where Kidd was standing and waiting. Garcia joined the shot.

"Mr. Kidd," he said, "can you tell us why you've decided to sell your collection at this time?"

Kidd grinned into the camera. In a drawl that sounded more Southern than it did Western, he said, "Oh, just tired of it, I guess." The word tired came out as "tahd."

"I've been told it's worth something like twenty million dollars," Garcia said. "What do you plan . . . ?"

"Well, I couldn't say just *what* it's worth, actually," Kidd said. "That's for the bidders to determine, isn't it?"

"What do you plan to do with all that money?" Garcia asked.

Kidd grinned. "Spend it, I reckon," he said.

Garcia smiled and—mindful that his television audience liked a little joke now and then—said, "Well, Mr. Kidd, try not to spend it all in one place." He looked directly at the camera and said, "This is Julio Garcia at Sotheby's . . ." and suddenly broke off mid-sentence, his eyes flashing off-camera. "Miss Kidd?" he called. "Excuse me, Miss Kidd!"

He almost moved out of frame, but the cameraman was swift and sure and he managed to follow him as he moved through the crowd to where a tall blonde woman was just leaving the lobby to enter the main room. The woman was wearing a mink coat over a dark blue Chanel suit. The blouse under the suit was a paler blue, with a stock tie. Her long blonde hair was swept back from an exquisitely beautiful face, her revealed sapphire earrings echoing the blue of the blouse and the deeper blue of her eyes. She was, Garcia knew from all he'd read about her, somewhere in her late thirties—thirty-six, maybe thirty-seven—but she looked a great deal younger, her complexion flawless, her face free of any makeup but lipstick and eye shadow. She turned as he approached.

"Miss Kidd, excuse me," he said, "Julio Garcia, Channel Five News. Could I have a moment of your time, please?"

Olivia Kidd arched one eyebrow and

looked down her nose, as though something unspeakably vile had crawled up onto the lapel of her mink coat.

"Miss Kidd," Garcia said, unfazed, "how do *you* feel about your brother selling all these valuable paintings?"

Outside the Luna Mare restaurant, two Fifth Precinct radio motor patrol cars were angled into the curb alongside an ambulance from Beekman Hospital and a police Mobile Lab van. The cardboard CRIME SCENE signs were already up on the striped barricades as Reardon and Hoffman pulled up in their unmarked, black Plymouth sedan. Hoffman had wanted to take Santa Claus along with them, give him a taste of something bigger than shoplifting. Reardon had turned the collar over to one of the blues on Mott Street. They were both pinning on their shields as they approached the patrolman outside the door of the restaurant, Reardon to the ribbed bottom of his black leather jacket, Hoffman to the flap pocket on his mackinaw. Reardon had taken off the blue watch cap and left it on the front seat of the car. A sharp wind was tossing his red hair. Hoffman was still wearing the peaked baseball cap.

"Medical Examiner here yet?" Reardon asked the patrolman.

"A few minutes ago," the patrolman said, nodding. He was thinking it was going to be a long, cold, fucking night standing outside the door here, and he hadn't put on his long johns.

"Who's the victim, do you know?" Hoffman asked.

"Owner of the place, guy named Ralph D'Annunzio. His wife and son are inside there. The son's name is Mark, I didn't catch the lady's."

Reardon nodded and shoved open the door.

The body was lying in a pool of blood near the bar. The body seemed incongruous. Minus the body, the restaurant would have looked and felt cozy and warm. A gray homburg and a pair of gray suede gloves were on the bartop. A man wearing a gray overcoat was crouched over the body. He looked up when Reardon and Hoffman came in.

"Reardon, Fifth P.D.U.," Reardon said.

"Dr. Norris," the man said, and went back to the body. A lab technician and a man with a Polaroid camera were waiting for Norris to get through with the body.

19

They were talking about girls. Reardon looked into the dining room. Christmas decorations all over the place, Christmas tree in one corner of the dining room on a table with a white tablecloth. A couple of uniformed cops were standing around looking bewildered, the way they always did at a homicide. A woman in her early fifties was sitting at one of the tables, weeping. A young man stood beside her, trying to comfort her, a stunned look on his face. Reardon figured this was the wife and the son. He nodded to Hoffman, who nodded back, and both men stepped around the body and went into the dining room.

"Mrs. D'Annunzio?" Reardon said.

She looked up at him, her face streaked with tears.

"I'm Detective Reardon, Fifth P.D.U., this is my partner, Detective Hoffman."

She nodded and then dabbed at her eyes with a lace-edged handkerchief.

"I'm sorry we have to ask you questions at a time like this," Reardon said, "but if you can tell us what happened . . ."

Mrs. D'Annunzio burst into tears. Her son—they assumed he was the son—patted her hand and murmured sounds of comfort, no words, only sounds. He, too, seemed as if he would burst into tears at any moment.

"Are you Mark D'Annunzio?" Reardon asked.

D'Annunzio nodded. He was in his late twenties, Reardon guessed, a tall, dark man with curly black hair and dark brown eyes. Thin, with a longish nose. Reardon was willing to bet he'd taken a lot of ribbing about that nose.

"Mr. D'Annunzio," he said, "can you tell us what happened?"

"They came in here with guns," D'Annunzio said.

"How many of them?" Hoffman asked.

"Two."

"When was this?"

"Half an hour ago."

"What'd they look like? White, black . . . ?"

"They were wearing ski masks."

"How about their hands?" Hoffman asked.

"Hands?"

"Were they white or black?"

"I didn't notice," D'Annunzio said. "Everything happened all at once. One minute everything was normal, and the next it . . . it . . ."

"Did they say anything?" Reardon asked.

21

"They said to be quiet and no one would get hurt. They asked me what my . . . no, wait. First they told us to put our hands up, and then they asked me what my name . . ."

"Excuse me," a voice behind Reardon said.

He turned. Norris, the Medical Examiner, was standing there with the gray suede gloves clutched in his right hand, and a small black satchel in his left.

"Talk to you a minute?" he said.

Reardon followed him through the arch and into the entryway. The photographer was already snapping his Polaroid pictures. The lab technician was looking at the corpse's hands.

"We're backed up at the morgue just now," Norris said. "All the bedbugs coming out of the woodwork for Christmas. You may not get your autopsy report for a few days. Meanwhile, the cause of death is obvious. You can put it down as gunshot wounds."

"Right, thanks," Reardon said.

Norris nodded, seemed about to say something else, and then simply drew on his gloves and went out. A sharp wind blew into the room before he closed the door behind him. Reardon walked back into the dining room again. Mrs. D'Annunzio was sobbing into her handkerchief. Mark D'Annunzio still had the stunned look on his face.

"What was that all about?" Hoffman asked.

"The autopsy report," Reardon said. "It may take a little longer than . . ."

"What do you mean *autopsy?*" D'Annunzio said. "Who said you could . . . ?"

"I'm sorry, Mr. D'Annunzio," Reardon said, "but it's mandatory in any trauma death."

"I don't want them cutting up my father," D'Annunzio said. He looked first at Reardon and then at Hoffman. "Who do I talk to about this?"

"I know how you feel," Reardon said, "but . . ."

"You *know* what killed him, why do you have to cut him up?"

"I'm sorry," Reardon said.

Their eyes met. D'Annunzio was holding back tears. Reardon put his hand on D'Annunzio's shoulder, gently, briefly. "I'm sorry," he said again. "Believe me."

D'Annunzio nodded, and then turned away to hide his tears. There was a brief, awkward silence. Hoffman cleared his throat.

"Mr. D'Annunzio," he said, "can you tell us what these men *sounded* like?"

"Sounded?"

"Yes. Were they speaking English?"

"Yes, they were. Yes," D'Annunzio said.

"Any regional accent or dialect?"

"Yes, but . . . I'm not sure what it was."

"Was it Hispanic?"

"No, I don't think so. No, it wasn't a Spanish accent."

"How about Chinese?"

"I . . . I don't know. It all happened so fast."

"*Could* it have been Chinese?"

"Maybe. No. I don't think so. I really don't know. You see, they . . ."

"What are you *doing?*" Mrs. D'Annunzio shrieked.

Her eyes were wide, fastened on the archway behind Reardon. He turned at once. The lab technician was still crouched over the body. In one hand he held a spoon-shaped piece of wood. In the other, he held an ink roller.

"Leave him *alone!*" Mrs. D'Annunzio shouted, and came out of her chair at once, rushing past Reardon and into the entryway. "Get away from him!" she screamed, grab-

24

CARMEL CLAY PUBLIC LIBRARY

bing for the technician's shoulder, almost knocking him off balance.

The technician, still crouching, flailed his arms to keep from toppling over backwards. Reardon was coming into the bar area now, immediately behind Mrs. D'Annunzio. The technician turned to him as the officer in charge.

"I'm only . . ." he started to say.

"Let it go," Reardon said.

"I *gotta* take his prints," the technician said. "This is a homicide."

"But let it go," Reardon said gently.

The technician shrugged. "Okay, pal," he said, "*you* explain it later, okay?"

"I'll explain it," Reardon said.

Mrs. D'Annunzio burst into tears again, and turned away from her husband's corpse. Reardon awkwardly put his arm around her. Hoffman was standing in the archway to the dining room now. Reardon glanced at him. Hoffman nodded.

"*Signora,*" Reardon said, "we'll come back another time, okay? Why don't you go home now? Mr. D'Annunzio, could you take your mother home, please? We'll talk to you later, all right?"

D'Annunzio stared at him, as if wonder-

25

ing whether he could trust his father's body alone with him.

"All right?" Reardon said.

D'Annunzio nodded.

HOMICIDES were rare in the Fifth Precinct.

By Reardon's count, there had been only eighteen of them this year, and the average was about twenty annually. That suited him just fine. He liked working down here; transfer him to an A-House like the Four-One in the Bronx or the Ninth right next door in Manhattan South, and he might have quit the force altogether. The Fifth was definitely not a high-crime area. This past year, there'd been something over a hundred burglaries, some eighty-five robberies, and forty-six arrests for grand larceny. In fact, the Chinese youth gangs here—involved as they were with extortion and felonious assault—constituted the most serious criminal threat. Fancy names, the gangs all had—Ghost Shadows, and Flying Dragons, Eagles, and Ching Yee. All punks in Reardon's estimation. But the activities of the gangs were limited to Chinatown, and that was only a small corner of the entire precinct territory.

Most people in the department referred to the detective unit at the Fifth as the "Chinatown Squad." Well, that was to be expected; the station house was smack in the center of Chinatown, on Elizabeth and Canal, sandwiched between a Chinese restaurant named Y.S. and a dime store. But the precinct territory was bordered on the east by Allen Street, on the west by Broadway, on the south by the East River and on the north by Houston Street, and the ethnic boil here was a volatile one. From Pearl to Canal, you had your Chinese. Bowery to Allen was largely Hispanic and black. From Spring to Houston, the streets were filled with Dominicans, Cubans, and Puerto Ricans. The Bowery was populated with vagrants of every stripe and color. And in Little Italy, which ran from Canal to Houston, an Italian restaurant owner had been shot dead at seven-thirty tonight—in a precinct where murders were rare.

Still, it was the "Chinatown Squad" and all the detectives at the Fifth carried a blue card printed in both English and Chinese. Reardon's card was a duplicate of the one Chick Hoffman carried:

第五分局偵探部
5TH PRECINCT DETECTIVES
依利沙伯街十九號
19 ELIZABETH STREET
偵探 DETECTIVE................................
（負責處理閣下之案）
(HAS YOUR CASE)
案件號碼 CASE No. ....
電話「三三四—〇七四二」 PHONE 334-0742

It was almost ten o'clock when they got back to the station house. They had started the evening tour at four that afternoon, expecting the usual run of occurrences great and small, but nothing so great as a homicide. There had been eighteen already this year, hadn't there? Well, now there were nineteen. As they mounted the low flat steps leading to the front door of the precinct, both men were thinking they didn't need this.

The black wooden numerals 1881—for the date the station house was completed and occupied—were set into the arched pediment over the entrance door. The Fifth had celebrated its centennial five years ago, the detectives opening a bottle of champagne (against departmental regulations, but what the hell) in the rec room on the third floor of the ancient building. Lieutenant Farmer hadn't known about the midnight celebration; they tried to keep as much as they possibly could from Lieutenant Farmer. Beneath the arched pediment was a wooden panel with the words "5th Precinct" on it. Beneath that, another date: 1921. Reardon guessed that was the last time the precinct had been painted. Over the door itself was a brown sign lettered in yellow with the words:

BE ONE OF THE GOOD GUYS
JOIN THE 5TH PCT.
AUXILIARY POLICE

The door was set with a glass panel, odd for a police station, but no one down here expected anybody to try forcible entry. A sign in the lower half of the glass panel read ALL PERSONS MUST STOP AT DESK. The same words were repeated below this in Chinese. And below that in Spanish.

Reardon shoved open the door.

The muster room was cold. The Fifth still had a coal-burning furnace in the basement, maybe the only precinct in the entire city that was so blessed. It was impossible to keep the place warm in the wintertime. In the summertime, because there was no air-conditioning, it was impossible to keep it cool. Reardon guessed he preferred winters here at the Fifth. At least you could put on more clothes. In the summer, no matter how far down you stripped, you couldn't slip out of your skin.

Sergeant McLaughlin sat behind the high muster desk on the right of the room, the telephone to his ear, a huge American flag on the wall behind him. McLaughlin was in his shirtsleeves. He weighed two hundred and fifty pounds, and he was probably the only man in the precinct who constantly complained that it was too hot in here. "Just a second, Mike," he said into the phone, and then, to Reardon and Hoffman, who were crossing the room toward the steps at the far end, "Your Santa Claus is kicking up a storm back there."

"Back there" was what the cops called the 124 Room, which housed the precinct clerk, the computer, and the now virtually defunct Arrest Process room with its small detention cage and its fingerprinting table. Nowadays, most arrests were brought to Central Booking at Headquarters, not six blocks from the precinct itself. But where property was involved, as in robbery, burglary, or narcotics arrests, the perps were taken first to the precinct itself—where they were printed and where all the paperwork was done—before they were taken to Headquarters for formal booking. There were no holding cells at the Fifth. The only detention cage was in the 124 Room. Santa Claus was in that cage now, screaming his head off about his rights.

"Send him to the North Pole," Hoffman said.

"When you gonna book him?" McLaughlin asked.

"Later," Reardon said. "We've got a homicide."

Inside the 124 Room, the clerk was sitting at the computer, performing whatever ritual was necessary to make the damn thing work. Santa Claus kept yelling and ranting, but the clerk never looked up from the keyboard. The computer's true and honorable designation was FATN—Reardon didn't know what the letters stood for. All the cops at the Fifth called it Fat Nellie. It was used to check warrants, car registrations, and so on, and it stored information from every precinct in the city. Only three men at the Fifth knew how to use it. In the detention cage, Santa Claus said, "I want a fucking lawyer!"

On the phone in the muster room, Mc-Laughlin said, "So how's it going up there, Mike?"

Hoffman and Reardon started up the steps to the second floor.

Behind them, Santa Claus was still yelling.

Their footfalls echoed on the iron-runged staircase.

The second-floor corridor opened almost immediately onto a half-wall behind which was a small room with metal filing cabinets, desks, and chairs. An American flag hung on the far wall, smaller than the one over the muster desk downstairs. A wooden cabinet with glass-paneled doors was against the wall under the flag. The inside of the cabinet was stacked with books. Its top was decorated with departmental trophies from when the room was used as part of the clerical office. The room, at ten o'clock on a cold night in December, was empty. A handsomely painted sign set high on the half-wall read—first in Chinese and then in English:

CHINATOWN PROJECT

The Chinatown Project had been started initially to assist Chinese-speaking citizens with criminal complaints. Civilians speaking

33

Chinese were now available at the precinct on a twenty-four-hour basis, but nowadays they seemed to be helping the residents of Chinatown with *all* their problems, including photocopying. A hand-lettered sign taped to the lower part of the half-wall read:

XEROX COPIES
MON TO FRI

Reardon and Hoffman turned to the right. They had both been turning to the right for a good many years now.

To the right was a doorway over which hung a sign reading:

DETECTIVES

An arrow was under the sign. It pointed to the left.

A smaller sign was beneath the arrow:

5TH PCT.
INVESTIGATING UNIT

There was another arrow on this sign, and it too pointed to the left.

The detectives walked through the doorway and turned to the left.

This was home to them for a goodly part of each day. Up the staircase, turn to the right, walk through the doorway, turn to the left and into the small office that housed the Precinct Investigating Unit, a title now nonoperative. One of these days, Reardon thought, somebody is going to change the signs around here. Meanwhile, the 5th Precinct Investigating Unit was now known as the 5th P.D.U., which stood for 5th Precinct Detective Unit, but anybody who answered the telephone said, "Fifth Squad," as a hangover habit from the old days. The NYPD changed its titles, and its rules and regulations, and its procedures as often as it changed its underwear. The only thing that never changed was the look of a squadroom. Detective squadrooms looked the same in every precinct in the city, no matter *what* they were called. Flaked and peeling apple green paint. Grilles over all the windows. The windows themselves encrusted with the grime of—in the case of the Fifth —more than a century. Bulletin boards with wanted notices. Clipboards hanging from nails on the walls. Metal filing cabinets: DO NOT REMOVE ANY FILE WITHOUT PERMISSION. An electric wall clock with a dangling wire leading to a wall outlet. Naked hanging light

35

bulbs. No detention cage here in the Fifth's squadroom; that was downstairs. Three teams of detectives worked out of this room, day and night. Four men to a team, day and night. This room never rested. This room was home to Hoffman and Reardon and ten other detectives like them. There were fifteen men working out of the Detective Unit: a lieutenant, two goldshield sergeants, one Detective/1st Grade, one 2nd Grade, and ten 3rd Grades.

Detective Gianelli was on the phone when Hoffman and Reardon walked into the room. Detective Ruiz was at another desk, reading. Gianelli was forty years old, with curly black hair, a swarthy Mediterranean complexion, and a handlebar mustache. Ruiz was twenty-eight, light-skinned, as slender as a toreador. Neither of the men greeted Hoffman and Reardon.

"So what do you mean?" Gianelli said into the phone.

"Any calls for me?" Reardon asked Ruiz.

Ruiz did not look up from his book. "Who you expecting?" he asked. "The Commissioner?"

"I don't *want* to know about twists, lands, and grooves," Gianelli said into the phone. "I don't under*stand* twists, lands, and grooves."

"Impossible to get a straight answer from this guy," Reardon said to Hoffman. "Yes or no, Alex?"

"No, your Honor," Ruiz said.

"All I want to know is what kind of gun it was that fired the bullets," Gianelli said into the phone. "That's all I want to know." He listened. "So okay, tell me then," he said and picked up a pencil. "Yeah," he said, writing. "Yeah. Yeah. Yeah. Okay, thanks." He put the phone back onto its cradle. "These guys at Ballistics give me a song and dance everytime I call," he said to no one.

"Maybe they know you're a musician," Hoffman said.

"I send them some bullets, they start telling me about microscopes."

"Go blow your horn at them, Gabriel," Hoffman said.

"Who caught it out there?" Gianelli asked Reardon. "And don't call me Gabriel," he said to Hoffman.

"Guy named Ralph D'Annunzio," Reardon said. "Owns the Luna Mare."

"On Mulberry?" Ruiz asked, looking up from his book.

"Yeah."

"My name is Arthur," Gianelli said. "My *mother* calls me Arthur, my *father* calls me Arthur, the whole fuckin' *world* calls me Arthur. Only in this shithouse does anybody call me Gabriel."

"Sorry, Gabe," Hoffman said, and winked at Reardon.

"He just opened that a few weeks ago," Ruiz said. "Around Thanksgiving some- time."

"You know him?" Reardon asked.

"I ate there once," Ruiz said, and went back to his book. He was reading Cary and Eisenberg on corporations.

"Sixteen years playing trumpet for the NYPD band," Gianelli said, "nobody called me Gabriel. Only in this shithouse . . ."

"You shouldn't have been such a hero, Gabe," Hoffman said.

"I was stopping for gas!" Gianelli said.

"You shouldn't have stopped for gas, Gabe," Hoffman said.

"Who knew there was an armed robbery going down in there? Rotten thief smashed my lip and ruined my career."

"Ah, but you made the arrest," Hoffman said. "That's what counts."

"Who *needed* the arrest? Who *needed*

Detective/Third? I was happy playing trumpet. Now I'm here in this shithouse listening to a bunch of wise guys calling me Gabriel."

"Better here than the South Bronx," Ruiz said, looking up. "Who shot him?" he asked Reardon.

"Couple of guys wearing ski masks," Reardon said. "Is the lieutenant in?"

"On the phone with Headquarters," Ruiz said. "The Great White Feather does not like homicides in his precinct, Bry. You shouldn'ta caught a homicide tonight."

"Was that Santa Claus I saw downstairs?" Gianelli asked.

"That was Andy Bertuzzi," Hoffman said, "one of your *paisans*. Best shoplifter in the precinct."

"If he's the best, how come he got *caught?*" Gianelli said.

"If you want to read, go to the library," Hoffman said to Ruiz. "I need that typewriter."

"*I* need a law degree," Ruiz said, getting up.

"Next governor of the state here," Hoffman said.

"Four semesters to go," Ruiz said, and

took a chair across the room as Hoffman sat behind the typewriter.

"What's your game plan, Alex? Lawyer, then assistant D.A. . . . ."

"You said it yourself," Ruiz said. "First Puerto Rican governor of the state."

"Are you sure I didn't get a call?" Reardon asked.

"Positive," Ruiz said.

Hoffman began typing. "I'll do the paperwork," he said. "Why don't you go see her, Bry?"

"First I want to fill in the lieutenant," Reardon said.

"Ah, *finalmente*," Gianelli said, opening his arms wide to the doorway.

A ten-year-old Chinese kid stood in the doorframe, grinning into the room, his arms laden with brown paper bags. He was wearing blue jeans, sneakers, and what appeared to be at least three sweaters, one over the other, all in different colors.

"What took you so long, Tommy?" Gianelli asked.

"Busy night, Captain," Tommy said.

"Good, I'm starved," Hoffman said, and got up from behind the typewriter.

"Wait a minute, wait a minute," Gianelli said. "I didn't order for *you* guys."

"Did you bring chopsticks?" Hoffman asked.

"I forgot chopsticks," Tommy said.

"I didn't *order* chopsticks," Gianelli said. "You guys are supposed to be out on a fuckin' *murder*."

"We're back, Gabriel," Hoffman said. "Share and share alike."

"Listen, you guys . . ."

Ruiz was already digging into one of the bags. "Where's the fried rice?" he asked.

"Give the man his *arroz con pollo*," Hoffman said.

"Give the man his chopsticks," Ruiz said, "before he *steals* a pair."

"You know who this man is?" Gianelli said.

"Sure," Tommy said. "He's Detective Hoffman."

"Good kid, Tommy," Hoffman said, tousling his hair. "But next time, don't forget the chopsticks."

"He's Detective/First Grade . . ."

"*First* Grade, Tommy," Ruiz said.

". . . *Charles* Hoffman," Gianelli said, "who nine years ago broke the biggest armed robbery case this city ever had."

"Yeah, Mr. Hoffman?" Tommy said, wide-eyed.

"*Detective* Hoffman, please," Gianelli said.

"Detective First/*Grade* Hoffman," Ruiz said.

"Don't give the kid a bunch of bullshit," Hoffman said.

"Three hundred and fifty thousand dollars in that robbery," Gianelli said.

"Wow," Tommy said.

"Three hundred and fifty grand, kid," Ruiz said.

"In used bills," Gianelli said.

"*Used* bills," Ruiz said.

"And guess what, Tommy?" Gianelli said. "The money disappeared."

"Vanished," Ruiz said.

"Gone with the wind," Gianelli said. "The day Detective Hoffman quits the force, every cop in this city's gonna start following him."

"So they can find the stash, Tommy," Ruiz said.

Grinning, Reardon said, "Where'd you hide all those bills, Chick?"

"Yeah, yeah," Hoffman said. But he was not smiling.

"Richest man in New York here," Reardon said.

"Yeah, yeah," Hoffman said again.

"Pass the ribs," Gianelli said.

The door to the lieutenant's office opened.

Detective-Lieutenant Michael Thomas Farmer, fifty-five years old, iron-gray hair receding at the forehead, shirtsleeves rolled up to his biceps, blue eyes flashing, a deep scowl on his leathery face, stood in the doorframe.

"Come on in, Reardon," he said, and saw the men eating. "What the hell is this, a restaurant?" he asked. "You want to eat, go upstairs to the rec room. You get out of here," he said to Tommy. "Go play mahjongg." He turned abruptly and limped back into his office, slamming the door shut behind him.

"Great White Feather on warpath," Ruiz whispered.

"Put the wagons in a circle, Bry," Gianelli said, and took out his wallet. "What do we owe you?" he asked Tommy. Reardon already had his hand on the knob to the lieutenant's office. "I'll let you know what yours comes to," he said as Reardon opened the door.

A large map of the precinct dominated one wall of the lieutenant's office:

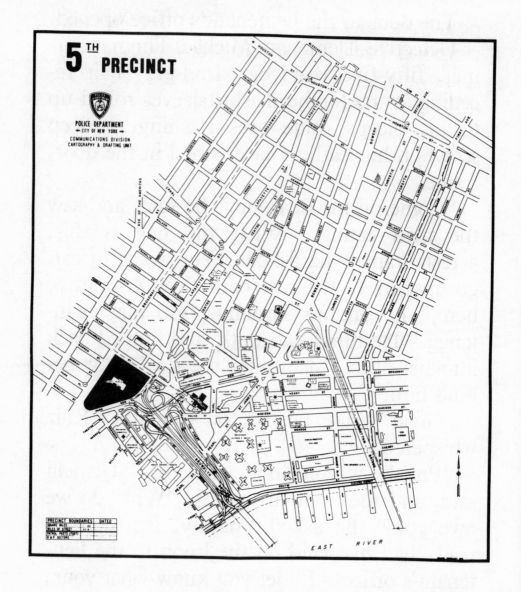

5ᵀᴴ PRECINCT

POLICE DEPARTMENT
CITY OF NEW YORK
COMMUNICATIONS DIVISION
CARTOGRAPHY & DRAFTING UNIT

The room itself was a virtual cubicle, a grilled window to the left of the single cluttered desk, clipboards hanging on the wall behind the desk, a yellowing refrigerator against the wall opposite the door. Farmer was at the refrigerator when Reardon came in. He took a container of milk from it,

44

poured a glass full to the brim, put the container back into the refrigerator, and carried the glass of milk back to his desk. He did not ask Reardon to sit. He shoved some papers aside, making room for the glass, and then said, without preamble, "I just got a call from Captain Healy at the lab. Seems a Detective Bryan Reardon of this precinct stopped one of his techs from fingerprinting a homicide victim." He sipped at the milk, pulled a face. "I hate milk," he said. "That true, Reardon?"

"Yes, sir," Reardon said.

"Rules and regs call for the fingerprinting of any homicide or suicide victim," Farmer said.

"Yes, sir. But the man's wife and son were there. They were upset to begin with, so I thought . . ."

"I don't like getting calls from captains," Farmer said.

"The man was shot down in their presence, sir. The mother and the son."

"I don't like departmental rank telling me I'm not running my squad by the book."

"Yes, sir."

"I'm going to tell you something, Reardon."

"Yes, sir."

45

"And I want you to listen."

"Yes, sir."

"Would you like to know why I limp? Would you like to know how I got this game leg?"

"I think I know how you got the limp, sir."

"I'll tell you how I got this limp," Farmer said, as if he hadn't heard Reardon. "Some dumb jerk didn't go by the book, that's how I got this limp."

"Yes, sir."

"He was supposed to post the color of the day, the color was *blue*, Reardon."

"Yes, sir."

"I was supposed to put a *blue* feather in my hatband so some dumb patrolman wouldn't mistake me for a cheap thief. And this clerk who *didn't* go by the book, he posted the color as *white*. So I put a *white* feather in my hatband, and some dumb patrolman *did* shoot me, and that's how I got this limp."

"Yes, sir."

"Do you understand that, Reardon?"

"Yes, sir."

"Have you heard that story before?"

"Yes, sir, that's how I understood you got the limp."

"*And* the desk job. *Because* of the limp."

"Yes, sir."

"You think I *want* a desk job?"

"No, sir."

"You think I *want* an ulcer? You think I *want* to drink milk, which I hate?"

"No, sir."

"If the regs call for a homicide victim to be printed, then by Christ the victim *will* be printed or you'll be walking a fuckin' beat on Staten Island! Do you think you've got that, Reardon?"

"Yes, sir, I've got it."

"Get that body fingerprinted. And let me see your report as soon as it's typed."

"Chick's working on it now, sir."

"Tell him," Farmer said. "I don't like unsolved murders in my precinct."

"No, sir, none of us do."

"Tell him," Farmer said in dismissal.

"Yes, sir," Reardon said, and went to the door.

Hoffman looked up as he came out into the squadroom.

"He wants the body printed," Reardon said. "Can you get the morgue on it right away?"

"I'll take care of it," Hoffman said. "Go on, get out of here."

"What about Santa?"

"I'll take care of him, too."

"You owe me two and a half bucks," Gianelli said.

Reardon took out his wallet.

"You sure you can handle this alone?" he said.

"*Go* already," Hoffman said.

The locker rooms were on the third floor of the station house. A toilet for policemen and another toilet for policewomen were on that same floor. Reardon washed his hands and face at the sink in the men's toilet, and then headed for the locker room to change out of his working clothes and into his street clothes. The locker rooms were behind a combined recreation room/training room with a pool table, a ping-pong table, a weight-lifting rack, and a large TV set—ostensibly there for the showing of departmental films, but tuned now to one of the local channels. A uniformed cop was shooting solitary pool as Reardon crossed the room.

On the television screen, the anchorman was saying, ". . . taped earlier tonight at the Sotheby gallery. Julio?"

Another man came onto the screen.

"We're here on York Avenue," he said, "where they are about to auction perhaps the finest and most extensive collection of Impressionist art in the world. The owner, Robert Sargent Kidd, is here with us at Sotheby's . . ." The camera panned to where a man in Western gear and a white Stetson hat was standing. The interviewer joined him as a title flashed across the bottom of the screen.

ROBERT SARGENT KIDD

"Mr. Kidd," the interviewer said, "can you tell us why you've decided to sell your collection at this time?"

"Oh, just tired of it, I guess," Kidd said, grinning.

"Eight ball in the side pocket," the cop at the pool table said to himself. He fired at the cue ball, said, "Very good, Tony. Ten ball in the corner," and shot again. "Excellent, Tony," he said, "we're putting you in for a commendation." Looking up, he said, "Watch this one, Bry. Six ball in the corner, off the three." He shot and missed. "Shit," he said.

A beautiful blonde woman was on the television screen now.

"Miss Kidd," the interviewer said, "how

do *you* feel about your brother selling all these valuable paintings?"

Another title appeared on the bottom of the screen:

MISS OLIVIA KIDD

The camera was close on the blonde's face now.

"My brother's paintings are my brother's business," she said. "It's his collection, he can do with it as he wishes."

"Turn that off, willya, Bry?" the cop said. "It's ruinin' my game."

Reardon moved to the television set.

"When do you expect you'll be going back to Phoenix, Miss Kidd?" the interviewer asked.

"I have no idea," the blonde said, and Reardon turned off the set.

Reardon knew this hospital well.

St. Vincent's. Seventh Avenue and Eleventh Street. Right in the heart of the Sixth Precinct, which ran north-south from West Fourteenth to Houston, and east-west from Broadway to the Hudson—sort of adjoining the Fifth at its northwest corner. Waited out here for her more times than he could count.

50

Cold winter nights like this one, where even the traffic seemed frozen in a stop-time crawl, sweltering summer nights with the fire hydrants open up the street and the kids romping in swimsuits under the spray. Autumn nights, when you wanted to kiss the star-drenched sky. And the spring, the scents of this city in the springtime, the scent of Kathy in the spring. Waited here to walk her home or to take her for a cappuccino or a beer farther downtown in the Village. Waited for her to step out of this gray-white building—what was now part of the Emergency wing, but what used to be the main building, the *only* building, in fact, before they started expanding in red brick next door and across the street—the sight of her in her nurse's uniform, blonde head bent as she came down the steps, lines of weariness around her blue eyes, his heart leaping each time he saw her. Her shifts were like a patrolman's—eight to four, or four to midnight, or sometimes the graveyard shift from midnight to eight A.M.—and he'd be here waiting for her, the way he was waiting now, waiting to take her hand in his and kiss the weariness from her eyes. He sometimes wondered whether it wasn't tougher dealing with sick people than it was with criminals. All

51

that pain and suffering. Nurses burned out as easily as cops, he was sure of that.

If she'd been relieved on time, same as cops, fifteen minutes before the hour, she should be coming through those doors at the top of the steps any—

There.

Kathy.

Blonde head characteristically ducked, that pensive look on her freckled Irish face, little white nurse's cap a bit askew, black cape billowing over the white uniform under it, slender, well-shaped legs in the white, flat nurse's shoes, his heart leaped.

"Kathy?" he said.

She was coming down the steps, almost to the sidewalk now. The traffic light on the corner changed, tinting the white cap red. She blinked at him, surprised, and squinted into the gloom.

"Hello, Bryan," she said.

No enthusiasm in her voice. The formal name "Bryan." Her voice dead.

He fell into step beside her.

"I've been calling all day long," he said. "Didn't you get my messages?"

"Yes, I got your messages," she said. "And I wish you'd stop trying to . . ."

"We're still married," he said. "You could at least return . . ."

She stopped dead in the middle of the sidewalk.

"The lawyers don't want any private communication between us," she said. "The lawyers . . ."

"*Fuck* the lawyers," he said.

"All right, fuck the lawyers," she said. "*I* don't want any private communication, either. I thought I made that clear to you."

She nodded once, briefly, punctuating the sentence, driving the point home with the nod. Her eyes met his, challengingly. Do you understand? her eyes said. Is it clear now? She began walking again, turning the corner onto Seventh Avenue, heading uptown. The night was very cold. A fierce wind hit them the minute they turned the corner. They walked side by side in silence, their shoulders hunched, the cape flapping wildly around her, like a bat caught in the wind.

"Where's Elizabeth?" he said.

"I don't have to answer that," she said.

"Yes, you do. She's my daughter. Where is she? I've been calling the apartment, there's no answer there."

"Talk to my lawyer," Kathy said flatly.

"I'm talking to you. Where's my daughter?"

She did not answer him.

"Kathy, what have you done with her?" he said.

"She's in Jersey, all right?" she said, sighing.

"Where? With your parents?"

"Yes."

"What the hell is she doing there?"

"I'm working again. You *know* that. I can't find baby-sitters who'll put up with the different shifts I have to . . ."

"Why didn't you discuss this with me?"

"Why? Is somebody on the squad moonlighting as a sitter?"

"I have a right to know what plans you make for my daughter."

"*Our* daughter," Kathy said. "And I'm not sure you *do* have that right."

They were approaching Fourteenth Street now, the subway entrance with its orange globes on the corner, the Chemical Bank behind it. The bus stop was on Fourteenth itself. She would catch the M-14 there, and it would take her crosstown to First Avenue—*if* she was heading home. He did not know if she was heading home. He reached for her arm.

"Kathy," he said, "can't we just . . . ?"

She pulled away at once, as though burned by his touch. They stood facing each other.

"I'm sorry," he said.

She did not answer him.

"Where are you going now?" he asked.

"Where do you think? Home."

"Let me come with you."

"No."

"Kathy . . . what's happening? Can you please tell me what's . . ."

"We're getting a divorce," she said. "I thought you knew."

"I mean . . . Jesus, do we have to snarl at each other like animals?"

People were coming up out of the subway now, a train must have just pulled in. They stood looking at each other as a crowd of strangers streamed past them into the night. The wind was fierce. Their eyes were watering. She kept searching his face.

At last she sighed and said, "I'm sorry, Bry. This is as difficult for me as it is for you."

"No, I don't think it is," he said.

"Believe me."

"Then call it off."

"No."

"Let's pretend it's eight years ago, Kath.

55

Let's pretend you're just out of Bellevue Nursing, and I'm a young cop investigating . . ."

"Bry, don't. Please."

"Do you remember that day?" he said.

Softly, she said, "I remember it."

"Detective Bryan Reardon, Miss," he said, re-enacting the moment for her. "I understand you were in the grocery store when the . . ."

"Please," she said.

". . . robbery took place," he said, his voice trailing. He looked into her eyes. "We might not have met at all," he said. "It was pure chance that . . ."

"I'm sorry we did," she said.

"You don't mean that."

"I mean it."

"Kathy," he said, "I don't want this divorce."

"I do," she said, and turned to start for the corner.

"Kathy, wait," he said. "Please."

She hesitated.

"Look at me," he said.

She would not meet his eyes. Her head was ducked against the wind. She kept staring past his shoulder, down the avenue.

"Look at me and tell me you don't love me anymore," he said.

She raised her head. A sharp gust of wind almost lifted the nurse's cap from where it was pinned to her blonde hair. Her left hand came up, caught it in time. He saw that she no longer wore her wedding band.

"I don't love you anymore," she said.

"Kathy," he said, "honey . . ."

"I don't love you, Bry," she said, more firmly this time, and started to turn again. "Goodnight," she said.

He reached for her at once, grabbing her by the shoulders.

"Don't *touch* me!" she said sharply, pulling away from him so fiercely that she almost lost her balance.

He backed off, his hands dropping. She glared at him for a moment, her face contorted, oh, Jesus, that beautiful Irish phizz. And then, without another word, she turned and went around the corner, out of sight.

He stood looking after her.

Then he put his hands in his pockets and walked off.

3

THIS goddamn city, a cop spent more time in court trying to make a case stick than he did on the streets making the arrest in the first place. Nine times out of ten, your man plea-bargained, walked away with a Mickey Mouse sentence, and was back on the streets again a few years later, working at the same old stand. Sometimes Reardon felt the courts were more in sympathy with the bad guys than with the guys who were trying to lock them up. Even the goddamn *buildings* down here were intimidating.

This morning, he had taken the subway to Chambers Street, and walked through City Hall Park, and then past the County Court Building where the words *The True Administration of Justice Is the Firmest Pillar of Good Government* (bullshit, he'd thought) were chiseled into the huge peristyle on the facade, and then to the Criminal Courts Building on Centre Street, where another chiseled legend seemed to mock further the efforts of law enforcement officers, this time reading *Where Law Ends, There Tyranny Begins*. So what else is new? he'd thought. What *could* you call what was happening in the streets today if not tyranny? Sometimes he thought he was in the wrong line of work.

And now, he sat in a wood-paneled courtroom with silvery winter light slanting through the tall windows, the jury box on his left, the judge in his solemn robes of justice on his right, and said again to Jurgens's defense attorney, because the attorney had repeated the question, "That's right, I made the arrest."

The defense attorney's name was Barrows. He was a rotund little man wearing a brown suit and a cream-colored shirt. His hair was the color of his dun-colored tie. He wore eyeglasses, and he often took them off to make a point, holding them in his hand and wagging them in a witness's face.

"On the basis of the girl's identification," Barrows said.

"Is that a question?" Reardon said.

"It is a question," Barrows said. "Did you arrest Harold Jurgens on the basis of Frances Monoghan's identification?"

"On the basis of her identification and on

other evidence," Reardon said. "His finger-prints were on the girl's handbag. Before he raped her, he . . ."

"Your Honor," Barrows said, "I move that last be stricken. We are here *precisely* to determine whether or not . . ."

"Granted," Judge Abrahams said.

"May I answer the question as regards evidence?" Reardon said.

"Please," Abrahams said.

"The handbag was patent leather," Reardon said, "we got some very good latents from it. The Fingerprint Section identified the prints as belonging to Harold Jurgens, a convicted rapist who'd previously served three years at Attica. On the basis of such evidence, I made application for an arrest warrant with a No-Knock provision . . ."

"Why the No-Knock?" Abrahams asked.

Reardon looked over to the defense table, where the accused—Harold Jurgens, a sallow-faced man in his mid-thirties—sat listening to every word.

"On information and belief that the man was armed and dangerous," he said. "Your Honor, when he raped her, he brandished . . ."

"Your Honor," Barrows said, looking pained.

"Sustained," Abrahams said. "Strike that."

"Mr. Reardon, isn't it true," Barrows said, "that you asked for the No-Knock provision so that you could gain an advantage over Mr. Jurgens?"

"Yes, I wanted an advantage," Reardon said, "that's right. The man who raped Frances Monoghan . . ."

"Your Honor . . ."

"Let him finish," Abrahams said.

"Thank you," Reardon said. "The man was armed with a switchblade knife. He cut her across the face with it, disfigured her for life. Yes, I wanted an advantage when I went in there."

He glanced toward the jury box. Juror number five, an attractive woman in her late twenties, he guessed, was leaning forward intently, listening as carefully as was Harold Jurgens.

"And you fully *enjoyed* your advantage, didn't you?" Barrows asked.

"I don't know what that means," Reardon said. "What's the question?"

Barrows walked back to the defense table. He glanced at his client, and then picked up a glossy eight-by-ten photograph lying near

61

his briefcase. "Your Honor," he said, "I would like this marked as evidence, please."

"What is it?" Abrahams asked.

"A photograph taken of Harold Jurgens two weeks before the arrest. We've had it enlarged from a snapshot, I would like the jury to see it."

"Let me see it first, please," Abrahams said. Barrows handed the picture up to the bench. Abrahams looked at it and then turned to the assistant district attorney prosecuting the case. "Mr. Koenig?" he said.

"No objection," Koenig said.

"Mark it Exhibit One for the defense," Abrahams said, handing the picture to the clerk of the court.

"Thank you," Barrows said.

Reardon watched him as he walked to the jury box and handed the photograph to the elderly matron who was the foreman, forewoman, foreperson, whatever the hell they were calling them these days.

"This is what Harold Jurgens looked like two weeks before his arrest," he said. "Would you please look at it, and pass it on?"

He went back to the defense table and picked up another eight-by-ten.

"Your Honor," he said, "I would similarly like this marked as evidence, please. It's a blowup of the mug shot taken at Police Headquarters shortly after Mr. Jurgens was booked there." He approached the bench and handed the photo up to Abrahams.

"Mr. Koenig?" Abrahams said.

"No objection."

"Mark it Exhibit Two," Abrahams said.

Barrows carried the second picture to the jury box, and handed it to the foreman again. She glanced at Reardon as she accepted it. Seemed to be taking his measure. The picture started down the line. As juror number five accepted it, she looked squarely at Reardon.

"That is what Harold Jurgens looked like shortly after his arrest," Barrows said. "You will notice that his left eye is discolored, his lip is bruised and swollen, and there are cuts and lacerations all over his face."

He looked at Reardon. Reardon looked at Koenig, sitting at the prosecutor's table. He was doodling on a lined yellow pad. Barrows came back to the witness box.

"Mr. Reardon," he said, "have you seen these pictures?"

"I've seen the mug shot," Reardon said.

"Then allow me," Barrows said, and walked to his briefcase and opened it. "Your

Honor, may I show him prints of those photos?"

"Yes, yes," Abrahams said impatiently.

Barrows took two eight-by-tens from his briefcase and carried them to the witness box. He handed them to Reardon. Reardon looked at them. The identical photos the jury had just seen. Juror number five was staring at him more intently now.

"A remarkable difference, wouldn't you say?" Barrows asked.

Reardon said nothing.

"Mr. Reardon?" Barrows said. "Would you like to comment on the difference between the photographs? You *do* see a difference, don't you?"

"I see a difference, yes."

"How would you account for the difference, Mr. Reardon?"

"I have no way of accounting for it."

"Was Mr. Jurgens's face bruised and lacerated when you broke into his apartment at . . . ?"

"I didn't *break* in," Reardon said at once. "I went there with a warrant."

"*Was* his face bruised and lacerated?" Barrows insisted, taking off his glasses and shaking them at Reardon. "*Was* his eye discolored? *Was* his lip swollen?"

"No," Reardon said.

"But the mug shot attests that these bruises, these lacerations, these marks of violence were there *after* Harold Jurgens was questioned at the Fifth Precinct."

"If you're suggesting . . ."

"I am stating as a *fact*, Mr. Reardon, that a confession was *coerced* from the accused."

"That's a lie!" Reardon said. "I never touched . . ."

"Did you not say in the presence of Police Officer Anthony Aiello that prison was too good for Mr. Jurgens?"

"I said that, yes."

"Did you not say, again in the presence of Officer Aiello, that Mr. Jurgens should be dragged through the street behind wild horses?"

"I said that, too."

"And when you were alone with Mr. Jurgens, allegedly *questioning* him, did you not then decide to take the law into your own hands, and . . . ?"

"No, I did *not*," Reardon said tightly.

"Did you not, in fact, use in your *questioning* a back-room, rubber-hose technique forbidden by the very laws you are sworn to uphold?"

"I did *not*."

"Then how do you account for the differences in those two photographs?"

"He wasn't mugged and printed at the Fifth," Reardon said. "That was done at Headquarters, where he was booked. He was in with a lot of other prisoners there. Most criminals don't particularly appreciate either rapists or child molesters. I don't know how he got those bruises, but it's entirely possible . . ."

"No further questions, your Honor," Barrows said.

Koenig rose at once from the prosecutor's table. "No questions," he said.

Reardon stepped down from the witness box. Juror number five was still watching him. He sat beside Koenig and whispered, "You *could* have objected, you know."

"Why?" Koenig said, and smiled. "He convinced me."

Not far from where Reardon, on the phone with Lieutenant Farmer, was complaining that Koenig had let their case go down the toilet, two men sat in the corner office of a brokerage firm in the Equitable Building on Broadway, between Cedar and Pine, almost directly across from the huge black Merrill Lynch building at One Liberty Plaza.

66

Lowell Rothstein was thirty-eight years old, darkly handsome, with wavy black hair and brown eyes he liked to think of as soulful. He was wearing a suit hand-tailored for him at Chipp's, and smoking a Dunhill cigarette he had just lighted with a gold Dunhill lighter. A gold Rolex watch ticked off minutes on his slender wrist. His partner, Joseph Phelps, was a year older, a plain-looking man going bald at the back of his head, wearing a rumpled gray flannel suit and black shoes that badly needed polish. He looked extremely worried. He sounded worried, too.

"Why does she want to see us?" he asked, and shook his head. "All the way from Arizona?" He shook his head again. "Her brother's here selling some paintings, isn't he? Do you think this is just a social visit?"

"The Kidds don't make social visits," Rothstein said.

Phelps glanced at the clock on his partner's desk. "What time did she say?"

"Eleven," Rothstein said. "Relax, will you?"

"The very rich make me nervous," Phelps said.

"The very *poor* make *me* nervous," Rothstein said. "Or at least the ones who can't *forget* they were poor."

"I was poor, yes," Phelps said. "Very."

"You're not poor now."

"I'm not rich, either. I still look at the right-hand side of the menu, do you know that?"

"What?"

"Where the prices are. My fondest wish is that one day I'll be able to go into a restaurant and order whatever I want—without first having to check the right-hand side of the menu."

"*That* poor you're not," Rothstein said.

"The stench lingers," Phelps said. "I live on Sutton Place now, I've got a summer home in the Hamptons, but I can still smell Sheepshead Bay. Money scares me, Lowell. Because it can all disappear in a minute."

"You're in the wrong business," Rothstein said.

"*What* time did she say? Did you tell me what time?"

"Eleven."

"It's already ten past."

"The privilege of the very rich," Rothstein said, and shrugged.

The buzzer on his desk sounded. He reached over and stabbed at a button.

"Yes?"

"Miss Kidd to see you," his secretary said.

"Send her right in, Jenny," Rothstein said. "Relax," he told his partner.

The door opened a moment later. Olivia Kidd, wearing her mink coat open over a dark green Chanel suit, came into the office, her hand extended.

"Lowell," she said, shaking his hand, "Joe," shaking his, "I'm sorry I'm late, the holiday traffic is impossible." She tossed her mink onto one of the leather upholstered armchairs, opened her dispatch case without preamble, and removed from it two sheets of paper. Handing one of the sheets to Rothstein, she said, "You've already had a quick look at this, Lowell, but you may want to go over it more leisurely now." She handed the second sheet to Phelps, who gave his partner a puzzled look. "Joe?" she said. "Read this carefully, won't you?"

She sat in the armchair, the mink spread under her, crossed her legs, and fished a cigarette from her handbag. Rothstein hurried to light it with his gold Dunhill. Phelps was already looking at the sheet of paper in his hand.

Across the top of it, he read:

KIDD FUTURES SCHEDULE: CMX VIA ROTHSTEIN-PHELPS, NYC

Beneath this, and stretched out across the page as column-headings, were the words:

PURCH ACCT	LOTS	TOTAL	DEL
DATE		OZ	MO

The room was silent as both men continued reading.

"What do you think?" Olivia said at last.

"I don't understand," Phelps said, looking up.

"What is it you don't understand, Joe?"

"Is this what you *want?* What you actually *want?*"

"Well, of course it is. Why would . . . ?"

"An average of six hundred contracts a *day?* Between now and Christmas Eve?"

"That's right."

"That's seven working days. You're talking forty-two hundred lots."

"Yes."

"Twenty-one million ounces."

"Yes."

"Divided among three accounts."

"*Corporate* accounts," Olivia said.

"Corporate or otherwise, there are rules, Olivia. Both Comex and the CFTC . . ."

"Yes, Joe, I know the rules."

"The Comex reportable position level is two hundred and fifty lots . . ."

"Yes, I know."

"And the CFTC requires that we file an oh-one form on anything over a *hundred* lots."

"So where's the problem, Joe, would you please tell me? Fourteen hundred lots in each account is well under the overall six-thousand-lot limit for any principal. We're not doing anything illegal here. It's all open and aboveboard."

"Eventually, we'd have to reveal the principals in each account. Comex would insist on that."

"We'll reveal them when we're asked to reveal them. Jessica's here, Sarge is here, I'm here. I don't see any problem. We are *not* going over the six-thousand-lot limit."

Phelps was silent for a long while.

"I assume there's a reason for this," he said at last.

"There's a reason for everything, isn't there?" Olivia said.

"May we know what it is?"

"We're feeling bullish," Olivia said, and smiled.

"Do you know how much cash we're talking here? To put up the margin deposits?"

"We already have it."

"We're talking three thousand a contract right now."

"More or less," Olivia said.

"That'll come to something like twelve, thirteen million dollars."

"Yes, I know."

"Do you plan to take delivery?"

"No."

"Well, thank God for *that*," Phelps said. "But I *still* don't like it. We send our man into the pit to buy that many contracts a day, he'll have a lot of sharp traders looking over his shoulder."

"Let them look," Olivia said, and shrugged.

"Lowell?" Phelps said. "Don't you agree with me?"

"I'd still like to know *why*," Rothstein said. "Is this something Joe and I might like to get into personally?"

"How can I possibly answer that, Lowell?"

"Well . . . when you say *we're* feeling

bullish, do you mean the *Captain* is feeling bullish, too?"

"Most decidedly."

"Then it might be worth looking into, eh, Joe?"

"I don't like gambling," Phelps said.

"We'll talk about it," Rothstein said.

"Gentlemen," Olivia said, and looked at her watch. "Hadn't you better start working on this?"

"Let me ask you something else, may I?" Rothstein said.

"Certainly."

"Will you be buying contracts only through Comex? Here in New York? Or will you be using foreign exchanges as well?"

"Why do you want to know that, Lowell?"

"Because that might change the whole complexion of it."

"In what way?"

"In a way that could determine whether Joe and I want to take positions ourselves."

"The way Mr. Dodge did?" Olivia asked.

Phelps looked from his partner to Olivia, puzzled again.

"Let me say this," Olivia said. "The exchanges we use are none of your business. But further, let me say *this*. Since Kidd

International owns twelve percent of Rothstein-Phelps, and since you've served us
exceptionally well over the years, I would
suggest that it might not be remiss for you
to take a flyer." She smiled. "If the price
went up to forty dollars an ounce by next
December, for example, you'd stand to make
a great deal of money on a *six*-dollar-an-
ounce investment." She smiled beatifically.
"Use your own judgment, gentlemen."

Rothstein looked at Phelps.

"But be discreet, won't you?" she said.

Rothstein smiled.

Phelps frowned.

"Is everything understood then?" Olivia
said. "You have the schedule, I want it implemented by the close on Christmas Eve."
She smiled briefly. "Lowell?" she said. "Joe?
Good day, gentlemen."

The restaurant on Pell Street was rather drab-
looking in contrast to the gaudier neon-fes-
tooned places surrounding it. The front plate
glass window, steamed over now and decorated with beaded curtains, was lettered in
black with the words THE RICE BOWL. The
entrance door was on the right, similarly
beaded, a menu Scotch-taped to the inside
of the glass. The street, at twenty minutes

to twelve, was already beginning to fill with people on their lunch hours.

A bell over the door tinkled as Reardon entered, but none of the waiters or diners so much as glanced at him as he closed the door behind him, cutting off the sharp wind that blew for an instant through the small room. A dozen tables, more or less, all of them without tablecloths. The overwhelming aroma of succulent food frying. A singsong babble of voices; most of the diners and all of the waiters were Chinese. He went immediately to the counter on his left, where a harried young Chinese was tallying a bill—on an abacus, he noticed—for a waitress who stood looking into the room, her back to the counter. Reardon said nothing until the man had finished his calculations, and handed the bill to the waitress. The man looked up at him.

"Benny Wong," Reardon said.

The man behind the counter said something in Chinese to the departing waitress. The waitress nodded. He turned to Reardon again, and in clipped English, said, "Who you, please?"

"Detective Reardon."

"Mr. Wong know you?" the counterman asked.

"He knows me."

The counterman picked up a telephone and dialed a single number. Into the phone, he said something in Chinese. He listened, and then spoke again. Reardon heard his name in an otherwise unintelligible rush of Chinese words. "Okay," the counterman said in English, and then put the receiver back on its cradle. "Someone be here," he said. "You wait."

Reardon nodded, reached into his pocket for a package of cigarettes, and was about to light one when the counterman said, "No smoke, please. Mr. Wong no smoke."

Reardon dropped the unlighted cigarette into a bowl on the countertop. A door opened at the far end of the room, to the right of the kitchen. A small Chinese man wearing dark trousers and a black tunic came to where Reardon was standing near the door.

"Mr. Reardon?" he said in virtually unaccented English. "I'm Gilbert Chan. This way, please."

Reardon followed him to the rear of the restaurant. He hadn't eaten anything since breakfast, and as he sniffed the savory aromas from the kitchen, closer now, he realized all at once just how hungry he was. Chan opened the same door through which

76

he'd entered the restaurant, and allowed Reardon to precede him into a small unfurnished anteroom. Another door was at the far end of this room. He opened it, and with a slight bow, said, "Please."

The room beyond would have come as a mild surprise to anyone who hadn't been in it before. It was furnished in what Reardon would have called British Barrister—booklined walls, a leather-topped desk, two leather armchairs, one behind the desk, one in front of it. Benny Wong sat in the chair behind the desk. With one fluid motion of his right hand, he offered the other chair to Reardon and dismissed Chan. Wong was, Reardon guessed, a man in his late sixties, looking much younger, though—the way affluent Chinese tended to—and dressed in a dark blue business suit, gold cuff links showing at his wrists. Black mustache over his lip. Slightly balding. No smile on his face. Deadly as a cobra.

He waited until Chan closed the door behind him.

"Don't tell me," he said to Reardon, "let me guess." Voice slightly singsong, but no pidgin English here, not for a man who'd been in America since 1926. "The restaurant on Mulberry, right? Last night, right?"

"You've got it," Reardon said.

"So naturally, you think back to 1982."

"Naturally."

"The Golden Star," Wong said. "Fifty-one East Broadway. Two, three o'clock in the morning. They march in with ski masks, stockings, paper bags over their heads, kill three people and wound eight others, including a very dear friend of mine," Wong said, and clucked his tongue. "This is not the same thing, Reardon."

"It's not, huh?"

"Positively not. That was gang shit back then. There were Free Masons and White Tigers in the bar. It was a fight over turf, that's all."

"How about *now?* Were any of the gangs putting the muscle on Ralph D'Annunzio?"

"How would I know?" Wong said.

"I think you would know," Reardon said.

There were two principal tongs in Chinatown. Originally offshoots of the secret societies in Guangdong Province, they now called themselves "businessmen's associations," but Reardon knew that between them the An Liang Shang Tsung Hui and the Hip Sing T'ang controlled all of the area's gambling parlors. The youth gangs, like sucker fish hanging on the underbellies of sharks, protected the parlors from hoods who might one fine night decide to hold them up. In addition, the gangs extorted protection money from the honest merchants in Chinatown—the Ghost Shadows working Mott Street, the Flying Dragons working Pell—for a reputed $5,000-$10,000 weekly take. If one of the gangs had decided to spill over onto Mulberry Street . . .

"You're thinking wrong," Wong said. "Believe me, you're thinking wrong. This was not Chinese."

"Ask around, will you?" Reardon said.

"Do I owe you something?" Wong asked, looking genuinely puzzled.

"No, just do me the favor, Benny."

"I'll ask," Wong said, "but believe me, I already know the answer. These were not Chinese."

Robert Sargent Kidd did not awaken until noon that Tuesday. The waiter who brought him his breakfast at the Park Lane Hotel advised him that the temperature outside was twenty-two degrees, and then told him to have a nice day. A copy of the *New York Times* was on the breakfast tray. The two-column story in the lower right-hand corner of the front page immediately caught his eye. The headline read:

FRENCH IMPRESSIONIST
COLLECTION
BRINGS RECORD $36.3 MILLION

Sipping at his coffee, Sarge read the story. A hundred and one paintings in all had gone under the hammer at Sotheby's last night, bringing prices ranging from $55,000 for an admittedly minor Monet to $4,600,000 for a truly superb Modigliani nude. A collection that had taken him years to assemble—Matisse, Van Gogh, Renoir, Seurat, Cézanne, Degas, Braque, Corot—gone in what now seemed an instant, though last night in that crowded room it had taken a painful eternity.

Sarge, you've got to get rid of those pictures.

His father talking.

I need the money they'll bring.

Andrew Kidd. They called him "The Captain." And, of course, the Captain had given his Sargent—or more appropriately his *sergeant*—an order. No simple request, this, oh no, an *order*. And when the Captain barked an order, you snapped to, by Christ, or there'd be hell to pay.

All of them gone now.

For thirty-six million and some change.

Gone.

For money.

To earn yet more money if the Captain's scheme worked. It would work, of course. His schemes always worked. And the Kidds would be richer. Much richer. All of them but Sarge, who would forever consider himself poverty-stricken now that his precious paintings were no longer in his possession.

He sipped at his coffee.

He looked out the window to the naked branches of the trees in Central Park.

Someday, he thought, I'd like to . . .

He did not know what he would like to do someday.

He knew only that his paintings were gone.

The D'Annunzio apartment was on Broome Street, in a red-brick building next door to the Arfi & Mazzola pharmacy. Directly across the street was the Church of the Most Holy Crucifix, which advised on a sign to the left of the entrance door that masses were given in English and in Spanish. To the right of the church, the Chia Sheung Food Products Company had set up shop. To Reardon, the ethnic mix on this single short street was representative of what was happening all over the precinct.

He took the steps up two at a time—a habit from when he was a teenager—walked down a narrow hallway on the third-floor landing, and knocked on the door to apartment 31. Mark D'Annunzio opened the door.

"I'm sorry to bother you," Reardon said. "Lieutenant Farmer told me you'd called . . ."

"Yes, come in," D'Annunzio said.

The front door opened into a small kitchen. Sink, stove, and refrigerator opposite the door. Frost-rimed, curtained window above the sink. Round table with an oilcloth cover nestled in the angle of the corner wall. Dust motes rising in a shaft of wintry sunlight. The house seemed empty and still.

"What I called about," D'Annunzio said, "sit down, would you like some coffee?"

"Thank you," Reardon said.

D'Annunzio went to the stove, where a coffee pot sat on a low gas flame. He took two cups from the cabinet, poured into each of them, and carried them to the table. "You take milk, sugar?" he asked.

"Black," Reardon said.

D'Annunzio sat opposite him. Both men sipped coffee as the dust motes climbed tirelessly in the silent house. Somewhere a clock ticked emptily.

"What I wanted to know," D'Annunzio said, "is how much longer they'll be. I mean . . . we have to make funeral arrangements . . ."

"I understand," Reardon said.

"I know it's the law, I know they have to do the autopsy, but you don't realize how upsetting this has been to my mother."

"I called the Medical Examiner's office before I came up here," Reardon said, nodding. "They'll be ready with their report sometime today. You can feel free to makewhatever arrangements you have to, Mr. D'Annunzio. I'll see that the bod . . . that your father . . . have you chosen a funeral home?"

D'Annunzio nodded bleakly. "Riverside," he said. "On Canal Street."

"I'll have them contact the morgue. Don't worry, I'll take care of it."

"The relatives, you know, they keep phoning, wanting to know when it'll be."

"Tell them it'll be tomorrow."

"So many relatives," D'Annunzio said. "And friends. He had a lot of friends, my father. When something like this happens . . ."

He let the sentence trail.

Reardon listened to the ticking clock.

"How about enemies?" he said. "I know

this was a robbery, on the face of it we've got a robbery here, but sometimes things aren't exactly what they seem. And I keep thinking of what you said. That one of them asked you your name."

"My father's name, too."

"They wanted *his* name, too?"

"Yes. Then they told him to move over near the bar, and while he was going they . . . they shot him in the back."

"Would you know if your father ever received any threatening letters or phone calls?"

"No, nothing like that."

"Any trouble with the waiters? Or anybody else working for him? Anyone who might have been bearing a grudge?"

"No."

"Did he owe money to anyone?"

"Paid all his bills on the dime," D'Annunzio said. "Food and beverage suppliers, garbage collection, linen, all on the dime."

"Who handled *that* for him, would you know?" Reardon asked. "Garbage collection and linens."

"Why? Are you thinking the mob?"

"I'm just trying to touch all the bases."

"No, I don't think this was anything like that," D'Annunzio said. "They used to come eat in the restaurant all the time, ever since we opened. There's no reason the boys would've wanted to hurt my father, believe me."

"Mr. D'Annunzio, I have to ask this, please forgive me."

"What is it?"

"Were your mother and father happily married? Would there have been another man, or another woman, anyone who . . ."

"They've been married for almost forty years. My father never *looked* at another woman from the day he met her." He shook his head. He lifted his coffee cup, seemed about to drink, and then put it down on the table again. "It doesn't make sense, none of it. It was a robbery, like you say; on the face of it we had two guys coming in to stick us up. But then why didn't they take anything? And why did they kill him? *I* was the one reaching for the gun under the bar, why did they . . . ?"

"You had a gun on the premises?"

"A shotgun, I keep it under the bar. So when I'm reaching for it, the guy just says, 'No.' But when my father's coming over to the bar, they shoot him. The guy tells him to move over there, go there, whatever he said, and my father starts over to the bar, he's got his back to them, and they gun him down. It just doesn't make sense, does it?"

No, Reardon thought, it doesn't make sense at all.

"I'd like to take another look at the restaurant," he said.

By two o'clock that Tuesday afternoon, it was snowing heavily, and the lights in the ground-floor living room of the Seventy-first Street brownstone were on in defense against the gloom. The woman pacing the Bokharra was wearing high-heeled sandals and ruby-red, satin lounging pajamas that echoed the reds in the rug. The woman was angry. Her brown eyes flashed, and she tossed her long black hair with each stride she took. She was extraordinarily beautiful, but her fury contorted her face and her voice now was high and strident.

"I don't give a damn *what* you want!" she shouted.

Olivia was not surprised by her half-sister's tantrum. Although Jessica was twenty-four years old, she frequently behaved like a thirteen-year-old. Sitting calmly in a wing-back chair near the fireplace, the fire crackling and spitting, Olivia watched her and said nothing.

"The suite is booked for the seventeenth!" Jessica said. "That's tomorrow, and that's when I'm leaving!"

"Postpone it," Olivia said.

"No, I *won't* postpone it!" Jessica shouted. "My plane leaves Kennedy at eight in the morning, I'll be in Zurich late tomorrow night, and on the slopes in St. Moritz by Thursday—the same as I am *every* year!"

"Not this year, darling," Olivia said.

"Yes, this year, and next year, and the year after that, and whenever I *want* to!" Jessica said, and stopped dead before Olivia's chair, her hands on her hips, her lower lip thrust out challengingly.

Olivia shook her head.

"How'd you ever get to be such a spoiled brat?" she said.

"It runs in the blood," Jessica said.

"On *your* mother's side, maybe."

"Is it true that *your* mother was a barroom hooker?" Jessica said.

"Don't press your luck, Jessie," Olivia said. "We may share the same father . . ."

"Call him, go ahead, call him," Jessica said. "Tell him you're trying to get me to postpone my ski trip. See what he has to say about it."

"I'm here on his instructions," Olivia said.

"*He* wants me to postpone?"

"Or cancel entirely, you can take your choice."

"I don't believe it," Jessica said. "You're lying."

"I'd allow you to call him, but he may be napping. You'll have to take my word for it."

"*Your* word!" Jessica said, rolling her eyes.

"Yes. Which, incidentally, has never . . ."

"I had *your* word that this apartment was *mine.*"

"It is yours."

"A lovely townhouse in the Seventies," Jessica said, trying to mimic Olivia's deeper voice. "Three whole floors of your own, here's the key, Jessica. Just stay out of our hair in Phoenix."

"I never said that," Olivia said calmly.

"It's what you meant," Jessica said. "And I don't consider something *mine* if you and Sarge have keys to it, and can walk in whenever you like, no matter who's here with me. That's not *mine,* Olivia, that's only another holding in the fucking Kidd *empire!*"

"I stay at a hotel whenever I'm in New York," Olivia said. "You know that. And I've never . . ."

"You walked in this afternoon, didn't you?"

"I knocked first. Your privacy is sacrosanct, Jessie, you needn't worry. You can entertain . . ."

"Only my friends call me Jessie."

"*Jessica* then, fine. You can use this place to entertain as many of your adolescent disco pals as you care to, *Jessica*, provided you don't frighten the horses. The Captain's tired of bailing you out of trouble."

"I haven't heard any complaints," Jessica said.

"You're hearing them now. Stay out of the papers. Keep a low profile while you're in New York."

"Why can't I go to Switzerland?" Jessica asked.

"Because the Captain needs you here."

"Okay, *let's* call him, okay? Let's find out if he *really* . . ."

"If you want to risk his anger, go ahead." She nodded toward a desk across the room. "There's the phone."

Jessica hesitated, weighing this. She went to the bar and poured two fingers of cognac into a snifter. She came back to the fire, stood staring into the flames for a moment, her left hand on her hip, the cognac snifter in her right hand, a model's pose. Olivia could almost see the wheels spinning inside her gorgeous head. When she turned from the fire, her face was in repose. The anger was gone. Her voice was mildly beseeching, almost childlike.

"It's just that all my *friends* are there at Christmastime," she said.

"Yes, I know," Olivia said.

"I'll be missing all the parties."

"Give a party here."

"The parties are better in Switzerland."

"Enough, Jessie. If I have to tie you to that playpen . . ."

"Playpen?"

"Yes, that eternally reverberating four-poster bed upstairs, your *playpen*, darling sister. If I have to *tie* you to it to keep you here, I will, believe me."

She rose, walked to where her mink was draped over one arm of the sofa, and picked it up. Casually, she said, "And I'll also put someone outside your door to break both your legs if you try to walk out of here with a suitcase."

She smiled.

"Got it, *Jessica?*" she said.

Jessica scowled.

"Good," Olivia said, and shrugged into her mink.

A sign on the door of the Luna Mare restaurant read:

CLOSED DUE TO

DEATH IN THE FAMILY

A small black wreath hung on the doorknob under the sign. Inside the restaurant, Mark D'Annunzio sat at one of the tables, an open bottle of Chianti before him, a glass of wine in his hand. Reardon's wine glass was on the bartop. He was crouched behind the bar, looking at the safe. A clock on the wall read five-thirty. Outside, it was snowing fiercely. D'Annunzio had turned on very few lights, but the place seemed cozy and warm in contrast to the tundra beyond the plate glass windows.

"Before they shot your father," Reardon said, "did they take any money from the cash register?"

"No," D'Annunzio said. "Well, wait, I'm trying to remember. This was still early, there wasn't much cash in the register, anyway. But they didn't even go anywhere near it. They told us to keep quiet, and to put our hands up, and then they asked me what my name was, and they asked my father

91

what his name was, and they shot him. That was it. And ran out."

"You were standing about where I am now?" Reardon asked. "When they shot him?"

"Right about there."

"Did they know there was a safe behind the bar? Did they seem to know it?"

"I don't think so. How could they?"

He seemed on the verge of tears again. Reardon came around the bar, the wine glass in his hand, and sat at the table opposite him.

"You don't know what this restaurant meant to him," D'Annunzio said. "My grandfather came to this country in 1901, after the grape crop failed in Italy. He was a common laborer, didn't even speak the language, but he worked his fingers to the bone to raise a family and to make sure they never wanted for anything. Even during the Depression, my grandfather made sure his kids had clothes on their backs and food in their bellies."

Reardon nodded. D'Annunzio poured more wine for him.

"There are people, you know," he said, "they come to this country, they only want to dump on it. Not my grandfather. He wanted to be a Yankee Doodle Dandy, applied for his citizenship papers practically the minute he got off the boat. Raised his kids to be Americans, never mind the other side."

He sipped at his wine. His eyes had a faraway look in them now. He seemed to be recalling a distant time, a less complicated time, a safer time.

"My father was the youngest," he said. "There are three older sisters and a brother in Washington."

He nodded. He said nothing for what seemed a very long time.

"This restaurant was his dream," he said at last. "He'd been saving for it all his life."

Another silence, longer this time.

"When he found this place, it was a dump, you shoulda seen the stove in back, you couldn't cut the grease on it with a machete."

He shook his head, a small smile on his lips.

"His dream. Put all his savings into fixing it up, got himself a mortgage, borrowed the rest he still needed. So now *this* happens. A man finally realizes his dream, and *this* happens."

He shook his head again. The smile was gone now.

"Mr. D'Annunzio," Reardon said, "you told me earlier that your father didn't owe anybody money."

"That's right."

"But you just said—unless I misunderstood you—that he *borrowed* the rest he needed."

"Yes."

"Do you mean privately?"

"I guess so. Because he got all he could from the bank, you know, and it just wouldn't stretch."

"How much did he borrow?"

"I don't know."

"Was it a sizable sum?"

"I don't know."

"Who'd he borrow it from?"

"I don't know. Anyway, what difference does it make? Did the money do him any good? He got his restaurant, he got his dream, but he . . . ."

And suddenly he was crying again. Reardon put his hand on his shoulder.

"I'm sorry," D'Annunzio said, sobbing.

"That's okay," Reardon said. "That's okay."

"He was such a good father to me," D'Annunzio said, fumbling for his handkerchief, "such a good man. Why'd they have to *do* this, those bastards!"

He blew his nose, and then looked directly across the table at Reardon.

"We'll never find them, will we?" he asked. "We don't know what they look like, we don't even . . ."

"I'll find them," Reardon said. "I promise you."

But he wasn't at all sure.

In a wine bar in the shadow of the Brooklyn Bridge, Rothstein and Phelps sat drinking a more expensive vintage than the one Reardon and D'Annunzio were sharing. Rothstein had ordered the wine, a 1969 Lafite-Rothschild Pouliac; Phelps would never have dared. Phelps seemed nervous sipping something so costly. He kept looking into the glass after each sip, as though mourning the loss of the dollars the vanishing liquid represented.

"Relax," Rothstein told him.

"I'm just afraid of taking such a big plunge," Phelps said. "I mean, personally. I mean, this would be *our* money, Lowell. This isn't the same as investing someone else's money."

"I think we can consider it a relatively safe investment," Rothstein said.

"Because the Kidds are taking such a heavy position?"

"Yes. And undoubtedly others as well."

"What makes you think so?"

"Things she said."

"Like what?"

"When we were discussing disclosure, she mentioned that the family was here in New York. I'm assuming she meant they'd be available to sign any documents required by the CFTC."

"Well, yes, but . . ."

"At the same time, she said there'd be purchases abroad. So I'm assuming those purchases are being made by *others*, with the Kidds in for varying percentages."

"You think the Captain is masterminding this?"

"Anything the Kidds do is masterminded by the Captain."

"Because it seems *reckless*, don't you think? All it takes is one smart guy at the exchange to realize . . ."

"They're not doing anything illegal, Joe. They're just trying to pick up some loose change between now and Christmas, that's all."

"Loose change! Forty-two hundred contracts? With a three thousand dollar deposit on each contract? Do you know what that comes to? It comes to an outlay of twelve million, six hundred thousand dollars!"

"That's right."

"Five thousand ounces in each contract is twenty-one million ounces, Lowell. If it *really* goes to forty dollars an ounce, those contracts will be worth eight hundred and forty million dollars. That's a profit of more than three quarters of a billion! In New York alone."

"To the Kidds, that's loose change. The question, Joe, is whether we want to follow their lead. That's the question."

"How much would you want to risk, Lowell?"

"Whatever we can raise. I personally would be in favor of hocking everything we've got. That's how sure I am."

"We could lose it all, you know."

"I know."

"All of it," Phelps said. "Back to Sheepshead Bay."

"Worse for me," Rothstein said.

"How so?"

"If you start with nothing, and you go back to nothing, you haven't lost anything.

If you're born with a silver spoon in your mouth, Lowell Rothstein, son of Jacob Rothstein the financier, and you suddenly end up without a penny . . . that can hurt, my friend, that can really hurt."

Phelps sipped at his wine.

"Chance of a lifetime here," he said softly.

"Both come out of it multimillionaires," Rothstein said. "We have to risk it, you know."

"I know that."

"Your glass is empty," Rothstein said, and signalled to the waiter. The waiter lifted the bottle from the wine cooler. He poured into both men's glasses.

"Thank you," Phelps said.

The waiter padded off.

"What'd she mean?" he asked.

"What'd who mean?" Rothstein said.

"Olivia. When she said you'd already seen the purchasing schedule."

"Did she say that?"

"That's what I thought."

"Lots on her mind, who knows?" Rothstein said, shrugging. He swallowed a long draught of the wine. "Ahhhh," he said.

"And who's Dodge?" Phelps asked.

"I don't know, who's Dodge?"

"Someone taking a position, isn't that what she said?"

"Who can follow Olivia?" Rothstein said, and shrugged. "Are we going into this or not?"

"I guess so," Phelps said. "I guess we've got to hope they know what they're doing . . ."

"Can't go wrong trusting the Kidds," Rothstein said.

"God, we could make a fortune!"

"Millions and millions and millions."

Phelps suddenly giggled.

"I'm going to ask for mine in silver dollars," he said.

"Be appropriate," Rothstein said.

"No, I mean so I can make a tremendous *pile* of them, and jump up and down on the pile, and pick up the coins, and let them trickle down on my head."

"All those coins, yeah."

"I love the smell of money. Do you love the smell of money?"

"I love it."

"But it scares me," Phelps said.

"No, don't be scared," Rothstein said, and raised his glass. "Joseph, my friend," he said, "Mr. Inside . . ."

"Lowell, my friend," Phelps said, raising his glass, "Mr. Outside . . ."

"Here's to us. In a week's time, we'll either be flat on our asses in the gutter . . ."

"Or we'll own the world," Phelps said.

"We'll own the world," Rothstein said, nodding. "Or at least a goodly part of it."

Solemnly, silently, the men clinked their glasses together.

4

WEDNESDAY morning, December 17, dawned cold and gray and windy. The old coal-burning furnace in the basement of the Fifth struggled valiantly against the Arctic temperatures, but the police station was cold, and the squadroom—because it was on the second floor and the furnace's fan wasn't powerful enough to propel heat very far—was only slightly warmer than the streets outside. Gianelli, sitting at his desk typing, was still wearing his overcoat. Reardon was wearing a sweater under his suit jacket. He had put on long johns before leaving for work this morning. Lieutenant Farmer, hunched now over the report Hoffman had typed on the night of the murder, was in his shirtsleeves. Gianelli wondered if the lieutenant was some kind of polar bear or something.

"Where does it say anything in Chick's report about them asking the old man what his name was?" Farmer asked.

"It doesn't," Hoffman said. He was standing at the water cooler, debating whether he wanted a drink of water or not. It seemed too cold in here to drink water. He was still wearing the mackinaw he'd worn to work this morning.

"I only found out last night," Reardon said.

"Maybe that's why they shot him," Gianelli said, looking up from his typewriter. "Maybe they didn't like the name Ralph." Across the small room, Ruiz was talking to an old lady who had come to the precinct to report a disturbance the night before. Like all of the detectives except Farmer, he was dressed for the squadroom tundra, wearing a short car coat with a fake fur collar.

"Why shoot a man who's doing everything you're telling him to do?" Reardon said. "He was moving over to the bar, just the way they told him."

"So what?" Farmer said.

"You say this happened at midnight?" Ruiz asked the old lady.

"Yes, twelve o'clock sharp," she said. She was wearing a woolen hat pulled down over her ears. She was wearing a black cloth coat. She was wearing leg warmers over her pantyhose, but she didn't look like a Broadway dancer.

"If you come in to rob a place, why do you shoot a man without robbing anything?" Reardon asked.

"He's got a point, Loot," Gianelli said.

"Knocked on the door and said he was your husband, huh?" Ruiz said.

"That's right," the old lady said.

"Stop looking for mysteries, Reardon," Farmer said.

"I'm saying . . ."

"There are no mysteries in police work. There are only crimes and the people who commit those crimes."

"Maybe it *was* your husband," Ruiz said. "Was your husband home at the time?"

"My husband's been dead for twenty years," the lady said.

"Oh," Ruiz said. "Okay, let's take down some information, okay?"

"You've got two hungry punks here who tried to rip off a restaurant," Farmer said. "And panicked. And killed the owner. That's what you've got here."

"If they were so hungry . . ." Reardon said.

"Run it by the book," Farmer said. "Ask your questions, check your M.O. file, find out which punks just got paroled after doing time for armed robbery. You got a man commits an armed robbery, he's going to do it again and again 'cause it's the only line of work he knows."

The phone on Hoffman's desk rang. He picked up the receiver.

"Fifth Squad," he said. "Detective Hoffman."

"*I* wouldn't have shot a man before I cleaned out the register," Reardon said. "Not if I went in there to steal."

"Me, neither," Gianelli said.

"Uh-huh," Hoffman said into the phone. "Just a second, okay?"

"Who says thieves have to make sense?" Farmer asked, and tossed the D.D. report onto Reardon's desk. "Get a copy of this to Homicide," he said. "And Reardon . . ."

"Bry? For you," Hoffman said.

"*Find* those punks," Farmer said, and limped into his office. Reardon picked up the extension phone.

"Hello?" he said. "Oh, Martin, good, glad you got back to me."

"What apartment was this?" Ruiz asked the old lady.

"Apartment fourteen," she said.

"And you say this was around midnight."

"Midnight exactly," the lady said.

"Well, what I want to know is does she have the right to send my kid to Jersey," Reardon said into the phone. He listened. "Her parents there," he said, and listened again. "Sixty-five, something like that. Her father used to work for the phone company, he's retired now." He listened again.

"Has this happened before?" Ruiz asked.

"All the time," the lady said.

"What?" Ruiz said.

"What?" Reardon said. "Well, how the hell do I know if we can show they're unfit?"

"What do you mean by all the time?" Ruiz asked.

"Every night," the lady said.

"*Every* night?"

"At midnight. I think he's in love with me."

"Uh-huh," Reardon said into the phone. "Uh-huh. All right, how about this after-noon sometime? No, I can't right now, Martin. How about lunch? Well, when *are* you free? Okay, two o'clock, I'll see you then, fine," he said, and hung up.

"Do you know who this man is?" Ruiz said.

"Yes. He's John Travolta," the lady said.

Ruiz looked at her.

"He's in love with me," she said.

"Who was that?" Hoffman asked Reardon.

"My lawyer," Reardon said. "The fucking asshole." He glanced quickly to where the old lady was now telling Ruiz about Travolta jumping off the screen one time to kiss her.

"What's the problem now?" Hoffman asked.

"I'm trying to see my *daughter*, that's the problem."

"Calm down," Hoffman said. "I'm not the one who sent her to Jersey."

"Yeah," Reardon said, but he was still steaming.

Hoffman picked up the report from where Farmer had dropped it on the desk. "There's something missing from this," he said.

"There's a *lot* missing from it," Reardon said.

"Calm down, willya?"

"There's a goddamn family been busted up for no reason at all," Reardon said.

"Whose family are you talking about, Bry?" Hoffman asked. "The D'Annunzios . . . or yours?"

Reardon stared at him.

Ruiz said, "I'll call Mr. Travolta personally and tell him to stop bothering you."

"No, don't tell him to stop bothering me,"

the lady said. "Just tell him to stop doing it so late at night."

"I'm sorry," Reardon said.

"Just don't let it get to you, okay?" Hoffman said.

"What *about* the report?"

"Remember the people we were questioning on the street?"

"Yeah?"

"Where was Sadie?"

"Who?"

"Sadie. The shopping bag lady. She's usually in that doorway across from the restaurant, isn't she? That's where she *lives*, Bry. That doorway is her *home*."

"Maybe she went south for the holidays," Reardon said. "Found herself a warmer doorway on Chambers Street."

"I think we ought to look for her," Hoffman said.

"Tell him to bother me around nine, nine-thirty," the old lady said as she left the squadroom.

New York City's Bowery was a desperate place at any time of the year, but today, with soot-stained snow piled against the gutters and a harsh wind blowing, it seemed more forbidding than usual. The drunks appeared paralyzed. Normally, they would be out in the middle of the street, offering to wipe the windshields of cars stopped for traffic lights, hoping to pick up a quarter here, a nickel there. Or they would be on the sidewalks, making their pitch to whatever pedestrian happened to pass, people here to shop the various wholesale supply houses that lined either side of the avenue. Below Delancey, you had your stores selling lighting fixtures and a handful of stores selling glassware and cutlery. Above Delancey, the restaurant supply stores took over in earnest—kitchen equipment, cash registers, china, plumbing, pizza ovens—and in the midst of all this, an advance scout probing enemy terrain, was a lone Chinese chicken market. The drunks, the homeless of this city, sat huddled in doorways, staring glassy-eyed into the cold, all of them candidates for freezing to death. The thermometer outside one of the banks on Canal Street had read twelve degrees when Reardon and Hoffman drove past it. It felt colder than that now that they were out of the car.

"It's the wind-chill factor," Hoffman said.

They played the canvass by the book, the way Farmer would have liked it.

"Lady in her sixties. Her name's Sadie.

The shopping bag lady. Sadie. You seen her around?"

"What's her last name?" a drunk asked. He was sitting in a doorway near the Bowery Mission. He had tied newspapers around his trouser legs. He had wet his pants, and the urine had soaked through the newspapers.

"We don't know her last name. She's Sadie. She's around all the time. Everybody knows Sadie."

"Don't believe I've had the pleasure," the drunk said.

They continued along the Bowery.

"Cold," Reardon said.

Hoffman nodded. His eyes were tearing.

Another doorway. This one near Grand Street.

Another drunk.

"Sally, did you say?"

"Forget it."

And yet another.

And another.

The wind howling through the Bowery with a vengeance.

Nearing the northernmost boundary of the precinct now, the Salvation Army–Booth House between Rivington and Stanton. A man there told them he'd seen Sadie on Monday.

"Monday when?" Hoffman asked.

"The afternoon sometime."

"She didn't come in Monday *night*, did she? After seven o'clock?"

"Not while I was here," the man said. "Why? What'd she do?"

Doubling back on the other side of the avenue now, a hotel near the corner of Broome Street, the room clerk telling them she'd taken a room there on Monday night.

"Is she still here?" Reardon asked.

"No, she only had cash enough for the one night."

"When did she leave?" Hoffman asked.

"Early yesterday morning."

"Did she say where she was going?"

"Yeah, Paris, France," the clerk said drily. "There's lots of garbage cans in Paris, France."

It was warmer in the car, even though the heater wasn't functioning properly. They cruised the streets, looking. Plenty of shopping bag ladies, but none of them Sadie. Plenty of men lying in doorways. Plenty of people passing by them hurriedly. The wind lashed the snow piled against the curbs, sent eddies into the air so that it seemed it was snowing again.

"Lost souls," Hoffman said. "Every fucking one of 'em. Some of these guys, they're probably doctors, lawyers, maybe, lost themselves in a fuckin' bottle."

"You want to break for lunch?" Reardon asked.

"Let's hit a few more places," Hoffman said.

"You bucking for Commissioner?"

"Fat chance. In this city, unless you're Irish or black, you haven't got a prayer above Captain."

"You mean *I* might make Commissioner?" Reardon said, grinning.

"Sure, go talk to your rabbi."

The men fell silent. The heater rattled and clanged.

"Fuckin' jungle out there," Hoffman said.

They continued riding in silence.

"You talk about promotions," Hoffman said, "that robbery bust ain't helping me, either."

"What do you mean?"

"That missing cash."

"Come on," Reardon said.

"They think I *bagged* that fuckin' loot," Hoffman said.

"Nobody thinks that."

"They don't, huh? I'm fifty years old, I broke that case nine years ago. Nine fuckin' years, Bry. I was Detective/First at the time, and I'm *still* Detective/First. Somebody up there's got his eye on me, Bry. There's a folder up there at Headquarters, it's marked Chick Hoffman, and under my name it says 'Hold.' I'm in a holding pattern, Bry. I could find Judge Crater tomorrow, and I *still* won't get a promotion. You know what it feels like to be in a job you know you do pretty damn good, and there ain't no future in—"

"Up ahead," Reardon said.

"What?"

"There she is."

Sadie was standing in front of a building near Hester Street, picking through the garbage can out front. They pulled the car to the curb. Hoffman was already on the sidewalk as Reardon turned off the ignition. Sadie looked up as Hoffman approached, recognized him right off as a cop, and seemed about to run.

"Hello, Sadie," Hoffman said. "How you doing?"

Sadie held her ground, her eyes shifting to Reardon as he came up.

"Got a few minutes?" Hoffman said. "We'd like to talk to you."

"I'm busy just now," Sadie said.

"Come on, we'll buy you a drink," Reardon said.

"Why not?" Sadie said at once.

At a little before one that afternoon, the Cathay Bar on Bayard Street was virtually empty. Three Chinese men sat at the bar on stools, but that was it. There were two empty shot glasses in front of Sadie. She had downed each of the shots in something like two seconds flat, and was working on the third one now, savoring it this time, lingering over it.

"Where were you Monday night, Sadie?" Reardon asked. "How come you weren't in your doorway?"

"I was out with some friends," Sadie said.

"Doing what?" Hoffman asked.

"We went to a movie."

"What movie?"

"I forget the name. It was cowboys."

"Cowboys, huh?"

"Yeah, cowboys," she said, and smiled, pleased with her answer. Her blue eyes were shrewd in her face. She peered out at them from behind a scarf wrapped around her head and under her chin. She sipped at her whiskey again, gauged what was left in the shot glass, wondering how long she could keep them here buying drinks for her.

"How come you haven't been back to Mulberry Street?" Reardon asked.

"I been there," she said.

"Not in your usual doorway."

"Yeah, but I been there."

"You don't like that doorway anymore?" Hoffman asked.

"I like it fine," Sadie said, and shrugged. "But there's plenty other doorways this city." She looked at the shot glass hesitantly and then, apparently deciding she could take a chance on their generosity, swallowed the rest of the whiskey in a single gulp. She looked into the empty glass mournfully. She looked up at the detectives. Her eyes were startlingly blue. Reardon suddenly realized that she must have once been a very beautiful woman. He signalled to the bartender, pointed to Sadie's glass. The bartender was not accustomed to giving table service, but he knew the Law when he saw it. He hurried over with a bottle.

"Leave the bottle," Reardon said.

"So how come?" Hoffman said.

"How come what?" Sadie said, pouring for herself.

"How come you ain't been back to that doorway?"

"I got tired of that doorway," she said,

drinking. "I like to try different doorways every now and then."

"You haven't tried a different doorway for the past three years," Reardon said.

"Well, time for a change, right?" Sadie said, again pleased with her answer, her blue eyes twinkling.

"Where you living now, Sadie?"

"Well, I found a nice doorway on Kenmare the night after the . . ."

She stopped dead.

"The night after the what?" Reardon said.

"Snowstorm," she said at once.

"You talking about last night?" Hoffman said.

"Musta been."

"Or *Monday* night?"

"No, no. Monday night, I slept at the Chelsea."

"How come no doorway?"

"Well, I had a little money, so I figured . . ."

"Were you afraid to sleep in a doorway on Monday night?"

"Why would I be afraid?"

"You tell us," Reardon said.

"No, I wasn't afraid."

"What were you afraid of, Sadie?"

"Did something scare you, Sadie?"

"Did you see the shooting, Sadie?"

"I didn't see no shooting Monday night," Sadie said.

"Who said the shooting was on Monday night?"

"You just asked me . . ."

"Where were you on Monday night, Sadie?"

"I told you," she said. "At the movies."

"Which movie?"

"The cowboys."

"Not the *picture*, the *theater*," Hoffman said. "What theater was it?"

"The one on Bowery and Hester."

"The Music Palace?"

"Yeah."

"That's a Chinese theater," Hoffman said.

"It only shows Chinese pictures," Reardon said.

"Yeah, it was Chinese cowboys," Sadie said.

"You were in your usual doorway on Monday night, weren't you?" Reardon said.

"You saw the shooting, didn't you?" Hoffman said.

"What'd you see, Sadie?"

"*Were* you in your doorway as usual?"

"Nossir," she said, and poured herself another drink.

"You've got nothing to be afraid of,"

Reardon said. "If you saw something, you can tell us."

"Sure, and get in trouble," Sadie said.

"A man's been killed," Hoffman said. "We want to lock up whoever did it."

"Sure, and they'll be out in six months."

"They?" Reardon said.

"How do you know there was more than one of them, Sadie?"

"I don't know *how* many there was. I didn't see nothing."

"Sadie, if we catch these men, we'll send them away for a long, long time. You don't have to worry, Sadie. If you saw something . . ."

"I don't want no trouble," Sadie said. "I got a good life, I don't want no trouble."

"*Did* you see them?" Hoffman asked.

Sadie looked down into her shot glass.

"Sadie?" Reardon said. "Please help us."

She kept staring into her glass.

"I got a good life," she said.

The detectives said nothing.

"I don't want trouble," she said.

They waited.

At last she looked up. There were tears in her eyes.

"I saw them," she said.

"Where were you?" Hoffman asked.

"In my doorway. They pulled up in a car."

"How many of them?"

"Three. One stayed in the car."

"Were they wearing masks?"

"Not when they pulled up."

"What'd they look like?"

"They were Puerto Ricans."

"All three of them?"

"All three."

"What kind of car were they driving?"

"A brown Mercedes-Benz."

Hoffman looked at Reardon.

"Armed robbers in a Mercedes-Benz?" he said. "You sure it wasn't a Chevy?"

"I know my cars," Sadie said. "It was a Mercedes-Benz."

"Did you happen to notice the license plate?"

"No. I mind my own business."

"Was it a New York plate?"

"I didn't see it."

"Three Puerto Ricans in a Mercedes-Benz," Reardon said.

"Grand Larceny, Auto," Hoffman said bleakly.

"Okay, Sadie, thanks," Reardon said, and both men got up.

"Could you leave the bottle, please?" Sadie said in a very small voice.

It was close to one-thirty in the afternoon when Sarge let himself into the brownstone on East Seventy-first Street. He took his key from the latch, put it back into his trouser pocket, and then hung his overcoat on the brass rack just inside the ground-level entrance door.

"Jessie?" he called.

There was no answer.

He draped his muffler over the coat, called "Jessie?" again, and walked into the living room. There was the aroma of dead ashes in the room. And stale cigarette smoke. Unwashed brandy snifters were on the coffee table in front of the fireplace. A woman's high-heeled shoe rested on its side on the hearth.

Sarge walked to the staircase leading to the upper stories.

"Jessie?" he said again, and started up the carpeted steps. A stained-glass window on the first-floor landing, sunlight streaming through it. To the right, the dining room and kitchen. He went up to the second floor, where the bedrooms were. An oak door at the end of the hallway, a brass doorknob. He twisted the doorknob, opened the door a crack.

"Jessie?" he whispered.

She was asleep in the canopied four-poster bed on the other side of the room, quilt pulled to her chin, long black hair spread on the pillow. He stepped into the room, stood watching her silently for a moment, the exquisite nose and high cheekbones, the fair complexion, exactly the picture of their mother when she was young. "Jessie?" he said again.

She stirred.

Sleepily, she said, "What time is it?"

"Half past one," Sarge said.

"Crack of dawn," Jessica said, and rolled over, her eyes still closed.

He stood watching her.

"Late party last night," she mumbled into the pillow.

"You ought to get up, though," he said. "Day's half gone already."

"*What* time did you say?" Her eyes still closed.

"One-thirty."

"Mmm," she said. One eye opened. "I feel awful," she said, and eased herself to a sitting postion. "Oh, boy, do I feel awful."

"I'll make you some coffee," Sarge said.

"I don't want any coffee," Jessica said.

She threw back the quilt, swung her long legs over the side of the bed, and sat there a moment, her hands folded in her lap, head bent, long black hair hiding half her face. She was wearing a pale blue babydoll nightgown. She curled her toes, stared at her feet.

"Has Olivia gone back to Phoenix?" she asked.

"Early this morning."

"Good riddance," she said, and got off the bed. She was wearing no panties under the nightgown. There was a flash of dark pubic hair as she came off the bed, stretched, yawned, and then padded silently to the bathroom. Sarge heard her spitting into the sink. He heard the shower starting.

"What's going on, Sarge?" she asked.

"What do you mean?"

"What?"

"I said . . ."

"I can't hear you. Come in here, will you?"

He went to the bathroom door, stood in the doorframe. She was reaching into the shower stall, testing the stream of water with her right hand.

"Why can't I go to Switzerland?"

"Because you're needed here," Sarge said.

"Since when am *I* needed anywhere? It's my *signature* that's needed, isn't it?"

"Well . . . yes. Or perhaps not. It depends. Your signature won't be needed unless it's asked for. But in that event, the Captain wants you here in New York."

"Are we buying something?"

"Yes."

"What?"

"I'd rather not say."

"But is that why you sold all your paintings?"

She pulled the nightgown over her head, stood there naked a moment, her back to him, and then stepped into the shower.

"Is it?" she asked.

"Let's say we needed some ready cash," Sarge said.

He could see her soaping herself behind the frosted glass door of the shower stall. He remembered once—when they were both children—the beating his father had given him because he'd been in the bathroom while Jessica was bathing. Six years old, she was then. Playing with a rubber toy in the bathtub, suds all around her. Sarge sitting on the toilet bowl, the lid down, watching her as she bathed. Eight years old at the time.

"So you were the one who had to make the sacrifice, huh?" Jessica said.

"It wasn't such a sacrifice."

Wanted to kill his father that night. Lay in bed, aching everywhere, planning how he would kill his father.

"Don't lie to me," Jessica said. "I know what those paintings meant to you."

Soaping herself. Distorted image behind the frosted glass. Hands gliding over her body.

"Was it the Captain's idea to sell them?"

Water splashing. Her voice sounding hollow in the stall.

"Yes."

"Really needs money that badly, huh?"

"No, he simply felt they were the most expendable asset." He shrugged. "This isn't a big deal, Jessie."

"Tell me what it is," Jessica said.

"I'd rather not," he said.

"Why?"

"Knowing can be dangerous."

She turned off the water. He heard her sighing deeply. Behind the glass, she ran her hands over her body again, sweeping droplets from it. She opened the stall door then, and stepped onto the tiled floor, naked, reaching for a towel. Tardily, she said,

"Turn your back." And then, the towel wrapped around her already, she said, "Never mind."

She started out of the bathroom, paused where he was standing in the doorframe, reached up to touch his cheek gently, smiled, and then went into the bedroom. He turned to watch her.

"What's *Olivia* giving up?" she asked.

"Well . . ."

"Nothing, right?"

She went to her dresser, opened the top drawer, took from it a pair of rose-colored, lace-edged panties and a matching garter belt. She rummaged in the drawer, searching for a pair of similarly hued nylons.

"The Captain wouldn't *dream* of asking *her* to sell her precious horses in Kentucky, would he?"

"Well, the horses aren't worth all that much," Sarge said.

"Still, he didn't ask her, did he?"

"No, he didn't."

Jessica went to the bed, dried herself, tossed the towel aside, and fastened the garter belt around her waist. She did not ask him to turn his back, and he did not. He remembered the first time he'd seen her breasts. Thirteen years old, she was, the Captain would have killed him. Standing only in panties at the bathroom sink, breasts cupped in her hands, looking at herself in the mirror. *Are they too small?* she'd asked. He'd assured her they weren't too small.

"Of course not," she said, sitting on the bed again and extending one leg, pulling a nylon onto it, smoothing it up over her calves. "*You* have to sell your paintings, *I* have to give up my trip to Switzerland, but Olivia just goes her merry way."

He said nothing. He watched as she put on the other stocking, clasped it to the garter belt, and stepped into her panties. Again, the flash of dark pubic hair. He remembered once—this was later, when they were teenagers—watching her dress for the beach. "My summer trim," she'd said, smiling, and then stepped into the bikini.

She went back to the dresser, took a half-slip from it, and put it on. No bra. She had not worn a bra for as long as he could remember. She walked to her dressing table, sat, crossed her long legs, picked up a hairbrush and began brushing out her hair.

"I've still got all my pre-Columbian stuff," Sarge said, shrugging.

"How kind of him to let you keep it," Jessica said. She was looking at herself in the mirror, stroking her hair with the brush, preening for the mirror, sitting straight upright, firm breasts moving only slightly to the rhythm of the brush strokes. She smiled at him. "Tell me what the big deal is," she said.

"I can't," he said. "Not till after Christmas."

"What's so special about *before* Christmas?"

"Big secret," Sarge said, smiling.

"Surely you can trust your own sister with a secret," she said. Right hand still moving. Rhythmic brush strokes. Breasts jiggling.

"Not this one," he said.

"Tell me, Sarge," she said, her eyes meeting his in the mirror.

"Can't."

"You used to tell me everything," she said, a pouting look on her face. "Tell me, Sarge."

He shook his head. "No use even asking, Jess."

"Meanie," she said, and smiled again. Putting down the brush, she turned suddenly on the stool, her long legs together, toes pointed, hands on her thighs. "When are *you* going back to Phoenix?" she asked.

"I've got to stay in New York," he said. "Same as you."

"For what?"

"The money from Sotheby's, for one."

"And your signature?"

"Well . . ."

"If needed?"

She rose, walked past him to the closet, selected a simple sheath, pulled it over her head, smoothed it over her hips. She knelt to pick up a pair of matching high-heeled shoes. She sat on the edge of the bed, crossed her legs, put on first one shoe, then the other.

"Want to go dancing with me some night this week?" she asked.

"I'm not much good at that disco stuff you do," he said.

She rose again, walked to where he was standing.

"I'll teach you," she said, and kissed him dangerously close to his mouth.

This was the old city.

This was where the Dutch had been. Narrow streets lined with tall buildings, but Reardon could still visualize horse-drawn carts rumbling over these cobblestones. Historic New York. Now the bastion of high finance and the law.

The law offices of Martin Bennett (né

Berman) were in a building on Beaver Street, not far from the Fraunces Tavern. Bennett owned the building, and most of his time was spent supervising leases and collecting rents. Reardon had once done a favor for him, tracking down an errant client by using the Identification Section's base file at Headquarters, and Bennett was now handling the divorce action gratis. Reardon was willing to take a freebie wherever and however it was offered—unless it was linked to criminal activity. But sometimes he wondered if he wouldn't be better off with an attorney more skilled in matters matrimonial.

Bennett was a man in his late fifties, perpetually smiling, eternally puffing on one or another huge-bowled pipe with a curving stem. He rather resembled a sharp-nosed Sherlock Holmes, minus the deer-stalker hat and the ability to reach conclusions on the basis of sparse information. His brows were thick and shaggy; Reardon suspected he never clipped them, further suspected he thought of them as a sort of trademark, like Michael Jackson's white glove. His desk was always piled high with papers. Infallibly, he could reach to the bottom of any stack, or the middle, or a spot a third of the way down, and pull from the untidy sheaf the exact document he wanted. A conjuror's trick. No Sherlock Holmes, but something of a magician in his own right. Sitting behind his barrier of yellowing papers, a cloud of thick smoke floating above his head, he puffed on his pipe and serenely reported on the latest development in the case of Reardon v. Reardon. The clock on the wall behind his desk read 2:10 P.M.

"Why didn't you tell me this on the phone this morning?" Reardon asked.

"Because I didn't *have* it this morning," Bennett said. "Her lawyer called ten minutes ago."

"And said they've got a court order?"

"Right. Forbidding you to see either Kathy or your daughter." Bennett puffed on his pipe. "Have you been making a pest of yourself, Bry?"

"A pest?" Reardon said. "She ships my daughter to Jersey, her parents live way the hell over near the Pennsylvania border . . ."

"The order says you've been harassing her," Bennett said.

"I haven't. Who signed it?"

"A judge named Santangelo. We'll have it here in half an hour. I sent a messenger for it." Bennett paused. He puffed on his pipe again. He looked quizzically at the bowl, and

129

then struck a wooden match and held it to the dottle. Great clouds of smoke surrounded his head, drifted up toward the old tin ceiling in the book-lined room. No, he wasn't Sherlock Holmes, after all. He was somebody out of *Great Expectations*. "They found out about your rape case," he said, puffing, the match still held to the bowl of the pipe, his eyes looking up over the bowl.

"What do you mean?" Reardon said. "*Who* found out? Found out *what?*"

"Kathy, her lawyer, who knows? About your roughing up that guy after . . ."

"What? Who the hell . . . ?"

"It's a matter of public record," Bennett said.

"Public *record?* I testified I never laid a *hand* on that punk!"

Bennett shrugged and tossed the charred matchstick into an oversized ash tray brimming with pipe cleaners and other matchsticks and the gummy residue of dottles past. "Santangelo apparently read the record and believed what he wanted to believe," he said. "As far as he's concerned, you're a violent man who's been harassing a woman who wants a divorce. What can I tell you, Bry? He signed the order."

"So what does that mean?" Reardon asked tightly.

"It means you stay away from them. Period."

"No way."

"Bry . . ."

"No fucking *way!*"

Reardon did not get to the funeral home on Canal Street until almost three o'clock. The shortest day of the year was still four days away, but because of the overcast it seemed as if darkness had already come. The feeling of gloom persisted inside the chapel, lined with sconces of artificial light pretending to be eternal flames or some damn thing, banks of flowers imitating spring, but neither flames nor flowers able to disguise the fact that this was a chamber of death.

At an Irish wake, you told the bereaved, "I'm sorry for your trouble."

He was here to tell the D'Annunzio family that he was sorry for their trouble.

The chapel was crowded with family and friends. Ralph D'Annunzio's body lay in an open coffin at the far end of the room. He had been shot four times, but in the back, and the undertaker's cosmetic art had not been needed to cover any face wounds.

He looked very dead, nonetheless. Whenever anyone at a wake said to Reardon, "He looks so natural," or "He looks like he's sleeping," Reardon silently thought, *Bullshit*. They looked *dead* is what they looked. He hesitated in the doorway, searching for Mrs. D'Annunzio or her son. He spotted Mark D'Annunzio talking quietly with a small group of people, and as he started toward him, Mark saw him and came to him instead, his hand extended.

"Mr. Reardon," he said, sounding surprised. "Thanks for coming by."

"Are you all right?" Reardon asked, taking his hand.

"Well, you know," Mark said.

"I brought these with me," Reardon said, and handed Mark a manila Evidence envelope. "Your father's personal effects. I thought you might like to have them."

"Thank you," Mark said, and took the envelope.

"Mr. Reardon?"

He turned. Marie D'Annunzio, the dead man's wife, now the dead man's widow, dressed in black, no makeup on her face, eyes vaguely out of focus, tear stains on her cheeks, hand extended. Reardon took her hand in both his own.

"*Signora,*" he said softly. "I'm so sorry."

I'm sorry for your trouble, he thought.

"Thank you," she said.

Awkwardly, he held her hand between his own.

"He brought papa's things," Mark said.

"Thank you," she said again. Her eyes met Reardon's. "Have you learned anything yet?" she asked.

"Not very much," Reardon said. He released her hand. He didn't know what to do with his hands. "You wouldn't know anyone who drives a brown Mercedes sedan, would you?" he asked.

"*Cosa?*"

"That's a car, Mom," Mark said, and then shook his head. "I can't think of anybody," he said.

"Would your father have had any business dealings with Puerto Ricans?"

"Mom?" Mark said.

"No," she said.

"Did any Puerto Ricans come to the restaurant this past week?"

"I don't remember any."

"To talk to your father, to eat, whatever."

"That wasn't a Spanish accent, Mr. Reardon," Mark said. "I can tell you that."

133

"We have a witness who saw three Puerto Ricans," Reardon said.

"I don't see how that can be," Mark said. "Mom? Did they sound Spanish to you?"

"No, not Spanish," Mrs. D'Annunzio said.

"Can you remember what they *did* sound like? It wasn't Chinese, was it?"

"No, not Chinese," Mark said.

"No," Mrs. D'Annunzio said.

"Well," Reardon said, and sighed. "Mrs. D'Annunzio, when I was going through your husband's wallet . . . it's right there in the stuff I brought back . . . I found a credit-card receipt for an airline ticket. It was dated the fourteenth of December, that would've been the day before the holdup. A Sunday. Would your husband have had any reason to fly anywhere on that day?"

"Yes," Mrs. D'Annunzio said, nodding. "His brother lives in Washington."

"Is that where your husband went?"

"Yes. We're closed on Sundays. He figured that would be a good time to go."

"To see his brother?"

"Yes."

"Would you know why?"

"No."

"What's his brother's name, can you tell me?"

"John D'Annunzio."

"He's the maitre d' at a fancy restaurant there," Mark said. "I have the name and address at the house, if you want them."

"Yes, please," Reardon said, "and his home address and phone number, too, if you've got those. I'll stop by later." He paused. "If there's anything I can do for you, anything you need . . ."

"Thank you," Mrs. D'Annunzio said, and took his hand again.

He kept thinking *I'm sorry for your trouble.*

5

PUT Stuyvesant Town and Peter Cooper Village together, Reardon thought, and they'd be a fair-sized town in some parts of the country. That was the amazing thing about this city. You tried to explain to somebody from Brindleshit, Wyoming, that you could fit his whole damn *town* into any given New York neighborhood, and he sucked wind through his teeth and looked at you like you were crazy. The two housing developments on the East River ran north and south for a total of seven blocks, almost a third of a mile, and then another three blocks—*longer* blocks because they were running east to west—between First Avenue and the river. Red brick buildings—well, they looked more brown than they did red—bordered on the north by Bellevue, where Kathy had done her nurse's training, and on the south by another conglomeration of buildings that formed yet another town-sized development;

the Jacob Riis Houses, the Lillian Wald Houses, the Baruch Houses. Choice waterfront real estate for the lower middle class. When he was living in Stuyvesant Town, it wasn't too bad a commute to the station house. Walk up Fourteenth Street to the IRT subway stop on Third Avenue, take the downtown local to Canal—only four stations away, Astor Place, Bleecker, Spring, and then Canal—walk up the block to Elizabeth Street, and there you were. Your home away from home.

This apartment, the sound of tugs on the river, Greenpoint on the other side, a glimpse of the Queensboro Bridge farther uptown—the cops in this city remembered the names of the bridges by putting them in alphabetical order, starting with the Brooklyn Bridge, farthest south, and then the Manhattan, and then the Williamsburg, but the system went to pot when you got to the Queensboro on Fifty-ninth Street—this apartment used to be his home. It no longer was. Kathy lived here now. And his daughter. When she wasn't with her goddamn grandparents in Jersey.

"I shouldn't have let you in," she said.

It was seven-thirty in the morning. A bleak gray Thursday, the eighteenth day of

December, a week before Christmas. She was dressed for work, except for her shoes. She was sitting in what used to be his favorite easy chair, lacing up her flat white shoes.

"My lawyers told me . . ."

"That's just what I want to talk about," Reardon said, "your lawyers. Martin tells me they've got a signed court order . . ."

"I don't know about a court order," Kathy said. "I'm leaving this entirely to them, Bry. And I wish *you* would too." She gave the lace a tug on the word "you." She had a habit of emphasizing language with gestures, adding force to vocabulary.

"No, I'm not leaving it to any lawyers," Reardon said. "Not where my daughter's concerned." He hesitated and then said, "Have you put a private eye on me, Kath?"

"Of course not," she said, and rose, and went into the kitchen. A pot of coffee was brewing on the stove. She poured herself a cup, and did not offer him one.

"Then how'd they find out about my testimony yesterday?"

"I don't know what you're talking about."

Sipping at the coffee. Probably went against her grain not to be able to extend a hospitality that was second nature to her. But making a point. This is *my* home now.

You do not belong here. The coffee is mine. The cups are mine. You are not wanted here.

"They're claiming I roughed up a punk who raped . . ."

"I don't want to hear it," she said.

"They're claiming I'm a violent man who's harassing. . ."

"You *are* harassing me!" she said. "You come in here at seven in the morning . . ."

"Seven-thirty . . ."

"Yelling and screaming . . . I'm not even *awake* yet!"

"The hospital told me . . ."

"You shouldn't have called the hospital."

"I had to talk to you."

"There's nothing to talk about."

"There's the fucking *court* order to talk about!"

"I told you I don't know anything about a court order." She put down the coffee cup, went to where her cape was draped over a chair, her nurse's cap lying on the seat. She picked up the cap, pinned it to her hair. "I have to go," she said. "I'll be late."

"The court order says I can't see you or Elizabeth anymore," Reardon said. "Why'd you do that, Kath? Do you really hate me that much?"

"I don't hate you," she said.

"Then why'd you do it?"

"I didn't do *anything*, damn it. I've been leaving it to the lawyers. If they asked for a court order . . ."

"They did. And they got it."

"I'll tell them to tear it up, okay? Or whatever the hell you do with something like that."

"No, it's not that simple."

"What do you want from me, Bry? I'll call my parents, okay? I'll tell them you can see Elizabeth no matter *what* the order says."

"Fine," he said, and paused. "*Did* you know about that order?"

"I told you I didn't."

"You told me a lot of things, Kath."

"Bry, I've got to leave." Putting on her cape, not looking at him, she said, "Please don't come here again."

"I used to live here," he said.

"You don't anymore."

Reardon sighed. "Okay, call them," he said.

"When I get to the hospital," she said, and looked at her watch. "I'm already late."

"Tell them I'll be there this afternoon. As soon as I'm out of court."

"I'll tell them."

"I miss her, Kath," he said gently, and paused again. "I miss you, too."

Ignoring this, she went to the door, opened it, and waited for him to go out of the apartment before she locked the door behind her.

In the hallway, she said, "I hope I can catch a taxi."

It was cold even in Phoenix. The forecasters said an Arctic front was sweeping down over most of the country. The sun was shining here, but it was cold. For Phoenix, anyway. Thirty-four degrees. The rambling house had not been built for such weather. The mean maximum wintertime temperature was supposed to be sixty-five degrees. Thirty-four was incredible. The house was centrally heated, but somehow psychology worked against reality when the temperature dropped so low. It wasn't *supposed* to be this cold here. When it got this cold, there seemed no way to keep the house warm, empirical knowledge to the contrary. Expectations, Olivia thought. Tell someone you're serving him pineapple juice, hand him a glass of fine white wine instead, and he'll spit it out because he was expecting pineapple juice. The black eggs. Somewhere, she forgot where, chickens laid eggs with black yolks. The locals ate those eggs, but nobody else would. They expected *yellow* yolks. The black-yolked eggs tasted exactly the same, but sorry. Expectations.

The house she'd grown up in could have been designed by Frank Lloyd Wright, would have been designed by him—money was no object—if he hadn't been busy with a hundred other projects when her father approached him. Low and rambling, with massive stone walls and large areas of glass, it sprawled over the Arizona landscape as if it were a part of it, there when the land was being formed. Arid land for the most part, though through the large pane of glass in the study Olivia could see a dozen or more horses grazing in a meadow that glistened like an emerald in sand. Beyond that, the open mouth of the abandoned copper mine, inoperative now, but a reminder. The study was distinctly Western in flavor, the furnishings and carpeting echoing the earth tones of the landscape, the several pieces of Sarge's pre-Columbian sculpture—the major part of his collection was stored in New York—emphasizing the brownish-red tones.

Andrew Kidd sat behind a desk in that study.

He was in a wheelchair.

He was wearing a blue robe. A blanket was over his lap. His face was pale, his blue eyes rheumy, the skin on his hands virtually translucent, strewn with liver spots. Sunlight touched his bald head as he looked over the papers on his desk. Seventy-eight years old. Olivia could remember when they used to ride the fields together, his blond hair blowing in the wind, his hands strong on the reins.

"You're not drinking your tea," she said.

"I don't like drinking through a straw," he said.

"It'll take the chill off, Daddy."

"You get old, it always seems too cold. Why do you suppose that is?"

"It *is* cold," she said.

"Not as cold as it seems. I hate being old, Livvie."

"You're not old."

"Too damn old," he said. "Where the hell did the time go?" He glanced through the window, where in the distance the ugly copper mine dominated the horizon. "I came out here in 1922 without a cent," he said, "started working for the railroad. Won this patch of godforsaken land in a poker game, thought it was worthless, would've preferred a hundred dollars in cash instead." He nodded, remembering. "Who'd have dreamt there was copper on it?" He nodded again. "I'll never plow that first mine under as long as I live." He turned to her. "I hope you'll leave it there after I'm dead, Livvie."

"You're the only one in the world who calls me Livvie," she said.

"You're the only one who calls me Daddy. Something old-fashioned about 'Daddy.' And nice. Sarge calls me 'Father,' Jessica calls me 'Pop.' Everybody else calls me the Captain, started calling me that when I bought out Lambert Shipping forty years ago. The Captain. Sarge resents it. Thinks I named him Sargent to keep him in his place, the captain and the sergeant. He's wrong. I named him after the painter, John Singer Sargent, best portrait artist who ever lived. Little did I know my only son would turn out to be a *collector*. Was he upset?"

"A little."

"Well, he shouldn't be. I wasn't about to divest the *firm* of anything, not for a small-potatoes deal like this one. What'd he realize on the sale, anyway?"

"A bit over thirty-six million."

"And the margins worldwide? What'll they be costing us?"

"Just about that."

144

"Well, he can buy his pictures back after Christmas. Hundreds more if he feels like."

"I'm sure he knows that."

"How'd Jessie take what you told her?"

"Badly."

"She isn't worth a hill of beans, that girl, as much a nitwit as her mother was, dancing her life away, whoring it away. Only worthwhile thing about her is her signature. Didn't much like your calling off her trip, huh?"

"Not much, Daddy."

"Hell with her. Shoulda whipped her little ass ages ago, taught her how to sit on a raw bottom. Taught Sarge, though. That time in the bathroom with her." He shook his head. "His own sister naked as a sparrow, and him sittin' on the crapper watching her, all eyes. Blistered his bottom till he couldn't walk straight. The shame of it."

He scowled, remembering. And then his face softened.

"You're all I've got, Livvie. I love you to death."

"And I love you," she said softly.

"Ah, I hope so," Andrew said, "I hope so."

He looked through the window again, toward the copper mine in the distance.

"Do you think I'm greedy?" he asked.

"Yes," she said, and smiled.

"There's my girl," he said, returning the smile. "Never lies to me, does she? I'm greedy, you're damn right. You and I both know what'll happen to the Kidd oil interests after Christmas Day. So why am I bothering with this other crap? Why make Sarge unhappy? For a lousy three, four billion worldwide? If indeed we net that much in the long run? Peanuts compared to what we'll realize on the oil alone. But I can't be bothered with Sarge's . . . do you know the story about the Texas oil man and the Chicano?"

"No," she said.

"This Texas oil zillionaire . . ."

"Like you."

"Yes, except I'm in Arizona. This Texas oil zillionaire is sitting at the back of a little chapel, praying, when this little Chicano comes in, goes to the altar, looks up at Christ on the cross there, and begins praying out loud. 'Lord,' he says . . . I wish I could do a Spanish accent, Livvie, but I can't . . . 'Lord,' he says, 'I really need your help. My wife just gave birth to our fifth baby, and she's very sick, and my son is in jail, and my daughter is a prostitute, and if you could find a way for me to get five hundred dollars, I would be very grateful. Five hundred dollars is all I need, Lord, that's all I'm asking for, can you please help me?' Well, the big Texan goes up to the altar, and he hands the little Chicano five hundred bucks, and he says to him, 'Here, don't bother *Him* with that shit.' "

Andrew burst out laughing.

"So what Sarge must be wondering is why *I'm* bothering with *this* shit. Well, if he should ask you, Livvie . . ."

"I don't think he'll ask me."

"I'm saying *if* he should. You just tell him it's greed. Good, old-fashioned *greed*. I want it *all*, Livvie, whatever I can lay my hands on. Before I die, I want to . . ."

"I don't want to hear you talk about dying," she said.

"We've all got to go sooner or later."

"Not you."

"No?" he said, smiling. "What'll you do? Have me stuffed and put me in the living room?"

"Don't *joke* about it!" she said angrily.

"There's what I mean, Livvie. The Kidd iron, the Kidd temper. We're alike, you and I, peas in a pod. God help anyone who ever tries to stand in your way."

She came to him, put her arm around his shoulders.

"Shall I pour you some hot tea?" she asked gently.

"No, I think I'd like to rest now," he said.

She adjusted the blanket on his lap.

"I love you, Daddy," she said.

"Yes, yes," he said, patting her hand. "My darling girl. My dear darling girl."

The jury in the Jurgens case came in at eleven o'clock that morning.

Reardon, sitting at the prosecutor's table with Koenig, watched the faces of the twelve men and women as they filed into the jury box, trying to read what was on them. Judge Abrahams turned to them as soon as they were seated.

"Ladies and gentlemen of the jury," he said, "have you agreed upon a verdict in this case?"

"We have," the foreman said.

"Please return the papers to the Court," the clerk said.

"Madam Foreman," Judge Abrahams said, "what is the jury's verdict?"

"We find the defendant not guilty," the foreman said.

Harold Jurgens broke into a wide grin.

Reardon turned to Koenig at once. "Poll them," he said.

"What for?" Koenig said.

"I want them to realize what they've done. I want them to feel individually responsible."

Koenig sighed and rose.

"Your Honor," he said, "may I respectfully request that the jury be polled?"

Abrahams nodded to the court clerk.

"Juror number one," the clerk said, "Alice Louise Phillips. How do you find the defendant?"

"Not guilty," the foreman said.

"Juror number two, Arthur Horwitz, how do you find the defendant?"

"Not guilty."

"Juror number three, James Kreuger, how do you find the defendant?"

"Not guilty."

"Juror number four, Miriam Hayes, how do you find the defendant?"

"Not guilty."

"Juror number five, Martha Sanderson . . ."

She rose. Brown hair cut shoulder length. Simple brown dress with a brooch at the neckline.

"How do you find the defendant?"

Her eyes turned toward the prosecutor's table. Her eyes found Reardon. She pulled back her shoulders, lifted her head defiantly, brown eyes boring into him.

"Not guilty," she said, and nodded for emphasis.

Her eyes held his.

"Juror number six," the court clerk said, "Alan Lehman . . ."

He was waiting for her in the corridor outside. *This* one he wanted to talk to personally. That fucking look she'd given him, this one he wanted to inform and educate. As she came out of the courtroom, he fell into step beside her. For an instant, she didn't know she was being paced, and then she turned to him with a startled little gasp and stopped dead in the marbled corridor.

"Are you proud of yourself, miss?" he said.

"What?" she said. The brown eyes opening wide, one hand coming up to the brooch at her neckline, protectively. Here she was, face to face with the maniac who'd beaten up a poor defenseless innocent man.

"It's okay, you can talk to me now," Reardon said, "it's all over and done with."

"Listen, mister . . ." she said.

"No, *you* listen," he said. "You've let an animal loose on the streets again, do you realize that?"

"I don't have to account to *you*, Detective Reardon, for the unanimous verdict of . . ."

"Took us six months to catch him, do you know that? He raped four women in that time. We finally got . . ."

"Listen, why don't you . . . ?"

". . . a positive ID, *plus* his fingerprints all over the lady's handbag . . ."

"Then why'd you have to *beat* a confession out of him?"

"You really believe that, don't you?"

"I believe it, yes," she said.

"You're wrong."

"I don't like what you stand for, Detective Reardon," she said. "If one citizen's rights are violated, then *every* citizen's . . ."

"Nobody's fucking rights were violated," he said heatedly. "The man's a habitual offender, a rapist who . . ."

"Tell it to the judge," she said in dismissal. "And watch your fucking language."

She moved away from him swiftly, high heels clattering on the marble corridor, little ass swinging indignantly in the simple brown dress.

Under his breath, he muttered, "I hope you're his *next* victim."

An hour and a half to get here, speeding all the way, hoping his detective's shield would serve him well if a zealous New Jersey highway patrolman stopped him, and too late to take her to lunch, anyway. "She's already *had* lunch," Kathy's mother informed him, and then made it clear that he was not welcome to sit around the house chatting with his own daughter, this despite the fact that the temperature outside had dropped to eighteen degrees and the wind was howling.

Where do you take a six-year-old kid who's already had lunch? He'd be working the four-to-midnight this afternoon, he had to leave Jersey no later than two-thirty, and it was already one o'clock. Could you sit in a Baskin-Robbins for an hour and a half, eating ice cream cones while outside it looked like Siberia? He settled on a roller-skating rink not far from her grandparents' house.

Organ music filled the vast auditorium. He had not been on skates since he was eleven or twelve, but it came back to him almost at once. Elizabeth was an ace. The image of her mother, straight blonde hair and intensely blue eyes, button nose, and freckles all over her Irish phizz, wearing now a plaid skirt and a blue sweater, little Peter Pan collar showing above its crew neck. They moved well together, danced like a famous Spanish ballroom team on wheels. She was telling him about Grandma and Grandpa. Organ music swelled behind them, a tune from the forties.

"They're okay, you know," Elizabeth said, "it's just that they're so *old*, Dad."

"Well, they're not *that* old, honey."

"No? I'll bet Grandpa's at least *forty*."

"At least," Reardon said, smiling.

"They don't like to *do* anything, you know what I mean? We just sit around on our asses all day."

"Watch the language, honey."

"What'd I say?"

"Skip it."

"So why do I have to be here?" Elizabeth asked. "I'm missing school and everything, Dad. I mean, did Mommy *have* to go back to work?"

"It's what she wanted, Liz."

"Are you out of money or something?"

"No, we've got enough money."

" 'Cause I thought we were *rich* and everything. I mean, detectives make lots of money, don't they?"

153

"Millions," he said.

"Well, not millions maybe. But hundreds and thousands of thousands."

"From the graft alone," Reardon said.

"Sure," Elizabeth said. "So why'd she have to go back to work?"

"Honey . . ." he said, "let's get a hot chocolate, okay?"

They skated to the railing, and then through the opening onto a carpeted floor. At the concession stand, he ordered a hot chocolate for Elizabeth, and asked her if she wanted anything else. She said she was still stuffed from lunch. He was ravenously hungry, that damn court appearance this morning, that little twerp Samalson or whatever her name was. He ordered a cup of coffee, two hot dogs, and a side of French fries. They sat at a table with benches, near the concession. The organ player was attempting rock now, a bad mistake. The place was virtually empty at this hour; Reardon guessed it wouldn't fill up until school broke.

"How's the hot chocolate?" he asked.

"Yummy," she said.

They were silent for a moment. The organ player was slaughtering a Stones' tune. A lone skater on the floor twirled like a break dancer.

"Honey," Reardon said, "there's something I've got to tell you. I want you to be a big girl now, and try to understand."

"I am a big girl," she said. Chocolate rimming her mouth. God, how he loved her!

"I know that."

"Bigger even than Suzie, and she's seven."

"Yes, sweetie. So please try to understand what I'm going to tell you."

"Sure, Dad." Her face suddenly solemn, blue eyes wide.

"Liz . . . your mother and I are separated." He looked into her eyes. "Do you know what that means?"

"No, what does it mean?" she said. That innocent face. Christ!

"It means . . . it means we're not living together anymore. All those stories she told you about me having to go down to Miami on an extradition case . . . they weren't true, Liz."

"Then where were you, if not in Miami?" Her eyes puzzled.

"In a hotel. In the city. In New York. I've been living in a hotel, Liz."

"Where?"

"On Twenty-sixth and Broadway."

"Can I come there sometime?" she asked.

"I don't think you'd like it much, Liz."

"When *will* you be going to Miami?"

"I'm not," he said. "That was a lie, Liz. I'm not going to Miami at all."

She stared at him.

"Liz . . . your mother and I are getting a divorce."

"Oh," she said.

The single word. Nothing more. Everything in that single word. And in her wide blue eyes.

"Do you know what divorce means?"

"Yes," she said. "Suzie's divorced."

"Her parents," he said.

"Whoever," she said. She was thoughtful for a moment. Then she asked, "Is that why I'm in New Jersey?"

"Until the lawyers work it out, yes."

"Work what out?"

"Well, the alimony payments, and child support, and . . . there's a lot to be worked out, Liz."

She nodded.

The organ player started "Tennessee Waltz."

"Who will I live with, Dad?" she asked. "After the divorce, I mean."

"Mom, I guess."

"I want to live with both of you," she said.

"Well . . . honey, I'd like that, too, but . . ."

"I love you both," she said, "and I want to live with both of you."

Another nod. A child's simple logic. You love two people, you live with both of them. Period.

"Honey," he said, "that won't be possible."

"Why not?"

"When two people break up . . ."

"Well, why do you and Mom have to break up?"

"I don't know. I really don't know, darling."

She looked into his face. She must have seen something on it—his pain and confusion perhaps, although he was trying very hard to hide it—because suddenly she threw herself into his arms. He held her tight, squeezing his eyes shut, clinging to her desperately.

6

A KEROSENE heater was going in the squad-room at four-thirty that afternoon, enabling the men to work in relative comfort. It was colder outside than it had been this morn-ing. The sun was gone now, the meshed windows showed as only frost-rimed black rectangles. Reardon had been fifteen min-utes late, relieving at four on the dot, rather than at the customary fifteen minutes to the hour. He was on the phone now, trying to get through to Washington, D.C. At his own desk, Gianelli was also on the phone. "Okay, I'll wait," Gianelli said, and rolled his eyes at Reardon. "Ballistics," he said. "I *hate* Bal-listics."

"I know I can dial it direct," Reardon said into his phone. "I've dialed it direct *three* times, and all I get is nothing. Nothing, yes. Zilch. Silence." He listened, and then said, "Well, *could* you please try it for me?"

"Ballistics and the telephone company ought to go partners," Gianelli said.

Haggerty, one of the Fifth's clerks, wearing a blue V-neck sweater over his uniformed shirt and a bulky blue cardigan over that, came into the office carrying a sheet of paper. "Here's the flyer went out," he said to Reardon. "It ain't much for anybody to go on. No year, no plate, just a brown Benz."

"Who got it?" Reardon asked.

"Every precinct in the city."

"I want the whole tri-state area covered."

"Yeah, I'm here," Gianelli said into his phone. "I been here *forever*."

"Won't do no good anyway, Bry," Haggerty said. "This's the week before Christmas, today's already the eighteenth. What cop out there is gonna be looking for cars?"

"A *what?*" Gianelli said into the phone. "I never heard of such a thing. All right, give it to me. Nice and slow, please."

"What they'll be looking for is presents for their wives," Haggerty said.

"Send it out, anyway," Reardon said.

"Or their girlfriends," Haggerty said. "They won't be looking for no brown Benz ain't even got a year or a plate."

"Hello?" Reardon said into the phone, and

159

waved Haggerty out. "Is this the Café de la Daine?"

"*Oui, bien sur,*" the voice on the other end said.

"This is Detective Reardon, I'm calling from the Fifth P.D.U. in New York. I'd like to speak to Mr. John D'Annunzio, please. Is he there?"

"*Oui, monsieur.*"

"May I speak to him, please?"

"*Un moment, s'il vous plait.*"

"Accommodate the *what?*" Gianelli said into his phone. "Well, *was* it? Then what are you wasting my time for?" He paused and then said, "What's the capacity? Right. Anything else? Okay, thanks." He slammed the receiver down on the cradle.

"Hello?" a man's voice said.

"Mr. D'Annunzio?" Reardon said.

"Yes?"

"This is Detective Reardon in Manhattan . . ."

"Yes?"

"I'm assuming you were notified of your brother's death . . ."

"Yes?"

"There are a few questions I'd like to ask you."

"What questions, Mr. Reardon?"

"I understand he went to Washington on the fourteenth of December. Did he go down there to see you, Mr. D'Annunzio?"

"Yes, he did," D'Annunzio said.

"That would have been a Sunday . . ."

"Yes, he came to the restaurant. We're open for dinner on Sunday night."

"Why did he come to see you, Mr. D'Annunzio? Can you tell me that?"

Farmer came limping out of his office. He put his hands on his hips and listened to Reardon's end of the conversation.

"Did he say who'd made this loan to him?" Reardon asked.

Farmer stood listening.

"What?" Reardon said. "I'm sorry, I didn't realize . . . well, what *would* be a convenient time for you?" He listened and then said, "I'll try you later then, thanks."

He replaced the receiver on the cradle, looked up at Farmer.

"D'Annunzio went there to borrow seventy-five hundred bucks. Told his brother he needed the money to meet a loan."

"Who from?" Farmer asked.

"He doesn't know. They're setting up for dinner, he wants me to call him back in an hour or so." He turned to Gianelli. "What'd Ballistics say?"

161

"Is anyone on this squad working anything but the D'Annunzio murder?" Farmer asked.

"Priorities, boss," Gianelli said.

"Priorities, my ass."

"The slugs were nine millimeter Parabellums. The gun . . . just a second." He looked at his notes. "Was a SIG P-210-5."

"A *what?*" Farmer said.

"Foreign pistol. Made in Switzerland, imported here by H.F. Grieder. It can be made to accommodate the 7.65 cartridge, but this one wasn't. The bullets were nine millimeters."

"I never *heard* of such a gun," Farmer said, and then turned at the sound of Hoffman's voice in the corridor outside.

"This city," Gianelli said, "you can pick up any gun you want for thirty-five cents."

Three young Hispanics came into the squadroom, their hands cuffed behind them. Hoffman and Ruiz were directly behind them. In this precinct, the Hispanics could have been anything: Puerto Rican, Cuban, Dominican, Salvadoran, Colombian. To the cops, with the possible exception of Ruiz, they all looked alike. These Hispanics did, in fact, look alike. All of them light-skinned. Each of them sporting a sparse mustache

162

over his upper lip. All in their mid-twenties. All wearing little black fedoras with narrow brims. One of them wore a brown leather jacket. The other two wore short cloth coats. They were all wearing pointed shoes; cockroach-kickers, the cops called them.

"Make yourselves comfortable, you bums," Ruiz said.

"Don't tell me I've actually got some working cops on this squad," Farmer said.

"Caught them sticking up a jewelry store on Canal," Hoffman said, and tossed three ski masks onto the desk. "This is what they were wearing."

Reardon looked at the ski masks.

Sadie had seen three Puerto Ricans wearing ski masks on the night of the murder.

"But no Mercedes-Benz, your Honor," Ruiz said.

"They don't speak English," Hoffman said.

"So they say," Ruiz said. *"Habla inglés, maricón?"* he asked the one in the brown leather jacket.

"No, señor policia," the man replied.

"How about your pals here?" Ruiz said, and turned to the ones in the cloth coats. *"Alguno de ustedes vagabundos habla inglés?"*

The other two answered almost in unison, shaking their heads.

"*No, nosotros no hablamos inglés.*"

"Sit down," Hoffman said, pointing. "Over there, on the bench."

The men sat, their eyes wide. The one in the leather jacket glanced at a Pimp Squad poster on the wall.

Hoffman beckoned Reardon and Ruiz to the other side of the room, where Farmer was standing.

"The guys who killed D'Annunzio were speaking English," he said.

"With an accent," Reardon said.

"But not a *Spanish* accent," Farmer said. "Your report . . ."

"It's worth a shot, anyway," Hoffman said. "The family mighta been too excited to tell what kind of accent. You want to take it from here, Bry?"

"Don't blow it," Farmer warned.

Reardon walked to the bench where the three Hispanics were sitting.

"Which one of you guys speaks English?" he asked.

The three men looked at him, bewildered.

"Nobody, huh?" He turned to Hoffman. "This might be real meat, Chick," he said.

"Looks that way," Hoffman said.

"You're *sure* you don't speak English, huh?"

No answer. Eyes open wide in their faces.

"Because if you do, you'd better tell me right now. Otherwise you're gonna be in hot water, believe me."

"*Que dice el?*" the one in the brown jacket asked Ruiz.

"Keep out of this, Alex," Reardon said. "Okay, listen," he said, hands on his hips. "A restaurant on Mulberry Street was held up this past Monday night. The owner was killed. You understand that?"

Blank stares.

"You don't understand it, huh? Okay, try to understand this. The guys who went in there spoke only Spanish. No English. Only *Spanish*, you got that?"

The men looked from one to the other.

The one in the brown jacket said, "*No entiendo. No hablo inglés.*"

"You don't *entiendo*, huh?" Reardon said. "Here's what I'm telling you, so you better start *entiende*-ing fast. If you speak English, you got nothing to worry about. Otherwise, we're gonna think you were the punks went in there shooting."

Silence. Puzzled frowns.

"Okay? I'll give you thirty seconds."

165

"*Que quiere el?*" the one in the brown jacket asked Ruiz.

"He's not gonna give you any help," Reardon said. "The only thing'll help you is to start talking English."

One of the men in the cloth coats said, "*Nosotros no sabemos que dice usted.*"

"Twenty seconds," Reardon said. "You guys have a possible murder rap hanging over your heads, never mind a two-bit hold-up." He looked at his watch. "Ten seconds," he said.

The telephone rang. Gianelli picked up the receiver.

"Fifth Squad, Gianelli," he said.

"Time's up," Reardon said, and turned to Hoffman. "They're either clean or they're stupid," he said.

"For you, Bry," Gianelli said. "On four. It's Mark D'Annunzio."

"Get Sadie in here," Farmer said. "Run a private little lineup for her."

The one in the brown leather jacket said, "*Usted tiene que decirnos nuestras leyes en español.*"

"*Cállate, pendejo!*" Ruiz said.

Reardon picked up the receiver.

"Hello, Mr. D'Annunzio," he said.

"He wants us to read him his rights in

166

Spanish," Ruiz said to Farmer. He turned to the three men sitting on the bench, and said, *"Yo les voy a dar sus leyes, pendejos!"*

"When was this?" Reardon said into the phone, and listened. "Uh-huh," he said. "Where are you? Uh-huh. Wait for me, I'll be right there."

He hung up.

"Bobby Nardelli was just there to see the D'Annunzio kid," he said. "Told him he wants the interest on the loan they made to his father."

Robert Alfred Nardelli was a small-time hood with three priors, two for burglary and one for assault. He was a sometimes enforcer for the mob's loan-sharking operation, and this bothered Reardon a lot. He had hoped the Monday night murder had nothing to do with the boys. Mark D'Annunzio had told him he couldn't see any connection between his father's death and the mob. "They used to come eat in the restaurant all the time," he'd said. So now he'd been visited by Bobby Nardelli, and Bobby wanted the interest on the loan they'd made. It looked shitty.

He found Bobby in the back room of a furniture store on Baxter Street. The store was the target of a Narcotics Squad stakeout that had been in effect since early August. Reardon supposed the unmarked truck out front had a narc in it, listening on a court-ordered wire. He also supposed Bobby knew the truck was NYPD issue. Nothing much slipped by the thieves in this city. You could bet your ass that the only words going in and out of the store on that telephone were between Bobby and the legion of girls who allegedly swooned everytime he swaggered into sight, God knew why.

Bobby was a man in his late twenties, some six-feet four-inches tall and weighing at least two hundred and twenty pounds. If you were going to have an enforcer, you could do worse than to pick a man like Bobby. His hands on the desk in front of him were huge, with the oversized knuckles of a streetfighter. A small scar ran from the tip of his right eyebrow to a point on the temple. He had eyes that could freeze a desert.

"He owed money," he said, and shrugged. "I went to collect it. Is that against the law? A man going to collect money that's owed him?"

"Did you know he was dead?" Reardon asked.

"No. What difference does it make?"

Bobby said. "Man borrows money, he don't pay it, then his *family* pays it. *Somebody* pays it, Reardon. We don't get stuck holding the bag."

"Who's we?" Reardon asked.

Bobby shrugged.

"How much did he borrow?"

"Seven K. And some change."

"When?"

"Couple of weeks before he opened his joint. I'm cooperating, right, Reardon?"

"Sure," Reardon said.

"He was short, the bank wouldn't let him have another nickel. They're charging interest almost as high as us these days, the banks. Can you believe it?"

"Who's us?" Reardon said.

Bobby shrugged again.

"This is a homicide we're talking here," Reardon said.

"So what do you want from me, your homicide?" Bobby said. "I'm a businessman. We lent the guy some bread, he knew what the interest rate was, he knew when the payments were due."

"What was the interest rate?"

"Does Macy's tell Gimbels?"

"When were the payments due?"

"Every Thursday. Today's Thursday."

"When did he make the last payment?"

"Last Thursday. When it was due."

"You're sure he paid you, huh?"

"I'm sure."

"You're sure you didn't go in there with a little muscle Monday night . . ."

"Positive."

"Who did?"

"You got me, pal."

Reardon sighed. "Okay," he said, "stay away from the D'Annunzio family. Your interest'll wait."

"No, it won't," Bobby said. "This ain't in my hands."

"Whose hands is it in?"

Bobby shrugged.

"You still working for Sallie Fortunato?"

"Who says I *ever* worked for him?" Bobby said.

"Come on, Bobby, cut the shit."

"That's news to me, my working for Sallie."

"Next time you talk to him," Reardon said, "which should be about three minutes after I walk out of here, tell him I'll be stopping by."

"I don't even know his number," Bobby said.

"Send a carrier pigeon."

"Besides," Bobby said, smiling, "who wants your truck outside listening?"

Salvatore Luigi Fortunato's B-sheet gave his age as sixty-four years old, his place of birth as Palermo, Sicily, and his various aliases as "Sallie," "Salvie," "Big Lou," and "The Accountant." He had done time only once, shortly after arriving in America, for Second-Degree Arson, presently defined as "intentionally damaging a building by starting a fire or causing an explosion," a Class-C felony for which he'd been sentenced to three years in prison, a year of which he'd served at Ossining before being paroled. He had managed to escape confinement since, presumably because he was connected with the mob, and could freely call upon their legal talent. Paunchy and graying, wearing a blue suit, a white shirt, black shoes, a dark blue tie, and rimless eyeglasses—which indeed made him resemble an accountant—he sat behind his desk in the small office at the rear of the Angela Cara pastry shop on Grand Street, and said, "Yes, I okayed the loan. So what?"

Two of his goons were in attendance. One of them was cleaning his nails with a toothpick. Reardon figured he'd seen this in a movie someplace. The other one was reading a copy of *Penthouse* magazine. Both of them feigned enormous indifference to the conversation.

"He came to you personally?" Reardon asked.

"No, no, he went to Bobby. Bobby called me, I said okay. It was peanuts, what's the big deal?"

"The big deal is he was killed."

"I'm going to give you a lesson in economics," Fortunato said. "You listening?"

"I'm listening."

"Dead men can't pay what they owe you."

"Is that the lesson?"

"It's the best lesson you'll ever learn."

"Thanks. But accidents sometimes happen."

"No, Reardon. Accidents don't happen accidentally. They only happen if they're *supposed* to happen. How long you been a cop? I have to tell you this?"

"Ralph D'Annunzio was killed, Sallie."

"None of my people killed him. Not accidentally or otherwise."

"Suppose, Sallie . . . . I'm just supposing now."

"Sure, go ahead, suppose."

"Suppose D'Annunzio wasn't meeting his interest payments . . ."

"You're already supposing wrong. He made the loan, what, a month ago? Sometime around Thanksgiving, it musta been, is that a month? Whenever. The point is, he's been meeting all the interest payments. So why would . . . ?"

"I have only Bobby's word for that."

"And mine."

"What if somebody went in there to collect, Sallie, and faked a robbery so it'd look like . . ."

"With *me* in the place? They'd have to be out of their minds."

Reardon looked at him.

"What are you saying?"

"I was *there* Monday night. I was sitting there eating when those punks came in." He indicated the goon reading *Penthouse.* "Jerry here wanted to bust it up, I told him to cool it. That's all I need, interfering with a stickup. You guys'd figure I was the one masterminded it."

"But you weren't, huh?"

"Come on, Reardon, why would I bother? For a lousy seventy-five hundred? When the man is meeting his payments? Come on." He sighed heavily, shook his head as though exasperated by the dullness of his student. "Anyway, I liked the guy," he said. "I been eating there ever since it opened. Nice clean place, good food." He smiled broadly. "I hate to eat places the Mafia goes, you never know when somebody's gonna start shooting."

"If you liked him so much, call off your dogs."

"Sure, I'll tell Bobby to cool it for a while. We can't *forget* the loan, Reardon, that's business. But respect for the dead is another thing. We'll give the family a little breathing space."

"Thanks," Reardon said.

"And *you* call off *your* dogs, okay? My people had nothing to do with this, I promise you."

"What'd these guys look like, Sallie? You were there, you saw the shooting . . ."

"Two of them with ski masks. Kinda slight of build. You checked the Chinese community? I wouldn't be surprised this was one of the Chinese gangs. Them Chinese punks need a swift kick in the ass."

"If you should hear anything, I'd appreciate your letting me know," Reardon said.

"Oh, sure," Fortunato said, his grin contradicting his words. "You'll be the *first* to know."

Reardon came out of the pastry shop, and walked to where he'd parked the unmarked sedan at the curb. He looked at his watch. Almost six o'clock. He was starting the car when the walkie-talkie on the seat erupted with the dispatcher's excited voice.

"Five P.D., all cars! Five P.D., all cars! Ten-thirteen on Rivington and Forsyth! Ten-thirteen on Rivington and Forsyth!"

Reardon picked up the walkie-talkie.

"Four-oh-three," he said.

"Go ahead, Bry."

"Who's the officer, do you know?"

"Chick Hoffman," the dispatcher said.

Rivington and Forsyth was in the extreme northeast corner of the precinct—walk two blocks uptown, cross Houston Street, and you were in the Ninth, which was no joy-ride. Everything down here overlapped, not only the precincts. Reardon sometimes thought of the city, especially *this* part of the city, as a jigsaw puzzle with interlocking pieces—the Village spilling over into Lower Broadway and Little Italy; Little Italy running into the Bowery and China-town; the Bowery becoming the Lower East

Side; Chinatown and Lower Broadway becoming Whitehall and Wall Street—a puzzle that remained a puzzle even when all the pieces were in place. Here on Rivington and Forsyth, this particular piece of the puzzle was now Hispanic, although an abandoned synagogue up the street had been organized in 1886 and erected in 1903.

The dispatcher had specified only Rivington and Forsyth, no address. A red brick building dominated one corner, the gold-lettered sign over its entrance arches identifying it as the N.Y.C. Adult Training Center. An empty lot was on the corner opposite, strewn with rubble and surrounded by a cyclone fence. Alongside this was a five-story tenement, the address over its door obliterated by spray paint. A Spanish "social club" now occupied what had been street-level stores flanking the entrance to the building. It was very cold there on Rivington and Forsyth at a little past six P.M. but the streets were thronged with citizens—the circus was in town. The circus consisted of an Emergency Service van and a dozen or more patrol cars angled into the curb. Most of the uniformed cops were crouched behind the protective cover of the cars or the van; all of them had pistols in their hands. The

Emergency Service cops—big fuckin' volunteer heroes—were casually strapping on ceramic vests. Reardon got out of the car, and walked over to a heavy-breathing, red-faced sergeant.

"Who called in the Officer-Assist, do you know?" he asked.

"Man on the beat," the sergeant said. "Heard shooting on the roof, went up there to find Hoffman pinned down behind a chimney."

"Thanks," Reardon said, and started toward the building.

An Emergency cop stopped him at the door.

"We've got it, Reardon. Go home," he said. He was wearing a ceramic vest, and he had a shotgun in his hands.

"That's my *partner* up there," Reardon said. "Go find yourself a jumper on a bridge."

He went into the hallway. A naked light bulb hanging from a broken fixture. The locks on the mailboxes broken. The glass panel on the inner door broken. The stench of urine. This was a city of minor assaults. The graffiti spray-painted on the subway cars and on the walls of buildings and monuments—Grant's *Tomb*, for Christ's sake, obliterated by graffiti! You saw enough graffiti, you began to think that's the way it *should* be, all that shit scribbled on the walls, you began to think that was the way it had *always* been. Beautiful art work, right? Fuckin' mayor smiling, smiling. You like our graffiti art work, folks? How'm I doin', folks? Ghetto blasters sitting on the shoulders of strolling kids, polluting the atmosphere, assaulting the ears the way graffiti assaulted the eyes. We don't care about this city, the assaulters said. Fuck your city. And fuck you. We *want* you to be afraid to wear a gold chain on Fifth Avenue. We *want* you to put bars on your windows, we *want* you to tremble in your beds at night. We want to assault you incessantly, assault you with the knowledge that the barbarian ponies are massing outside the barricades, assault you with fear of the unknown. This whole fucking city was an assault on the imagination.

A shot rang out the moment Reardon opened the metal door to the roof. He threw himself flat on the tarred surface, saw Hoffman crouched behind a chimney as more shots shattered the stillness of the night. He crawled over to him.

"Hello, Chick," he said.

"Well, well, the Cavalry," Hoffman said.

"Plus a thousand nine-one-one-cops pounding up the stairs."

"I hope they know how to handle a trigger-happy lunatic."

They both ducked as more shots came. Brick dust flew off the chimney.

"What happened?" Reardon asked.

"I was cruising, saw this guy come out of the building, thought he was running to catch a bus or something."

More shots.

"Crazy fuck won't let up for a minute," Hoffman said. "Anyway, he's running, and a gun falls out of his pocket, drops on the sidewalk. He stoops to pick it up, I'm already out of the car by then, the crazy bastard throws a coupla shots at me."

More shots. The men hugged the chimney wall.

"I've been counting," Hoffman said. "He reloads every seven shots. Got to be an automatic."

"Why'd he start shooting in the first place?" Reardon asked.

"Who the hell knows? Crazy."

A single shot this time.

"That's seven. Here's where he changes the clip. Want to count with me, friend?"

Silence.

Then two shots.

More silence.

Another two.

"That makes four," Hoffman said.

They waited.

Silence.

A single shot.

"Five," Reardon said.

"He's behind the pigeon coop," Hoffman said. "You take the right, I'll take the left."

On the street below, an ambulance siren.

Another shot.

"Six," Reardon said.

"Get set."

They braced themselves. It seemed an eternity before the last shot came.

"Go!" Hoffman yelled.

They broke from crouches into running strides, splitting into two targets as they came across the roof, Reardon on the right, Hoffman on the left. A small metallic *click* from behind the pigeon coop, a new clip being rammed home. Vaporized breath pluming from their mouths as they pounded across the tar. Reardon reached the corner of the pigeon coop. The man had his back to him.

"Freeze!" Reardon shouted, and the man whirled.

A Colt .45 automatic was in his right hand.

Reardon fired at once, taking the man in the shoulder. The man fell back against the pigeon coop. There was the frantic flutter of wings. The man slumped to the floor of the roof, lay in darkness against the wall of the coop. Breathing hard, Reardon reached down for him, rolled him over, cuffed his hands behind his back. A flashlight snapped on. Hoffman coming around the left-hand corner of the coop. He threw the beam into the man's face.

"You make him?" he said.

Reardon looked.

"Yeah," he said. "Harold Jurgens. The prick who got acquitted this morning."

He reached down for him.

"Up!" he said.

The door to the roof snapped open, metal banging against brick. A 911-cop peered into the darkness, a shotgun in his hands. "You guys okay?" he said.

"Move it!" Reardon told Jurgens, and shoved out at him angrily, almost knocking him off his feet again. "We're fine," he told the 911-cop.

"You're lucky," the cop said. "We've got a dead kid in the hallway downstairs."

7

THE television commercials all said, "Make it Jamaica again." Somebody up there must have been listening. Today was Jamaica in New York City. The tropics right here in the Big Apple. Fifty-four degrees outside, clear blue skies, not a hint of wind. In the squadroom, the detectives were sitting around in shirtsleeves. When Hoffman came in, he was wearing a sports jacket over a cotton turtleneck, no coat. He threw that morning's *Daily News* on Reardon's desk.

"Our boy made the front page," he said.

"Yeah, great," Reardon said, and looked at the headline:

RAPIST KILLS
12 YEAR OLD GIRL

"Wanna bet he walks again?" Reardon said sourly.

"Not this time," Hoffman said.

"Wanna bet?"

The phone on his desk rang. He picked up the receiver.

"Fifth Squad, Reardon," he said.

"Mr. Reardon?"

A woman's voice. Young, hesitant.

"Yes?"

"This is Miss Sanderson."

"Who?"

"Martha Sanderson." A pause. "I was juror number five." Another pause. "The Jurgens trial."

"Yes, Miss Sanderson?"

"I'm calling to apologize," she said.

"It's a little late for that, isn't it?" Reardon said.

"I saw the story in this morning's paper," she said, and paused again. "We were wrong . . . and I'm sorry."

"Yeah, well," he said, softening, "that's all right. Thanks for calling, I appreciate it."

There was a long silence on the line.

"Mr. Reardon," she said, "I really am sorry."

"I understand," he said.

"I'm not sure you do."

"Don't worry about it, okay?"

"I feel terrible about this, really, I do. I wonder . . . is it possible we could . . .

I'd like to explain further. I don't want you to think we reached our verdict without careful thought. And deliberation. It was a *wrong* decision, but I *do* feel I owe you an explanation."

"You've already explained, Miss Sanderson."

"I meant . . . in person."

"Well . . ."

"Do you think we could meet for a drink sometime later today? Or a cup of coffee? Something? Really, I feel I owe you something."

There was another long silence on the line.

"Mr. Reardon?"

"A drink sounds fine," he said.

"What's a good time for you?"

"I'm through here at four," he said, and looked at the clock.

"Could we make it a little past five?"

"Sure. Where are you?"

"I work for *Forbes* magazine," she said, "at Fifth and Eleventh. There's a place called Ringo's, on Twelfth. Could you meet me there at, say, five-fifteen? It's just off Sixth."

"Ringo's at five-fifteen. I'll see you there."

"I'm looking forward to it," she said, and hung up.

Reardon put the receiver back on the cradle.

"Must be a native New Yorker," he said. "She called it Sixth."

"Huh?" Hoffman said. He was reading the story on Jurgens's arrest.

"Instead of Avenue of the Americas."

"Still claims he had nothing to do with the little dead girl," Hoffman said. "Came running out of the hallway like a locomotive, but claims he never saw her in his life." He shrugged. "Maybe he *will* walk again."

"We shoulda nailed him on the roof," Reardon said. "Two in the heart."

His phone rang again. He picked up.

"Fifth Squad, Reardon."

"Reardon, this is Weissman at the Two-Four," a man's voice said. "I got your flyer on that brown Benz, and I . . ."

"Yeah?" Reardon said at once.

"Relax, this ain't a positive make," Weissman said. "But I been working a murder up here, guy on Central Park West got killed Monday night—about an hour before *your* guy caught it on Mulberry Street. A brown Benz figures in it. You want to come up here sometime today? We may have something in common."

185

Dave Weissman was a Detective/First Grade in his mid-forties, Reardon guessed, a bulky man wearing a sleeveless sweater over a sports shirt. The cops in this city frequently ran into one another, but this was the first time Reardon had ever met Weissman. Slightly balding at the back of his head, wearing eyeglasses, puffing on a cigar, he stood behind the slide projector and said, "This is what the apartment looked like." They were sitting in the Interrogation Room of the Twenty-fourth Precinct, uptown on West One Hundredth Street. The projector was set up on a long, scarred, wooden table. Weissman had hung a screen over the one-way mirror on the other side of the room.

"Place was a mess, as you can see."

The black and white slide showed the living room of an apartment in disarray. Sofa cushions strewn all over the floor. Chairs overturned. Open drawers and doors on the stereo unit and the long buffet. A floor lamp lying on its side.

"Whoever did it was obviously looking for something," Weissman said, and pressed the remote button he held in his right hand. There was a small click. Another slide came on. Black and white like the one before it.

"This is the bedroom," Weissman said.

A king-sized bed, a dresser opposite. The bed covers and pillows thrown on the floor. The mattress slashed. Clothing from the dresser drawers spilled onto the floor. Closet door open. Clothes on hangers thrown everywhere.

Another click, another slide.

"This is the victim."

What looked like a studio-posed photo flashed onto the screen.

"Peter Dodge," Weissman said. "Thirty-four years old. Single. I can let you have an eight-by-ten glossy of this, if you think you can use it. It's a recent picture."

"Yes, I'd like one," Reardon said.

Another click. The picture of the dark-haired, smiling man on the screen was replaced by a shot of the same man, naked and lying on a blood-spattered, tiled bathroom floor.

"This is the way we found him," Weissman said. "Starkers, his hands tied behind his back with a wire coat hanger. He was a lawyer. Partner in a small firm called Lewis and Dodge."

Another click.

"Here's the wall safe in the bedroom closet. Obviously forced him to open it, but didn't take any of the contents. We checked with his insurance agent, got a list of all his valuables."

Click.

"Silverware chest in the dining room. Nothing missing."

Click.

"This is the library. Some valuable paintings on the wall, all of them still there."

He snapped off the projector.

"That's about it."

He walked to the wall switch. Fluorescent light flooded the room.

"How was he killed?" Reardon asked.

"With a knife. How'd they get your guy?"

"Four slugs from a Swiss pistol. They shot him in the back."

"Nice people," Weissman said. "Before they killed *my* guy, they beat him half to death."

"How many of them?"

"Three, according to the doorman."

"And driving a brown Benz?"

"That's what the man said." Weissman rolled up the screen. "I'll tell you, Reardon, this one baffles me. All the signs of a burglary, but nothing stolen. All the signs of a weirdo torture killing, but this guy Dodge was straight as an arrow." He shook his head. "I *hate* mysteries, don't you?"

"What time did the doorman say they went in?"

"Five-thirty, six, in there. What time was yours?"

"Around seven."

"Plenty of time to get down there, even with the holiday traffic."

"*If* it was them."

"You got anything looks better?"

"Not at the moment." He stood up, extended his hand. "Thanks, Weissman, I'll keep in touch." He looked at the wall clock. "Christ," he said, "is that the right time?" He checked his own watch. "Mind if I make a call?" he said.

"Be my guest," Weissman said, and hefted the projector off the table. Reardon followed him into the squadroom. "Any one of those desks," Weissman said.

Reardon went to the closest desk, lifted the receiver on the phone there, got a dial tone, and dialed Directory Assistance. "In Manhattan," he said into the phone. "A place called Ringo's on West Twelfth." He waited. He jotted a number onto a pad on the desk. "Thank you," he said, and pressed the cradle button, and then dialed the number the operator had given him.

"Ringo's," a man's voice said.

"Yes, would you know if there's a Miss Sanderson there?"

"Who?"

"Martha Sanderson. I was supposed to meet her at five-fifteen, would you know if she's . . . ?"

"It's already five to six," the man said.

"I know. Is she still there?"

"Hold on a second, willya?"

He waited.

The man came back onto the line some three minutes later. "If it's the one I think she was, she left about ten minutes ago," he said.

"Okay, thanks," Reardon said, and hung up. "Shit," he said. He picked up the receiver again, waited for a dial tone, and called Information again. "In Manhattan, please," he told the operator. "Martha Sanderson."

"Would you spell the last name, please?" the operator said.

"S-A-N-D-E-R-S-O-N. I think."

"And the address?"

"I don't have an address."

"One moment, please."

He waited.

"Sir?"

"Yes?"

"That number is out of service at this time."

"Can you let me have the address there, please?"

"I'm sorry, sir, we're not allowed to give customers' addresses."

"I know that, but I'm a police officer."

"I'm sorry, sir."

"Check it with your supervisor, okay? My name is Bryan Reardon, Detective/ Second Grade, Fifth Squad."

"Well, sir . . ."

"Please check it, okay?"

"One moment, sir."

He waited.

"Fuckin' telephone company," he said to Weissman.

The operator came back onto the line.

"I can let you have that address, sir," she said.

"Thank you," he said, and moved the pad into place again.

The building on Eighty-fourth Street and First Avenue was a four-story brick tenement flanked on either side by vacant, bulldozed lots. Reardon looked up at it. A dim, flickering light behind one of the third-floor windows. All the other windows black.

Puzzled, he climbed the steps to the front door and stepped into the entryway. No lights. He struck a match, held it to the row of mailboxes. Only one mailbox had a name-tag on it.

M. Sanderson
Apt. 3B

He shook out the match, opened the inner door—no lock on it—and started for the stairwell. Utter blackness. He struck another match, began working his way upstairs. He had burned at least a dozen matches before he reached the third floor. He struck another one, and searched for the apartment. The match went out an instant after he found 3B. He knocked on the door.

"Yes?" a woman's voice said.

"It's me. Reardon," he said.

"Oh." Surprise in her voice. "Just a second, okay?"

He heard her fumbling with the lock and the night chain. The door opened.

"Hi," she said. "How'd you find me?"

"I'm a detective," he said, shrugging.

"Well, come in, okay?"

He stepped into the apartment. A loft-sized room, candles burning—the flickering light he had seen from outside—a cannel coal fire going in the fireplace.

"I waited a half-hour," she said, "and then figured you'd changed your mind."

"I'm sorry. I tried to call you there. Here, too, as a matter of fact. The operator told me . . ."

"Yeah, they cut off my phone. Would you like a drink? I have scotch." She paused, and then said, "Or would you prefer scotch? Or maybe scotch?"

"Scotch, thanks," Reardon said, smiling.

He watched her as she crossed to a table on the other side of the room. She was wearing a dark skirt, a white blouse, high-heeled pumps. He looked around the room. A low sofa. A beanbag chair. Pillows scattered on the floor. Paintings on the walls, barely visible in the candlelight.

"I hope you like it neat," she said. "And without ice. They turned off the water, too."

"Who's *they?*" Reardon asked.

"The people who own the building. They're tearing it down, but I refuse to move." She poured from a bottle of Johnnie Walker Red. "I'm the last of the Mohicans," she said. "All the other tenants have already knuckled under."

"You mean you're all alone here?"

"And here to stay," she said, and handed him his glass. She lifted her own glass. "Cheers," she said.

"Cheers."

They both drank.

"Have they served eviction papers?" Reardon asked.

"I tore them up. Sit down, okay?"

They moved to the couch.

"If they send a marshal," she said, "I'll throw him down the stairs. It's the principle of the thing. This is my *home*, you know? They've got no right to knock it down for a goddamn condominium. Do you know how much rent I'm paying here?"

"How much?"

"Two hundred a month. On a three-year lease." She sipped at her scotch. "Hell with them. If they drag me out of here, I'll camp outside with my furniture. The bulldozers can work around me."

"Well . . . good luck," Reardon said, and drank.

There was a long silence.

"So," she said.

"So," he said.

"What do I call you?"

"Bry," he said. "For Bryan."

"Good Irish name."

"And you're Martha."

"Martha? Oh dear God, no. That's what's on my birth certificate, but I've been Sandy ever since the first grade."

"Sandy then."

"And Bry."

There was another long silence.

"So," she said again.

"So," he said.

"I would have waited at Ringo's longer, but I have a standing rule. Half an hour and goodbye."

"The principle of the thing," he said, smiling.

"The principle," she said, returning the smile. "Listen, I feel awful about letting that man loose," she said suddenly. "It was just . . . well . . . I believed what the D.A. was saying about you. We *all* believed it."

"It wasn't true," Reardon said.

"I know that now. Or at least I *think* I do. You're . . . you don't seem to be the kind of man who could . . . well, I suppose that's wrong, too. I suppose, in your line of work, you're often forced to act violently. In violent situations, I mean. I mean . . . shit, forget it. Anyway, I'm sorry. I'm truly sorry."

"And I'm sorry for the way I behaved. In the corridor, I mean. After the verdict."

"Good, so we're both sorry," Sandy said, "so that's that, so what shall I make for dinner?"

"Well, I hadn't . . ."

"I thought . . ."

"Well . . ."

"Or do you have other plans?"

"No," he said. "No other plans."

"Then . . ."

"Yes, sure."

"Good. The choice is limited," she said, "I haven't got any gas, either. But we'll figure something out, okay? How does fondue sound?"

"Fine."

"And I've got some white wine chilling on the window sill."

"Sounds perfect."

"Good," she said, and rose from the couch. The kitchen was separated from the living room by a wall with a pass-through counter on it. He watched as she held a match to a kerosene lantern and then carried it to the kitchen table. "Candles are romantic as hell," she said, "but they don't give much light. Neither does this thing, for that matter. How'd the pioneer ladies manage?" She opened one of the cabinet doors, took out a bowl. "Do you think he'll go to jail this time?" she asked.

"I hope they throw away the key," he said. "Can I help you there?"

"No, I'm fine, just relax. More scotch?"

"I wouldn't mind."

"Just help yourself, okay?"

"Thanks," he said, and walked to the table against the living room wall. Pouring, he asked, "What do you do up there at *Forbes?*"

"I'm a researcher," she said. "Stepping-stone to bigger and better things. Are you sure fondue's okay?"

"Sure. Bigger and better like what?"

"Editor-in-chief, of course," she said, smiling. "I mean, after all, I didn't major in economics for nothing, did I? At Yale, no less."

"I'm impressed," he said, walking over to the passthrough counter, and sitting on a stool there.

"Don't be," she said, "it was a lark. Not too many girls there when I was a student, I thought I'd died and gone to heaven." She came to the counter, passed a fondue pot over it. "Could you light this thing, please?" she said. "Or maybe you ought to carry it over to the table first. Right in front of the couch there."

He took the pot, carried it over to the coffee table.

"How long have you been a cop?" she asked.

"Almost sixteen years. Do I just put a match to this?"

"Yeah, the Sterno. Don't blow yourself up. And before then?"

"I dropped out of C.C.N.Y. when my father died. I was twenty-one, joined the force to support my kid sisters. My mother was already dead. I missed Vietnam because my lottery number was a high one."

"Lucky you. How old *are* you, Bry?"

"Thirty-seven. And you?"

"Twenty-eight." She paused, and then said, "Ever been married?"

"I'm separated," he said. "You?"

"Twice," she said, surprising him. "I'll just make a small salad, okay?" she said. "This lettuce looks a bit wilted. Window boxes aren't all they're cracked up to be. The first time, when I was sixteen," she said. "My parents had it annulled. Next time just after I got out of Yale. To the sweetest man in the world, who decided his charms were being wasted on only one woman. I came home one day and found him in bed with two teenage girls and a Labrador retriever." She looked up from the salad bowl, smiling. "I exaggerate," she said. "But it was bad enough."

"When did that one end?"

"Four years ago."

There was a long silence.

"So," she said. "Are you hungry?"

"Starving."

"Let me take in the wine," she said, and went to the window. "Do you realize that when my grandparents first came here, *they* didn't have a refrigerator, either?"

"Ice boxes," Reardon said, nodding. "My grandmother had an ice box."

"I almost bought one," Sandy said. "But who'd deliver ice up to the third floor? Anyway, *are* there still ice men in this city?"

"I guess, yeah, but . . . well, I don't know, actually."

"It's nice and cold," she said, carrying the wine bottle to the passthrough and handing it to him. "If you want to put this on the table, too," she said, indicating the salad bowl, "I think I can manage the cheese and the bread." She picked up her tray, carried it around to the kitchen door, came into the living room, and went to the coffee table, where the Sterno can was flaming blue under the fondue pot.

"Good," she said. "Nice fire." She looked at him, and smiled suddenly. "This is fun, isn't it?" she said.

"Yes," he said.

And meant it.

8

He thought about her all the way to Washington.

Wondered if he shouldn't have tried hitting on her last night. Twice-divorced woman living alone—*really* alone—in a candlelit apartment, sipping wine, dipping bread in a cheese fondue, maybe she'd expected him to hit on her. The trouble was . . . well, she wasn't Kathy, that was the trouble. Nice-enough-looking woman, expressive brown eyes and hair the color of her name, generous mouth, good figure—but not Kathy. None of them were Kathy.

A month after the separation, he'd struck up a conversation with a hooker Mazzi had brought in. Young Chinese girl. Mazzi was a hairbag who should have become a minister instead of a cop. Reardon hated whenever the schedule broke so that Mazzi was in the squadroom with him. Always spouting Moral Majority crap. Some majority, the

Moral Majority. Majority of the *lip* was all. But there was Pope Mazzi the Third, as they called him, on his one-man crusade against immorality. Reardon suspected he *liked* arresting hookers, loved the short dresses tight across the ass and cut to show plenty of leg and breast, loved the heavy makeup and the dirty talk. He once suggested to Mazzi that he ask for a transfer to Vice, all these hooker busts he was making. Mazzi was shocked. Vice? Vice? He actually crossed himself. Twice for good measure.

The Chinese hooker was twenty-three, twenty-four, something in there. Mazzi had caught her soliciting two blocks from Headquarters, she had to be new at it. Or else dumb. This was still the summer, August, the latter part of August, she was wearing what she might have been wearing in Hong Kong or on Taiwan, red silk dress slit all the way to the thigh on her right leg, high-heeled red satin shoes, a stunner. While the Pope was typing up his report, Reardon started talking to her. He suspected she was an illegal alien, and he guessed she'd be in more trouble with Immigration than with the criminal court here, where hookers usually got off with a fine and a warning to keep it off the streets.

Not illegal at all, the way it turned out. Showed him her birth certificate, born right here on Bayard Street. Carried it with her because that was the first thing everybody thought, illegal Chink, ship her back to Shanghai or wherever. Not dumb, either. And not new in the life. She'd been hooking for three years, she told him. The money was good, certainly better than slinging moo goo gai pan in one of the restaurants down here. Said she'd been cruising near police plaza because she'd had good luck with cops lately. Cops understood hookers, she said. In a sense, cops understood *all* offenders better than they did straight civilians, wasn't that so? A symbiosis, she said. Reardon didn't know what the word meant. Also, cops were good tippers. Cops knew how hard you had to work to make a buck in this fuckin' city. Did Reardon know how many cops ended up marrying hookers? He told her he didn't know. He also told her she'd picked the wrong cop—"Hey, don't I know it already?"—when she asked Mazzi if he wanted to have a good time. Mazzi thought a good time was playing bingo in church on his night off. Mazzi thought a good time was watching the Disney channel on his cable TV. Mazzi was the Pope of Chinatown—

"Do you know the Pope story?" Reardon asked her. He felt comfortable with this girl, he didn't know why. Figured he could risk telling her a dirty joke, even though Mazzi was sitting almost within earshot, his fingers flying over the typewriter keys. Separated for a month that August, hardly able to say two words in a row to *any* woman, and here he was talking to a hooker and actually enjoying himself.

"The Pope decides to take a walk outside the Vatican," he said, lowering his voice because he didn't want Mazzi to get up on the pulpit, "and as luck would have it, he runs into a hooker."

"Uh-oh," the girl said. Her brown eyes were wide in her face.

"The hooker says, 'You want a blowjob, a hundred thousand lira,' and the Pope throws up his hands and says, 'I don't know, I don't know, no, I don't know,' and runs back to the Vatican. He sits in his office for a long time, thinking over what just happened, and then he buzzes the mother superior and asks her to come in. 'Mother Superior,' he says, 'what's a blowjob?' And the mother superior says, 'A hundred thousand lira, same as outside.' "

The girl burst out laughing.

Mazzi looked up from his typewriter.

"Come see me tomorrow," she whispered to Reardon, "when all this bullshit is over with. It won't cost you a hundred thousand lira."

He went to see her the next day.

All business.

Cool as a cucumber.

First time he'd ever been to bed with anyone but Kathy in the past ten years.

Hardly said a word to him.

Well, yeah.

"Twenty-five," she said, " 'cause I like you. I usually charge fifty."

Great head.

Went out of there feeling worse than when he'd gone in.

So last night, there he was with a good-looking woman who'd been around the park once or twice, and all they'd done was eat the fondue and drink the wine, and then he'd told her he had to catch a plane to Washington the next morning, and she'd said she had to get up early, too, and they'd shaken hands, and she'd said, "Goodnight, Bry, it was fun," and he'd said, "I enjoyed it, Sandy," and that was that.

And he'd gone home to his fleabag hotel, and lain awake half the night thinking of Kathy.

Plane rides are no fucking good, he thought. They make you wonder about too many things.

The Café de la Daine was in Georgetown, on Wisconsin Avenue near Dumbarton Street. Reardon wasn't too familiar with Washington—he'd been here only once before, to give testimony in a Senate hearing —but he guessed this was one of the better parts of town. The restaurant at five to eleven that Saturday morning was alive with busboys setting the tables for lunch. One of them came over the moment Reardon walked through the front door.

Reardon showed him his potsie and his ID card. "Detective Reardon," he said, "New York City police. I'd like to see John D'Annunzio, please."

"I don't think he's in yet," the busboy said. "Let me check in back."

He disappeared into what Reardon supposed was the kitchen. Reardon looked around. Plush banquettes, white linen table cloths, polished silver, sparkling crystal. The kind of place he could never afford. The kind of place he maybe wouldn't ever set foot in even if he could afford it. The kitchen door opened again. A man in his late fifties, hair graying at the temples, brown eyes and shaggy brows, came walking swiftly toward him. He was wearing dark trousers and a white ruffled shirt, an untied bow tie hanging loose on its front. The resemblance between him and Ralph D'Annunzio was unmistakable. They could have been twins.

"What can I do for you?" he said, extending his hand.

"Mr. D'Annunzio?"

"John D'Annunzio, yes."

They shook hands briefly.

"I want to ask you a few more questions," Reardon said. "About your brother's visit."

"You came all the way from New York for that?"

"I've been having difficulty getting you on the phone, Mr. D'Annunzio. Both here and at home."

"Yeah, well, I took a few days off, went to Vegas," D'Annunzio said, shrugging. "Anyway, I told you everything I know."

"You said your brother came here to borrow money from you, is that right?"

D'Annunzio nodded. "Told me somebody was into him for seventy-five hundred bucks.

207

Said he wanted to clear the debt because the interest rates were killing him."

"How'd you react to that, Mr. D'Annunzio?"

"I told him to get lost."

"You told your brother . . ."

"Some brother. I don't see him for fifteen years, he shows up here and wants seventy-five hundred bucks. I work hard here, ten, twelve hours a day. You think that kind of money grows on trees?"

"Did he tell you who was holding the note?"

"I figured it was the shys, but who cares? Why? Was it them who killed him?"

"I don't know who killed him."

"Neither do I. This is what you came all the way here for?"

"I thought he might have mentioned something that . . ."

"Why? 'Cause I'm his long-lost brother? Bullshit. I mean, what kind of nerve is that, will you tell me? Fifteen years! He didn't even invite me to his son's confirmation, Mark, my nephew. By rights, I shoulda been godfather, am I right? My only brother? His only son? Ralph shoulda asked me to be godfather. Instead, he doesn't even invite me. Then he comes here and wants seventy-five hundred bucks. I told him to take a walk."

"How long was he here?"

"Ten, fifteen minutes? Who knows? As long as it took to say Hello, I need seventy-five hundred bucks, goodbye."

"Just like that, huh? After fifteen years?"

"What'd you want me to do, hold a parade?" He shook his head. "It was raining, I called a taxi for him. This was around eight-thirty last Sunday night. That's the last I saw of him."

"When you say you called a taxi . . ."

"I phoned one of the cab companies, right."

"Which one?" Reardon asked.

"Who remembers? I've got a dozen cards by the phone."

A call to the local police put Reardon on to the capital's equivalent of New York City's Taxi and Limousine Commission. It was called the Hack Office here in Washington, and it was located in room 2077 at 300 Indiana Avenue. But a phone call there netted only a taped recording saying that the office was closed on weekends and holidays. Reardon bought himself ten dollars' worth of change in a tobacco shop, closeted himself in a phone booth with the telephone directory's Yellow Pages open to *Taxicabs*, and began dialing every cab company in the city. Allied and Capitol and D.C. Express—the same question to each dispatcher—Dial and Globe and Mayflower—"Did you make an eight-thirty pickup last Sunday night at the Café de la Daine in Georgetown?"—Metropolitan and Omega and Potomac and finally, at a place called Regency Cab, he spoke to a dispatcher who seemed to remember a call from Georgetown around that time last Sunday night.

"Hold on a second, willya?" he said.

Reardon waited.

"This woulda been the fourteenth, am I right?" the dispatcher said.

"Last Sunday night, right," Reardon said. He could hear papers rustling on the other end of the line.

"Today's . . . what's today?"

"The twentieth."

"So that would've been last Sunday, right?" the clerk said.

"Right," Reardon said patiently. "Last Sunday. The fourteenth."

"Right," the dispatcher said. "Pickup at the Café de la Daine, right?"

"Right."

"To National Airport, right?"

"That's what I want to know," Reardon said.

"Right," the dispatcher said. "So let me see here. It musta been raining last Sunday, we got a lot of calls here. Was it raining last Sunday?"

"Yes," Reardon said.

"Which is why we got so many calls," the clerk said. "Sunday, Sunday," he said, riffling through the records, "Sunday, the fourteenth, right? Here we are." He ran his finger down the page. "De la Daine, Sunday, the fourteenth. Here it is, right. De la Daine to National. Eight-thirty P.M. pickup. Two passengers."

"Do you have the passengers' names?" Reardon asked.

"Do they list passengers' names in New York?" the dispatcher said.

"No, but . . ."

"Not here, neither," the clerk said. "All I got is a pickup at the restaurant, a deposit at National. That's what the man on the phone gave us."

"Who was driving the cab?" Reardon asked.

He found the driver at a little past noon

211

in the company garage on H and Third. He was eating a sandwich and sipping a Diet Pepsi. He told Reardon he always brought a sandwich from home, ate it here in the garage before he started his tour. He told Reardon he worked from one in the afternoon till ten at night. He didn't like to work past ten because that was when the monkeys came out. The monkeys liked to hold up cab drivers here in D.C. The cabbie had a wife and three kids, and he didn't want no monkey hitting him on the head with a lead pipe.

"Do you remember this particular call?" Reardon asked. "The Café de la Daine?"

"I get a lot of calls there," the cabbie said. "Nice restaurant, though I never been in it."

"Last Sunday night, around eight-thirty."

"It was raining last Sunday," the cabbie said.

"That's right."

"I'd have to look at my manifest," the cabbie said. "Under Title 15, we gotta keep a manifest shows all our pickups and deposits."

"Do you still have the one for last Sunday?"

"Oh, sure. What I do, I usually throw them away at the end of each month. I figure anybody's gonna make a complaint, by then they'da made it. So let me take a look, huh?"

He looked at the manifest. Reardon watched his finger running down the list of calls.

"Yeah, here it is. Café de la Daine, eight-thirty pickup. Yeah, I remember it now," he said, nodding. "But only because of the Arab."

"What Arab?" Reardon asked at once.

"Guy with a beard and this long white sheet, you know, and this thing on his head—what do you call those things they wear on their heads, the Arabs?"

"A turban?"

"Yeah, a turban."

"What about him?"

"He was one of the two guys I picked up at the restaurant."

"And you drove both of them to National Airport?"

"Straight to National. It's a ten-minute drive."

"What airline?"

"Eastern."

"Thanks," Reardon said, and went immediately to the pay phone on the garage wall. He knew the number of the Café de la Daine by heart; he'd dialed it often enough from New York. He recognized D'Annunzio's voice at once.

"Café de la Daine, good afternoon."

"Mr. D'Annunzio?" he said.

"Who's this, please?"

"Detective Reardon."

"Yes, Mr. Reardon?"

"I'm sorry to bother you again, but I wonder if you can tell me . . ."

"Mr. Reardon, we have a very busy lunch hour here. Can you . . . ?"

"Would you remember if there was an Arab in the restaurant last Sunday night?"

"A what?"

"An Arab. Man dressed in Arab garb, white robe, white turban. He would have taken the same cab your brother did."

"Oh, yes," D'Annunzio said. "He was here for dinner."

"What was his name?" Reardon said.

"I don't know. He was here with Senator Bailey."

"Senator *who?*"

"Bailey. Thomas Bailey."

"Thank you very much," Reardon said.

But, of course, both the Senate and the House had adjourned for the holidays sometime last week and even if this had not been a Saturday, the offices on Capitol Hill would have been empty.

As, in fact, they were.

Dead end.

In a strange city.

Reardon got the hell out of it on the next shuttle.

He was back in the squadroom by three-thirty that afternoon, and by four o'clock he had learned that Senator Thomas Bailey was one of the senators from Connecticut, and he had further learned where he lived and what his home phone number was. This last piece of information had come from a man in Albany who used to be a D.A. in New York, and who now worked under Commissioner Condon in the Division of Criminal Justice Services. Albany was a very political town, and Reardon figured it would not hurt to call his old D.A. drinking buddy at home, see if he could give him a lead on the senator. It took him twenty minutes to get back to Reardon.

At a little past four, Reardon dialed the senator's number in Norwalk, Connecticut. A woman answered the phone. Reardon identified himself as a working New York City detective and asked to speak to the senator, please. Bailey came onto the phone a moment later.

"How can I help you, Detective Reardon?" he asked. His voice sounded cigarette-seared, deep and husky.

"I'm sorry to break in on you this way, Senator . . ."

"No problem," Bailey said.

"But I'm investigating a homicide here in New York . . ."

"Uh-huh."

". . . and I wonder if I might ask you a few questions."

"Well, certainly go right ahead," Bailey said.

"Senator, did you have dinner at a restaurant called Café de la Daine last Sunday night?"

"In Washington, do you mean?"

"Yes, sir."

"I'm not even sure I was still *in* Washington last Sunday."

"The maitre d' seems to . . ."

"Yes, now that you mention it, I believe I did have dinner there, yes."

"Who was with you, Senator?"

"I was alone," Bailey said.

Reardon hesitated, and then said, "The

maitre d' seems to think there was an Arab with you."

"An Arab? I have a large Jewish constituency, Mr. Reardon. I do not make a habit of dining in public with Arabs."

"A man with a beard," Reardon said. "Wearing a white robe and a white turban. An Arab, Senator."

"Well . . ." Bailey said, and hesitated. "Perhaps someone of that description did stop at the table to say hello."

"Who was he?"

"I don't remember. There are always visiting dignitaries in Wash . . ."

"Oh, was he a dignitary?" Reardon asked at once.

"Mr. Reardon," Bailey said, "unless you have something specific in mind . . ."

"I have a homicide in mind, Senator. That's about as specific as anything can get. What was the Arab's name?"

"I didn't realize I was under oath before a Senate subcommittee."

"No, sir, you're not. But I'd hate like hell to have to tell the *New York Times* that you refused to cooperate in a homicide investigation."

There was a long silence on the line. At

last, Bailey said, "How on earth did you ever make the connection?"

"What connection?" Reardon said.

"Between what happened at La Guardia and me."

"What?" Reardon said. "What do you mean?"

There was another silence on the line.

"What homicide are you investigating, Mr. Reardon?" Bailey asked.

"A man named Ralph D'Annunzio was killed last Monday night at his restaurant in . . ."

"I don't know anything about that, I'm sorry."

"How about a man named Peter Dodge, who was . . ."

"Never heard of him. I'm sorry I can't be of more help, Mr. Reardon, but . . ."

"Senator, what homicide did you *think* I . . . ?"

"My wife and I are expecting guests very shortly," Bailey said. "You'll have to forgive me."

"What homicide were you . . . ?"

But the senator had already hung up.

In Arizona, it was two o'clock in the afternoon.

The temperature outside was sixty-two degrees Fahrenheit. A bit more reasonable, Olivia thought. Sunlight streamed through the study windows. Her father sat in a wheelchair behind his desk. He looked healthy and alert today, good color in his cheeks, a sparkle in his eyes. A lion closing in for the kill, she thought.

"Has Sotheby's paid Sarge?" he asked.

"We're already using the proceeds. Thirteen million was deposited to a discretionary account at Rothstein-Phelps, to cover the Comex purchases. The rest has gone to London and Hong Kong."

"You say he got something better than thirty-six million?"

"Thirty-six three," Olivia said.

"Which will pay for the margin on how many contracts?"

"I'm figuring roughly twelve thousand contracts at a margin of three thousand dollars each."

"Four thousand lots on each exchange?" Andrew asked.

"On average. On the Comex, for example, we're buying forty-*two* hundred lots. On the LME . . ."

"Yes, I get the picture. Any big jumps in the price yet?"

"At Friday's close, it was a little over six dollars an ounce."

"Any ripples from the CFTC?"

"Not yet. It doesn't matter, Daddy. This is all legal and aboveboard."

"More or less."

"Well . . . discounting the dummy corporations abroad, of course."

"Of course."

"But we're completely hidden there, Daddy. And in New York, we'll tell them whatever they want to know about our Comex purchases. If it comes to that."

"It may not, Livvie. It may not attract attention."

"Unless someone is terribly eager."

"What about that incident in the airport last Sunday night?"

"A group named Order of the Holy Crusade—or some such thing—is claiming responsibility for it."

"And the other two—the ones I call the 'accident' victims—what about them?"

"Accident victims indeed," Olivia said, smiling. "So far, no connection has been made."

"Good. It would seem we're well on our way then, wouldn't it?"

"I'd say so, yes."

Andrew nodded, pleased, and reached across the desk for his cup of tea.

"By the . . ."

Reaching for the tea.

". . . close Wednesday . . ."

Hand lifting the cup.

". . . we'll have . . ."

And suddenly he dropped the teacup.

And sat upright.

And gasped.

His face, almost ruddy an instant earlier, turned suddenly chalk white.

"Oh," he said, and shuddered.

"Daddy?" she said, alarmed, rushing around the desk to him.

"Oh," he said again, and toppled from his chair.

She knelt beside him at once, her eyes wide in panic. Over her shoulder, she shouted, "Charles! Come quick! *Charles!*"

Reardon left the squadroom at a little past six, took a taxi to his hotel, showered and changed his clothes, and then drove uptown to Sandy's apartment. This time, he took a flashlight from the car. He went up the stairs to the third floor, knocked on the door to apartment 3B, waited, and then knocked again.

"Yes?" Sandy called.

"Sandy," he said. "It's me. Bry."

"Oh," she said.

"Bry Reardon."

"Yes . . . uh . . . just a second, Bry."

He waited. He could hear footsteps approaching the door. Lock tumblers turning. The door opened a crack, the night chain stopping it. She did not take off the night chain. In the crack of the door, he saw her face, hair tousled, caught glimpses of naked flesh below.

"I . . . uh . . . was taking a nap," she said.

"I'm sorry," he said.

"That's okay, it's just . . . uh . . ."

Their eyes met. It's just there's somebody with me, her eyes said. It's just I was in bed with somebody, and this is a very inconvenient time for you to come knocking on my door. It's just go away, Charlie.

"Well, I . . ." He kept looking into her eyes, thinking maybe he was reading them wrong. But the night chain didn't move from its slot on the door, the night chain was as formidable as a moat. "I'll see you some other time, okay?" he said.

"Call me at the office, okay?" she said.

"*Forbes*, right," he said.

"Bry, I'm really sorry," she said. "I didn't know you'd be coming here, I . . ."

"No, no, hey," he said, "come on."

He looked at her a moment longer.

"Goodnight, Sandy," he said.

"Goodnight," she said.

He turned away from the door. He heard the door closing behind him. He heard the small oiled click of the lock tumblers falling.

The precinct was in Chinatown.

Chinatown was where he lived.

Chinatown was home.

A hundred thousand Chinese here, more or less, no one had an accurate count, and more of them arriving every day of the week. Cost an immigrant five thousand bucks for "key money" to a one-room apartment in a sleazy tenement. Twenty years ago, all your Chinese here were from only two counties in Guangdong Province. Today, you had maybe twenty provinces represented here. Not to mention all the Chinese immigrants from Southeast Asia. Chinatown had itself become a distant province of China. A third-world city right here in New York. A city unto itself, spilling over into southeast Manhattan, bursting its long-ago boundaries, displacing the Puerto Ricans, spreading like a vaporous cloud over Little Italy and what used to be the Jewish tenements on Henry Street, drifting all the way to Houston Street, moving restlessly, growing all the time. Another part of the city, rarely understood by anyone who didn't work here. Home.

He wandered the streets.

Well, he shouldn't have gone there. What the hell. Young, attractive woman, had he expected her to be alone on a Saturday night? Would've called first if she had a phone. Shit, why didn't she have a phone? Dumb.

Wandered the streets.

Crowded with tourists, the streets. Well, close to Christmas, lots of out-of-towners in the city, doing their Christmas shopping before they went back home to Iowa, wherever the hell that was.

Home.

He'd be alone this Christmas.

Well, fuck it.

He walked into Little Italy.

Only two blocks left of it now, the Chinese encroachment evident everywhere. Vegetable stands selling all kinds of exotic roots and herbs. Tea rooms with old bearded Chinese men sipping from cups they held in both hands. Dry-goods stores displaying lavish silks in their windows—the Chinese hooker in red silk, skirt slit to her ass. He stopped in front of the D'Annunzio building on Broome Street. He looked at his watch. He hesitated.

Well, shit, I don't want to bother them, he thought.

He looked up the street.

Well, he thought, and went into the building.

Mark D'Annunzio opened the door for him.

"Mr. Reardon, hey!" he said. "Come in, come in."

"I don't want to disturb you," Reardon said. "I was just . . ."

"What disturb?" Mark said. "Come on in."

He followed Mark into the apartment. There were dinner dishes on the kitchen table. Coffee cups. Mrs. D'Annunzio rose at once.

"Mr. Reardon," she said, "hello," and came around the table, both hands extended. "How nice to see you."

He took her hands.

"I was just passing by," he said, "thought I'd . . . uh . . . see how you're doing."

"Take off your coat," she said, "sit down."

"Well, no, I don't want to interrupt your meal."

"We're finished already, we were just having coffee. You can't take off your coat? Sit down for a minute?"

"Well . . ."

"Did you have supper yet?"

"Well, no, I was . . ."

"Mark, get Mr. Reardon a plate," she said, and went immediately to the stove. "The chicken's still hot," she said. "Do you like chicken?"

"Yes, I do," he said.

"*Cacciatore?*"

"Any which way."

"So take off your coat. What's the matter with you, standing there with your coat on?"

"Thank you," he said.

He took off his coat.

"Just throw it over one of the chairs," Mrs. D'Annunzio said.

"Thank you," he said again.

"Mark, get the wine," she said. "Red wine okay?" she asked Reardon.

"*Sì, va bene, signora,*" he said. "*Grazie.*"

"Ah, *lei parla italiano,*" she said.

226

"Solo un poco, signora."

"Ma lei parla molto bene!"

"I picked up a little when I was walking a beat here," Reardon said. "Years ago."

"Here you go," Mark said, pouring from a bottle of Chianti.

"Thank you."

Mrs. D'Annunzio took his plate to the stove, and heaped it high with chicken.

"That's enough for an army," Reardon said.

"Chicken is good for you," she said, putting the plate down before him. "Low cholesterol."

She sat down at the table beside him. When he did not pick up his fork at once, she said, *"Ma che cosa? Mangia!"*

He began eating. "Good," he said.

"What do you eat there at the station house?" she asked.

"Well . . . usually a sandwich. A hamburger. Some fries."

"You should eat better," she said, fussing at him. "And in this weather, you should wear a hat. Why don't you wear a hat, Mr. Reardon?"

"Never got in the habit, I guess."

"Because the heat escapes from your ears, you know."

"Come on, Mom," Mark said, laughing.

"*È vero*, it's true, don't laugh. How's the chicken?"

"Delicious," Reardon said.

"Sure," she said. "Come to the restaurant sometime, we make all kinds of chicken. *Cacciatore, valdostana, parmigiana . . .*"

"We're opening again on Monday, you know," Mark said.

"Is that wrong?" Mrs. D'Annunzio said, and sighed. "Is that too soon, Mr. Reardon?"

"No, *signora*, I don't think so."

"Life has to go on, Mom," Mark said.

"Yes," Reardon said.

Mrs. D'Annunzio sighed again. There was a long silence. Mark poured more wine for Reardon, and then said, "I don't suppose . . . you've learned anything yet."

"We're working on it," Reardon said. "We'll find them, don't worry." He took a sip of wine, and then said, "I didn't come here to ask you any more questions, believe me, but I just got back from Washington . . ."

"You went to Washington?" Mrs. D'Annunzio said, surprised.

"Yes, to talk to your brother-in-law. Actually to some other people, too, as it turned out. Tell me," he said, "when your husband came back from Washington, did he mention anything about an Arab?"

"*Cosa?*"

"*L'arabo*," Mark said. "The one who left his briefcase on the plane."

"What briefcase?" Reardon asked immediately.

"*La sua cartella da viaggio*," Mrs. D'Annunzio said, nodding. "He rushed off the airplane, he forgot it on the rack. Ralph chased after him, but then . . . when the man got shot . . . all the confusion . . ."

"Hold it, *please*," Reardon said. "What do you mean, he got shot?"

"In the terminal," Mrs. D'Annunzio said. "He got shot, you didn't read about it? The man who was sitting next to Ralph on the plane. Ralph tried to give the briefcase back to him, but . . ."

"Tell the truth, Mom," Mark said, and turned to Reardon. "My father panicked. There were cops all over the place, the man's chest was covered with blood, my father didn't want to get involved." He paused and then said, "This is New York, you know."

"Why didn't you tell me all this before?" Reardon said.

"I guess . . . I don't know . . . I didn't see

any connection between something that happened . . ."

"Let *me* figure out the goddamn connections, okay?" Reardon said angrily, and then turned immediately to Mrs. D'Annunzio and said, *"Scusi, signora."*

"I'm sorry," Mark said. "I should have realized."

"Did your father bring the briefcase home with him?"

"Yes."

"You saw it?"

"Yes."

"Where is it now?"

"I don't know," Mark said.

Canned music blared through the crowded room. Colored lights bounced off revolving mirrored balls, splintering reds and blues and ambers, sprinkling the faces and the gyrating bodies of the dancers. Mirrored walls multiplied the dancers by a hundred, speakers everywhere created an unimaginable din. You can't even hear yourself *think* in here, Sarge thought, and tried to steady Jessica, who'd had too much to drink and who was having trouble keeping her footing. He hated when she drank too much. Hated this place. Didn't know what to *do* to this damn music.

She went into a turn, solo-dancing, swinging out from him, her silver-sequined dress reflecting color, reflecting itself again in the mirrors, those damn mirrors were making him dizzy.

"Ooops," she said, and grinned a silly grin.

"Come on, let's sit down," Sarge said.

"Wanna *dance*," Jessica said.

"Later, Jess."

"Now," she said.

"Come *on*, Jess."

He took her elbow, leading her through the crowd, Jessica trying to pull away from him, jiggling her behind in time to the frantic beat, shaking her breasts. When they got back to the table, she picked up her drink immediately, and took a long swallow.

"Better go easy on the sauce," Sarge said.

"What for?" Jessica said. "In St. Moritz on a Saturday night, I'd be dancing and drinking and dancing and . . ."

"Excuse me," someone said.

Sarge turned to his right. A tall young man was standing there.

"Arthur Trevor," he said, *"New York Post.* I wonder if . . ."

"Buzz off, *New York Post*," Sarge said.

"Come on, Mr. Kidd," Trevor said, "you guys are news."

"It's the *Captain* who's the news," Jessica said.

"Jessie!" Sarge said sharply.

"That sterling leader of American industry . . ." Jessica said.

"What about him, Miss Kidd?" Trevor asked.

"Nothing," Sarge said. "Leave us alone, will you please?"

"I just want to know . . ."

"Do you want me to call the manager?"

"Hey, give me a break, okay? I'm a working stiff . . ."

"Give him a break, Sarge," Jessica said, and giggled.

"What kind of news has your father made now, Miss Kidd?" Trevor asked, leaning in on her.

"Listen, mister," Sarge said, "you want me to . . . ?"

"Went and had himself . . ."

"Shut . . ."

". . . a big old stroke out there in Arizona."

"Damn you, Jessie!"

"A stroke?" Trevor said. "Your father had a stroke?"

"Get the hell away from us!" Sarge said. He was on his feet now, hulking over Trevor. "You hear me? Move it!"

Trevor backed away from the table.

Jessica looked up at her brother.

"Did I say something wrong?" she asked.

9

SUNDAY MORNING, December 21, was bright, and clear, and extraordinarily mild. Nobody in New York could believe that Christmas was only four days away. Everyone began talking about the Hothouse Effect. Everyone started saying the polar ice cap was melting. Everyone began reconsidering plans made to spend the holidays in the Caribbean. New York was suddenly a nicer place to live in than it was to visit.

Except for cops.

There was only one thing worse than having to work on a Sunday, and that was having to work when the Sunday was a glorious one. Outside the old Fifth Precinct building on Elizabeth Street, men were strolling in shirtsleeves and women were wearing cotton dresses. In the squadroom upstairs, Gianelli stood at one of the grilled windows —open wide to admit air that was almost intoxicatingly balmy—and looked down into the street.

"When I was with the band," he said to Hoffman, "I didn't have to work on Sundays."

"Unless there was a parade," Hoffman said.

Reardon was sitting at his desk, the telephone receiver to his ear.

"Well, could you check the manifest for me?" he said, and listened. "What do you mean, there's no manifest? *Every* airline has a manifest."

"Parades ain't work," Gianelli said. "Parades are *fun*."

"Would you hold it down?" Reardon said, and then, into the phone, "I'm sorry, what was that?"

"People on the sidewalk cheering, and throwing confetti . . ."

"And throwing up," Hoffman said.

"Uh-huh," Reardon said into the phone.

"That wasn't work," Gianelli said. "This is work. This shitty squadroom is work. On a *Sunday*, no less."

"Okay, thanks," Reardon said, and put the receiver back on its cradle. "They don't keep a manifest for the shuttle," he said.

"People just walk on and off, pay for their tickets right on the plane."

"What's so important about this Arab, anyway?" Gianelli said.

"Maybe nothing," Reardon said. "Except he got shot. And I can't find anyone who knows who the fuck he *was*."

"So he shared a cab with D'Annunzio. So what?"

"You figure it was the nine o'clock shuttle, huh?" Hoffman said.

"Must've been," Reardon said. "They left the restaurant at eight-thirty, takes ten minutes to the airport, the last plane's at nine."

"And both of them got out of the cab at National, huh?"

"National Airlines?" Gianelli asked.

"No, National Airport."

"So what airline?"

"Eastern."

"They both got off at Eastern?"

"That's what the cabbie told me."

"And we know the Arab came to New York, 'cause this is where he got shot."

"And he left his briefcase on the plane," Reardon said.

"Which D'Annunzio picked up, and now nobody knows where it is."

"Terrific," Hoffman said.

"Feel like taking a ride out to La Guardia?" Reardon asked.

La Guardia Airport was thronged with traffic that Sunday morning. Sunday was a good day to see people off.

"You get a Puerto Rican going back to the island," Hoffman said, "he takes the whole family to the airport for the big farewell scene. Grandma, Grandpa, all the aunts and uncles, the cousins, the screaming babies, they're all outside the gate kissing this cane-cutter carrying a cardboard suitcase. You'd think the dumb fuck was goin' off to fight the fuckin' Russians."

"Don't let Ruiz hear you say that," Reardon said.

"Fuck Ruiz, too. He prob'ly has his whole family seein' him off at the *subway* station every morning."

They parked the car in the short-term parking lot, and began walking toward the terminal.

"Place is a fuckin' madhouse today," Hoffman said. "I'll bet you got people here today just came to see the planes takin' off and landin', you know that? Something free to do on a nice Sunday. This city, you tell a guy it's free to jump under a subway car, he'll do it. 'Cause it's free. Look at all these fuckin' people, willya?"

The taxi dispatcher outside Eastern Airlines was busy signalling to cabs and loading passengers.

"You picked a day, all right," he told them when Reardon identified himself.

"What do you know about this Arab who came in on Eastern's nine o'clock shuttle from Washington last Sunday night?" Reardon asked.

"Come on, you gotta be kidding," the dispatcher said, and turned to a man and a woman standing at the curb. "Where you going, mister?" he asked.

"The Parker Meridien," the man said.

"Manhattan?"

"Yes," the man said.

The dispatcher signalled to the next cab in line.

"The guy got shot, it was in all the newspapers the next day, don't you read the newspapers?" the dispatcher said. "Manhattan," he said to the cabbie. "Parker Meridien. Load the bags fast, okay?" He turned to Reardon again. "Or you're supposed to be a cop, don't you talk to other cops? Who were here when the guy got shot?"

"Well, it's a big city," Reardon said.

"Were you working last Sunday night?" Hoffman asked.

"I was working," the dispatcher said. "Where to, lady?"

"Brooklyn," the woman next in line said.

The dispatcher signalled to another cab. "I usually work from four to midnight," he said. "I took the day shift today because the other dispatcher's home sick. I don't know who the hell's gonna work the night shift, because it ain't gonna be me, I can tell you that. Brooklyn," he said to the cabbie. "These your bags, lady?"

"Yes."

"Two bags," he said, "load 'em fast."

"Were you working when the nine o'clock shuttle came in?" Reardon asked.

"Worked straight through to midnight," the dispatcher said. "Who's next here? There's supposed to be a line here."

"So what happened with the Arab?" Hoffman asked.

"Make a line here, okay?" the dispatcher said to the crowd. "I can't help you unless you make a line. There's no sense shoving, 'cause there ain't no cabs right this minute, anyway. First come, first serve. Where you goin', mister?"

"Manhattan."

"Okay, you're next up, soon as we get a cab here."

"Did you see this man we're talking about?" Hoffman said.

"Are you kidding?" the dispatcher said. *Everybody* saw him. He was comin' out of the terminal when they opened fire on him."

"Who?"

"Two guys in business suits, who. Who knows who? Have they been caught yet? Does anybody even know who was shot? Who, he asks me."

"Got shot where? Right out here on the taxi line?"

"He come out of the terminal like a ship under sail, you know?" the dispatcher said. "Sheets flying in the wind. He comes over to me, is *coming* over to me, when bam, bam, bam, a dozen shots ring out, he's dead before he hits the sidewalk."

"Then what?" Reardon said.

"Then we got people scrambling in all directions, and cops all over the place, and an ambulance pulling in, and off he goes."

"To where?" Hoffman asked.

"To Elmhurst General, is where. Here we go, mister, you said Manhattan, didn't you?"

The three-column headline on the front page of Sunday's *New York Times* read:

FINANCIER SUFFERS STROKE

Beneath that, the subhead read:

Andrew Kidd in Serious Condition

The newspaper was on the desk in Phelps's study. He kept looking at the headline as he dialed Rothstein's number. He let the phone ring six times, seven, eight, where the hell *was . . . ?*

"Hello?"

"Lowell, it's Joe."

"Yes, Joe."

"What took you so long to . . . ?"

"I was in the shower. What's the matter?"

"Have you seen the *Times?*"

"No. What is it?"

"Kidd had a stroke."

"What?"

"A stroke, a stroke, what are we going to do?"

"I'll call Phoenix right away," Rothstein said.

"Get back to me, will you?"

"Yes, Joe, as soon as I know what's . . . ."

"Lowell . . ."

"Joe, I'll take *care* of it, okay?"

The emergency room at Elmhurst General Hospital was uncommonly crowded for a Sunday morning. One of the two interns on duty was a hawk-faced Indian with a sallow complexion and an extremely harried look. Hoffman wondered why all the goddamn interns in this city came from Calcutta. Dr. Brajabihari Hemkar—as his little nametag read—told them that Saturday night was usually their busiest time, something the detectives already knew. In this city, Saturday night was when the werewolves came out to howl and drink blood. But this was Sunday morning, 10:05 A.M. by the wall clock, and in addition to the usual number of kids who'd overturned a scalding pot of water or stuck a fork into a toaster, there were two stabbing victims and a gunshot victim, all three of whom added immeasurably to the sense of confusion in the waiting room and the harried look on Dr. Hemkar's face.

"What is it you wanted to know?" he asked, and glanced nervously toward the entrance door where a uniformed police officer had just come in with a man who was bleeding down the left side of his head.

Neither Reardon nor Hoffman was wearing anything that would indicate they were police detectives, no shield or ID card pinned to the collar, nothing that would have told the uniformed cop they were on the job. But he recognized them at once for fellow officers, and immediately said, "His wife hit him with a baseball bat."

"Very nice," Hoffman said, nodding.

The man kept bleeding. His eye was swollen half-closed. Dr. Hemkar asked a nurse to get Dr. Shaffer, and then took the detectives aside and said, "I hope we can make this fast, really. As you can see . . ."

"Just a few quick questions," Reardon said. "We're trying to track down a man who was brought here from La Guardia last Sunday night. He would've been wearing traditional Arab . . ."

"Yes, what about him?" Hemkar said, and then turned to a young man who came from a room near the admissions desk. Through the open door, Reardon could see a woman lying on a table, the front of her blouse covered with blood.

"Can you take this one, Jake?" Hemkar said.

"World War III today," the other intern said. "Come with me, please, sir."

"His wife hit him with a baseball bat," the uniformed cop said again.

"Thank you, officer. This way, please, sir."

"You need me anymore?" the uniformed cop asked Hemkar.

"No, thank you, that'll be fine," Hemkar said, and sighed heavily, and turned to the detectives again.

"Do you remember the man?" Hoffman asked.

"Yes, I do."

"As we understand this," Reardon said, "it was a D.O.A., is that right?"

"Correct," Hemkar said.

"Who was he?" Hoffman asked.

"Who knows?" Hemkar said. "There was no identification on the body."

"No wallet?"

"No passport?"

"Nothing," Hemkar said. "I had a nurse call the Hundred and fourteenth Precinct the moment I realized he was dead. Two detectives were here within the hour."

"Then what?" Reardon asked.

"They called Queens General, and the morgue wagon picked up the cadaver sometime later that night. Around eleven, eleven-thirty, I think it was."

"For autopsy?"

"As required in any trauma death," Hemkar said, and nodded.

The Chief of Staff at Queens General Hospital was a portly little man with a white goatee and rimless eyeglasses. He sat toying with a letter opener as the detectives told him what they had learned at Elmhurst General. A triangular-shaped nameplate on his desk read DR. ERNEST PATTERSON. A mustard stain was centered like a tie tack on his blue tie.

"What we're interested in knowing," Reardon said, "is whether or not any bullets were recovered during autopsy."

"We never did an autopsy," Patterson said.

"According to Dr. Hemkar, your wagon made the pickup at . . ."

"Indeed," Patterson said. "But it was forced off the road somewhere between Elmhurst and here."

"*Forced* off the . . . ?"

"Yes, sir, at gun point," Patterson said.

"*Gun* point?" Hoffman said.

"Yes, sir. The body was removed from the wagon at gun point. What I'm saying, sir, is that the body never *got* here. It was

245

transferred to the automobile that forced the wagon off the road."

"What *kind* of automobile?" Reardon asked at once.

"I believe our driver described it as a brown Mercedes-Benz," Patterson said.

It was ten minutes to eleven when Rothstein finally got through to Phoenix. Charles, the Kidd butler, answered the phone. Rothstein recognized the man's voice immediately, pseudo-British, somewhat high and nasal.

"Charles," he said, "this is Lowell Rothstein. I just read about . . ."

"Yes, Mr. Rothstein?" Charles said. "How are you, sir?"

"Fine, thank you. How's the *Captain*, that's the question. May I speak to Miss Kidd, please?"

"Miss Kidd is not taking any calls," Charles said, and hung up.

Two doctors hovered over him, one of them taking his pulse.

Olivia sat beside the bed, holding her father's other hand. He looked gray and gaunt. Spittle bubbled onto his lips as he spoke.

"Historically true," he said, and nodded. "Oil through the roof, then silver and gold . . ."

She watched the doctor. His strong fingers on her father's thin wrist.

"Well?" she said.

"He's weakening, Miss Kidd. His pulse rate . . ."

"Then *give* him something!" Olivia said.

"There's nothing more I can give him. You have to understand . . ."

"If you let him die . . ." Olivia said warningly.

"Miss Kidd, please. We've done everything possible. The best we can hope for now . . ."

"I don't want to hear it!"

Her father chuckled.

"Kidd fire and iron," he said. "Nothing'll stop you, Livvie . . ."

He tried to sit up, fell back against the pillows again.

"Livvie?" he said.

"I'm here, Daddy."

"Don't go 'way," he said.

"I won't," she said.

"Noise, Livvie," he said, "so much noise in my head, I . . . Livvie?"

"Yes, Daddy."

Her father shuddered. She gripped his hand tightly.

"Got to do it for me, Livvie," he said, "too much noise. Christmas Eve, nail it all down, Livvie." He opened his eyes wide. "Livvie? Where are you?"

"Here, Daddy."

"Wind tunnel," he said. "Noise . . . voices." He shook his head. "Silver used to be on a par with gold," he said, and laughed. "Says so in the Bible, go read it. Could be again, who knows? Still, small potatoes, the oil's the thing. Finish it for me, Livvie. Finish it all on Christmas . . . big . . . Christmas . . . big . . ."

His voice trailed.

"Daddy?" she said.

His eyes were still wide open.

"Daddy!" she said, alarmed.

One of the doctors shook his head.

"Oh, my God!" she said, and threw herself onto her father's chest, holding him close and tight.

Reardon didn't have to meet Kathy and Liz till one o'clock, when Kathy had promised he could have his daughter for lunch. On the phone, she had actually said, "You can have Liz for lunch," which sounded cannibalistic but he hadn't dared laugh, not at the language separation and divorce forced upon people. He was glad he had a little time. He still hadn't shown the D'Annunzios the picture he'd got from Weissman up at the Two-Four.

Mark D'Annunzio was out, his mother didn't know where.

She'd been crying, Reardon could see that.

She offered him a cup of coffee.

He sat at the table with her and asked her how it was going.

She told him she didn't want to open the restaurant tomorrow. She said Christmas was on Thursday, they'd be closed then, anyway, and if they *did* open tomorrow they'd close early on Wednesday, wouldn't they? Christmas Eve? So what was the sense of opening tomorrow? It was too soon, opening tomorrow. It wasn't showing the proper respect.

Reardon told her that when his mother died, his father went to work the very next day.

He did not tell her that he'd hated his father from that day to the day he got killed by a bus on Columbus Avenue, coming out of a saloon, drunk, crossing the street against a light. Hated him all that time, and then suddenly stopped hating him. Figured him for a poor old drunk instead. Maybe a poor old drunk he loved.

"Well," Mrs. D'Annunzio said, and sighed.

He guessed she was thinking *Well, the Irish.*

He showed her the picture. The picture that looked like a studio shot. Peter Dodge smiling into the camera. Not the picture with his hands tied behind his back with a wire hanger and blood all over the white tile floor. "Has this man ever been in the restaurant?" he asked.

Mrs. D'Annunzio squinted at the picture. She took her eyeglasses from the pocket of the black sweater she was wearing over a black dress, put them on, and held the picture closer to her face.

"You kidding me?" she asked.

"Do you know him?"

"Sure," she said. "He's the lawyer made the contract."

"What contract?" Reardon said at once.

"For the restaurant. To buy the restaurant."

"Peter Dodge is your lawyer?"

"Well, Ralph's. Ralph was the one talked to him. I only met him once or twice."

"When did you see him last?" Reardon asked.

"Not too long ago," Mrs. D'Annunzio said. "A few days, maybe."

"When?"

"Let me see," she said. She was silent, thinking. "Could it be?"

"Could what be, Mrs. D'Annunzio."

"I think he came in Monday. For lunch Monday."

"The day your husband was killed?"

"Yes. I saw my husband talking to him, in fact. Yes. It was Monday. I'm sure."

Their eyes met.

"Does it mean something?" she asked.

"Maybe," he said.

They were waiting outside the Rice Bowl restaurant as agreed, mother and daughter looking very blonde and blue-eyed in the sunshine, one prettier than the other, Liz carrying a handbag like a proper lady, six years old, her face breaking into a wide grin when she saw him. Reardon walked over. He felt a little guilty about having a *real* lunch, even if it was only with his daughter. Usually the detectives grabbed a bite on the run. He also felt a little guilty about taking her to the Rice Bowl, where he hoped to catch Benny Wong, ask if he'd heard anything in the Chinese community. He took his daughter's hand, held it in his own. She looked up at him shyly, like a teenager on her first date.

"You're early," he said to Kathy.

"You said one o'clock."

"It's only ten to."

"Well . . . I thought . . . I have to drive her back to Jersey, you know, I'm working the midnight tonight. So I figured if you were a little early . . ."

"Sure," Reardon said, "no problem." He hesitated. "Why don't you join us?" he asked.

"Thanks, no, I . . . uh . . . there are some things I wanted to look at. While I'm down here. I never get to Chinatown anymore."

"Come on in, have a cup of tea, anyway."

"Yeah, come on, Mommy," Elizabeth said.

"Bry, I don't want to make this a family get-together, okay?" Kathy said.

"A lousy cup of tea?"

"I'll see you in an hour," she said, and turned and walked off.

"Mommy's getting to be a pain in the ass," Elizabeth said.

She ordered spare ribs, egg rolls, and wonton soup. She told him that Mommy had made her promise she would eat vegetables, and she asked *him* to promise that he wouldn't tell her she was eating all this *good* stuff instead. Benny Wong came over to the table while they were breaking open their fortune cookies.

"Got anything for me?" Reardon asked.

"Like I told you," Wong said, "it wasn't a Chinese thing. This your daughter?"

"Yeah," Reardon said.

"What's your name, honey?" Wong asked.

"Liz. What's yours?"

Wong laughed. "Come by the counter before you leave," he said, "I'll give you a box of lichee nuts. You like lichee nuts?"

"I don't know what that is," Elizabeth said.

"That's delicious is what it is," Wong said. "Lichee nuts. Stop by the counter, you hear?"

As soon as he left the table, she handed Reardon the slip of paper that had been inside her fortune cookie.

"What does it say, Dad?" she asked.

"It says . . . you will have good news."

"Good," she said. "Maybe you'll come see me for Christmas."

"Maybe," he said.

"Do you think so?"

"Well . . . I . . . honey, I . . . I really don't think so. I think Mommy plans to spend Christmas in New Jersey. With Grandma and Grandpa."

"So why don't *you* come there, too?"

"Well, I don't think Mommy would want me to, Liz."

"Don't *you* want to?"

"I want to, darling. With all my heart."

"I think this is dumb," Elizabeth said.

"Yes," he said, "it's dumb."

The Six O'Clock News was on television when Reardon got to Stuyvesant Town. He had quit work at four, had called the apartment on the off chance that Kathy was home from Jersey by then, had gotten no answer, and had gone to a bar on Canal Street to have a few drinks and to chat up the barmaid, a girl with an enormous bosom and a very wide mouth. Hoffman had told Pope Mazzi the Third that the girl—whose name was Jeanine—gave blowjobs in the men's room. Told Mazzi that was why she had such a big mouth. With such thick lips. Mazzi said it was because the girl was an octoroon, which he said was part nigger. He couldn't remember how many parts.

Jeanine had red hair and sort of greenish eyes—hazel, Reardon guessed you would call them—and she didn't look like any black girl Reardon knew, but maybe Mazzi was right. Or maybe Hoffman was right, maybe you *could* get a big mouth with thick lips from giving blowjobs in the men's room. He was tempted to ask her if she gave blowjobs in the men's room. He was tempted to ask her if she was a macaroon, like Mazzi said she was. He called the apartment again at five-thirty, and when Kathy answered, he hung up. Didn't want to *ask* if he could come over, risk refusal, just wanted to pop in on her.

She opened the door after he'd rung the bell twice.

She was wearing a blue robe. Barefoot. Hair pulled back in a pony tail. She stood in the doorframe, blocking it. He could see the television set going in the living room. The Six O'Clock News.

"What is it?" she said.

"I want to talk to you," he said.

"Have you been drinking?" she asked.

"I had a drink," he said.

"You smell like a brewery."

"*Two* drinks, okay?" he said. "Did you take Liz back to Jersey?"

"I took her back."

"Do you think that's smart, shuttling her back and forth like . . . ?"

"I'm working tonight. Damn it, Bry, I don't have to give you a detailed report on what I do with my own daughter."

"May I come in, please?" he said.

"Why?"

"I'd like to come in, please."

"Have you ever had the feeling . . ."

"Kathy . . ."

". . . that you're on a merry-go-round that just won't stop?"

"I want to talk about Elizabeth."

"Bry . . ."

"Please," he said.

"All right," she said, sighing. "Come in. For a minute."

In the living room, the television newscaster was saying, ". . . new negotiations now under way. This would mean an increase in grain export to the Soviet Union, provided the terms of the nuclear reduction agreement are implemented as outlined."

"Did she say anything to you this afternoon?" Reardon asked.

"She said a lot of things."

"In Phoenix, Arizona," the newscaster said, "the billionaire financier, Andrew

Kidd, died this morning after suffering a massive stroke yesterday. He is survived by three children. Olivia Kidd—seen here at Puerto Vallarta last winter . . ."

Reardon glanced at the screen. A tall blonde woman wearing a bikini was standing on a balcony overlooking what he supposed was the Pacific Ocean.

"She's six years old," Kathy said.

"Robert Sargent Kidd, who is in New York this week . . ."

"She doesn't understand . . ."

"Can you please turn that off?" Reardon said.

Kathy snapped off the television set. There was a long silence.

"Look," Reardon said, "forget about *me*, okay? Forget how *I* feel about this . . ."

"I wish you'd let me," Kathy said.

"Just think of *her*, okay? Just think of what this's doing to *her*."

"She'll get over it. This isn't the first time in history . . ."

"It's the first time it's happened to her, Kath. She loves us both. We're asking her to . . ."

"Nobody's asking her to stop loving us." She went to the television set again, and dug into the handbag resting on top of it.

257

"She's not getting the divorce, *we* are," she said, and pulled out a package of cigarettes.

"I thought you quit smoking," he said.

"I thought so, too," she said, lighting a cigarette, and then dropped her lighter back into the bag. She blew out a stream of smoke. "Bry," she said, "let's be sensible, okay? I know why you're here, I know what you're going to ask. For the hundredth time. But can't you understand? It'd be worse for Liz if we stayed together. Don't you realize that?"

"We could make it work," he said.

"Not after what happened," she said softly.

"That was two years ago."

"It was yesterday!" she said sharply.

"Kathy . . ."

"You're not the one who still has nightmares about it!" she said. "Look, I don't want to talk about it, it's bad enough I have to live with it."

"But you *don't* have to live . . ."

"No? How do I scrub off the filth, Bry?"

"Look, you're right, let's not . . ."

"How do I get the stink out of my nostrils? How do I forget the humiliation and the . . . ?"

"Kathy, let's *not* talk about it, okay? You know how you get when . . ."

"Your friends the cops!" she said angrily, and stubbed out the cigarette. "Oh, gee, Mrs. Reardon, we're so sorry about what happened. But did you do anything to provoke it? Were you walking in a suggestive manner, did you swing your hips, did you shake your . . . ?"

"Kathy, honey, please, there's no sense . . ."

"No sense at all, right! *He* runs off with a few scratches on his face—did you resist him, Mrs. Reardon, did you try to *prevent* what was happening—and *I'm* left with his fucking baby inside me!"

Silence.

Boom.

The boom of silence.

The same words again. His baby inside me. And the silence following the words.

She reached into her handbag again. She pulled out the package of cigarettes again.

"So what does a nice Irish-Catholic girl do?" she said. "Strict upbringing, bless me, Father, for I have sinned, what does she do? She has an abortion, Bry, and then she spends the rest of her life living in terror."

She shook another cigarette free. Her hands were trembling.

"Look at this," she said, "look what

you're doing to me. Will you please get out of here?"

He came up behind her as she searched in the bag for her lighter.

"Kathy," he said, "what's done is done."

He gently touched her shoulder.

"The important thing . . ."

She whirled on him, her eyes blazing. A gun was in her right hand.

"Where'd you get that?" he said.

"Where do you get guns in this city?" she said. "You're the cop, Bry, you tell me."

"Put it down," he said.

"No." The gun was shaking in her fist. "I carry it in my bag all day long, and I sleep with it under my pillow at night. If any man ever comes near me again . . ."

"I'm not any man," he said softly. "I'm me."

"You're any man," she said. "Don't touch me again, Bry, or I'll blow your fucking head off."

They stood not four feet apart, staring at each other. It could be four thousand miles, he thought.

"So that's where it's at," he said.

He hadn't thought that's where it was at. Not until now.

"That's *exactly* where it's at," she said.

The gun was steady now. It was pointed at his head.

She'll shoot me, he thought. Jesus, she'll shoot me.

They kept looking at each other.

He thought, I'm a stranger to her.

"Okay," he said at last, and started for the door.

"Don't come back, Bry," she said.

"I won't," he said.

"I mean it."

"I know you do."

He reached for the door knob. He opened the door.

"Kathy," he said, "good luck, honey."

He stepped into the hallway.

So softly that she could not possibly have heard him, he said, "Goodbye, honey."

10

He was shaving when the telephone rang. In the mirror, he could see his lathered face and the room behind him. Single bed. A scarred dresser. A naked light bulb hanging in the center of the room. A torn shade on the window. Another light bulb over the sink. His face covered with lather, a razor in his hand. He put the razor down on the sink and went to the phone.

"Hello?" he said.

"Hi, it's Sandy."

He nodded. "Hello, Sandy," he said. He had drunk too much last night after leaving Kathy. Far too much. There was a sand turtle in his mouth. His eyes were bloodshot. The Monday morning blahs. Exacerbated by almost a full fifth of bourbon. He did not want to be talking to Sandy Sanderson. He did not want to be talking to anyone. This was his day off. He planned to go to the library and check out the newspaper stories on the unknown Arab who'd been shot at La Guardia and spirited off to Christ knew where. He planned to visit the law offices of Lewis and Dodge. He planned to come back to the hotel and finish off the rest of the bourbon.

The case was getting to be a pain in the ass.

He didn't know what D'Annunzio had to do with the Arab who'd been shot too many times in the chest and whose body had been stolen from a meat wagon on the way to the morgue. He didn't know what D'Annunzio's murder had to do with the murder of his lawyer, Peter Dodge, who'd been stabbed to death all the way up on Central Park West on the same day he'd had lunch at the Luna Mare.

"I had a tough time tracking you down," Sandy said.

"My day off," he said.

"Who's the man at the precinct who kept calling me 'Your Honor?' "

"Must've been Alex Ruiz."

"Wouldn't give me your home number till I told him you were investigating a burglary for me. I don't think he believed me, actually."

"But he gave you the number."

"He gave it to me. Where's the Lorimar Hotel?"

"Twenty-sixth and Broadway."

"Sounds charming."

"Oh, yes, lovely."

There was a long silence on the line.

"The reason I'm calling," she said, and hesitated. "I always seem to be apologizing to you." Another pause. "I'm sorry about the other night."

"Well, I would have called before coming over," he said, "but . . ."

"I know. No telephone. Anyway, I'm sorry."

"It was my fault," he said.

Why the hell was *he* apologizing to *her?* She was the one who'd had somebody in the apartment with her. Shit, he thought.

"Here we go again," she said. "Apologizing to each other. Let's make a deal, okay? No more sorrys."

"Sure," he said.

Another long silence. So what now? he thought. Get off the phone, lady. I got shaving cream all over my face.

"Want to have a drink later?" she asked.

He hesitated. He shrugged. "Sure," he said.

"Your place or mine?"

"Have you given up on Ringo's?"

"I got stood up there once," she said. "My place at six, okay?"

He almost said forget it. Instead, he said, "I'll bring the wine."

"Never mind wine, just bring a flashlight," Sandy said. "See you later."

There was a click on the line. He looked at the receiver. He shook his head, put the receiver back on the cradle, and then went to the sink.

He looked at himself in the mirror for a long time.

Then he began shaving again.

He did not get to see Phillipa Lewis until almost two o'clock that afternoon. Repeated calls to the law firm of Lewis and Dodge netted only the information that she was out of the office and would not return until after lunch sometime. He spent his own lunch hour in the Forty-second Street Library, reading through the back issues of last week's newspapers.

The *Times* story on the dead Arab told him nothing he didn't already know. Unidentified man shot at La Guardia Airport, body hijacked from the ambulance on the way to Queens General. A longish story, but

265

buried at the back of last Monday's newspaper. Both the *Post* and the *News* had made bigger deals of the shooting and the subsequent hijacking of the body. MYSTERY ARAB KILLED, the *News* headline read. ARAB SLAIN, CORPSE STOLEN, blared the *Post* headline. Now, with both newspapers in front of him, he recalled having seen them last Monday. But the Jurgens trial had started that morning, and he'd been too busy to read either paper. And that night, of course, he'd caught the D'Annunzio murder. In this city, your corpses fell all around you, like cold rain. A cop needed an umbrella, was all. He expected the story would make the covers of both *Time* and *Newsweek* in the immediate future. Hot story like this one, he was surprised it wasn't on the stands already. He often wondered if *Time* and *Newsweek* were in secret partnership. Otherwise, how could you explain the same cover stories week after week after week, even when the issue wasn't a strictly topical one? Sometimes the world got too difficult for Reardon. Sometimes he thought it was *all* a big fucking conspiracy.

If, for example, Senator Bailey had in fact dined with the unknown Arab on the night of his murder, why hadn't he come forward to identify him?

Or had there been *two* Arabs on the nine o'clock shuttle from Washington?

Or three? Or a dozen?

None of them the one who got shot.

But Bailey had asked him, "How on earth did you ever make the connection?"

And then had said, "Between what happened at La Guardia and me."

They'd been talking about homicide. They'd been talking about the Arab.

So Bailey came up with La Guardia.

And now it turns out an Arab was shot and killed at La Guardia, and his body was still drifting around out there someplace, and Bailey didn't know anything about anything.

A big fucking conspiracy.

Reardon would have preferred running down a burglar.

He was waiting in the reception room when Phillipa Lewis walked in. An attractive woman in her early forties, he guessed. Wearing a gray topcoat over a trim gray business suit. He introduced himself, told her why he was there, and she immediately looked at her watch. Politely, but not overly enthusiastically, she invited him into her office. Sitting behind her desk—blonde hair pulled tightly back, red earrings, blue eyes —she listened as he explained that he was working a homicide possibly related to the murder of Peter Dodge.

"Even now," she said, "it's hard to get used to the word *murder*. Well, it was a shock to all of us here. As I'm sure you realize." Vassar out of Rosemary Hall, he guessed. "He seemed so extraordinarily *up* that day," she said in the same somewhat nasal voice, talking through her pretty little uptilted nose. "He'd been away for the weekend, skiing in Vermont—Stratton, I believe. Peter was an avid skier. He came back Monday morning and could talk about nothing but how excellent conditions had been. Fresh powder, sunshine . . . do you ski, Mr. Reardon?"

"No, I don't."

"A lovely sport," she said.

"Who made the lunch reservation for him that day, would you know?"

"Well, his secretary, I would imagine."

"At the Luna Mare."

"Yes. He loved Italian food."

"What time did he get back here?"

"At about two. And rushed right out again."

"Oh? Where'd he go?"

Phillipa hesitated. "I'm not sure I should tell you," she said.

"Why not?"

"It was a personal matter."

"A woman?"

"No, no," she said, and smiled.

"Then what? The man was *murdered* that night, Miss Lewis. Anything you can tell me . . ."

"Well, I've already told Detective Weissman all he wanted to know."

"Yes, but at the time Detective Weissman didn't have all the facts."

"What facts?" she said.

"One," Reardon said, and began ticking them off on the fingers of his left hand. "Mr. Dodge had lunch that day at a restaurant named Luna Mare. It's my understanding that your firm wrote the contract for the purchase of that restaurant."

"Yes, that's true. Peter did."

"All right, two. He was killed sometime between six and six-thirty that night, possibly by three men who were driving a brown Mercedes-Benz. Three, approximately an hour later, the owner of the Luna Mare was killed, by two men who got out of a brown Mercedes-Benz. I'm looking for a connection, Miss Lewis. Peter Dodge was

D'Annunzio's lawyer, but what's the connection *beyond* that?"

"Where he went that afternoon has nothing to do with his murder."

"How do you know that?"

"Or with this man who owns the Luna Mare."

"Let me judge, okay?"

"I mean, this simply isn't the connection you're looking for."

"Where did he go, Miss Lewis? Would you please tell me?"

Phillipa sighed. "It's just . . . he confided this to me, and I'm not sure I should . . ."

"What'd he confide?"

It seemed a long time before Phillipa answered. Reardon waited.

"That he'd bought some silver contracts."

"Some what?" Reardon said.

"Silver contracts. That's where he went. To buy silver contracts."

"I don't know what that means."

"He bought silver contracts, Mr. Reardon. Heavily and long."

"I still don't . . ."

"It means he hoped to make a large profit."

"And this is what he confided to you?"

"Yes. That he'd bought the contracts."

"These silver contracts."

"Yes." She paused and said, "He urged me to follow suit."

"He was giving you some sort of tip, is that it?"

"Well, yes, if you want to put it that way."

"To buy silver contracts."

"Yes. Heavily and long."

"I guess I know what heavily means . . ."

"Well, yes, heavily."

"But what does *long* mean?"

"Well, that would take some time to explain," Phillipa said, and looked at her watch. "I'm sorry, but I'm already late for an appointment uptown. One buys futures, you see. Silver is a commodity, like soybeans, hog bellies, grain . . . really, I am sorry, but I do have to leave."

"One more question," Reardon said. "Where did he buy these contracts?"

"At a firm called Rothstein-Phelps," Phillipa said.

A blonde, blue-eyed receptionist sat behind the switchboard at Rothstein-Phelps. Reardon wondered why every woman in the world was blonde and blue-eyed when your blonde, blue-eyed wife was divorcing you.

Well, Sandy isn't, he thought. Eyes the color of loam, hair a light shade of brown. But Sandy's got a boyfriend she lets into her bed.

"Rothstein-Phelps, good afternoon," the receptionist said. "One moment, please." She pushed a button, looked up at Reardon. "Yes, sir, may I help you?"

"Detective Reardon, Fifth P.D.U.," he said, flashing his shield. "I'd like to see either Mr. Rothstein or Mr. Phelps, please."

"Mr. Rothstein is out just now," the receptionist said. "Just a moment, sir, I'll see if Mr. Phelps is available." She pushed another button. "Alice," she said, "there's a detective here to see Mr. Phelps." She listened and then said, "He didn't say." She listened again. "Okay," she said and turned to Reardon. "It's just down the hall, sir," she said. "Through the door there."

Reardon opened the door and found himself in a beige-colored corridor, muted lighting overhead. He walked to a desk at the end of the hall, and showed his shield again to an elderly woman.

"Detective Reardon," he said. "For Mr. Phelps."

"Yes, sir, won't you go in, please?"

He went to the door she'd indicated, knocked, and then opened it. A stout little man sat behind a desk, a telephone to his ear. Dark suit, tie pulled down, top button of his white shirt open.

"Four cents a pound," he said, and gestured to a chair. "Eighty-eight dollars a ton," he said, and listened. "All right, get back to me." He put the phone down, stood, and extended his hand to Reardon. "Sorry," he said. Reardon took his hand. The palm was damp. "What can I do for you, Mr. Reardon? Sit down, please."

Reardon sat. He took out his notebook.

"A man named Peter Dodge was killed last Monday night," he said. "Would you know him?"

"Peter Dodge? No."

"His partner—a woman named Phillipa Lewis—tells me he had some business dealings with your firm on the afternoon of the murder."

Phelps shook his head. "I don't recognize his name as one of our customers."

"He bought silver," Reardon said.

"Oh? Did he?"

Eyes instantly alert.

"According to Miss Lewis. Silver contracts." He looked at his notebook. "Heavily and long."

"That's entirely possible," Phelps said,

and instantly reached for his telephone. He pressed a button in the base, said, "Alice, would you please check . . . ?" He looked up at Reardon. "When did you say this was?"

"Last Monday, the fifteenth."

". . . the list . . . the list of calls for Monday," Phelps said into the phone. "The fifteenth. And buzz Jenny for Mr. Rothstein's appointment calendar. See what he had scheduled for that date, would you? Thanks," he said, and hung up.

"You didn't sell those contracts personally, is that it?" Reardon asked.

"No, I didn't. But my partner may have. That's what I'm checking now."

"Would that have been unusual, Mr. Phelps? Buying long in silver?"

"Everyday occurrence," Phelps said.

Eyes alert again. Voice entirely too casual.

His phone buzzed. He picked up the receiver.

"Yes?" he said, and listened. "Uh-huh. Uh-huh. Okay, thank you." He put the receiver back on its cradle. "Yes, a man named Peter Dodge *was* here last Monday afternoon," he said to Reardon. "Lowell saw him. My partner, Lowell Rothstein."

"Did he buy silver contracts?"

"I'm sorry, I wouldn't know," Phelps said.

"If he talked to Lowell personally, then only Lowell would know about any silver position he took."

"Where can I reach your partner?" Reardon asked.

"He'll be out all afternoon. Can you try him tomorrow morning?"

"Sure," Reardon said, and paused. "Mr. Phelps . . . just how heavy is heavy?"

"Well," Phelps said, "I suppose that depends on how much loose change you have to spend, doesn't it?"

They were sitting in the living room of the Kidd brownstone on East Seventy-first Street.

Lowell Rothstein and all three survivors of the Kidd family.

"I was worried," Rothstein said, "I have to tell you. I didn't know whether or not your father's death might precipitate a change of plans."

"Nothing has changed," Olivia said.

"Well, fine then. We're to continue with the purchases as scheduled, is that it?"

"Yes," Olivia said.

"We have the money in our discretionary account . . ."

"Good."

". . . where either Joe or I can draw checks as needed. The price has gone up just a bit, and we've seen some raised eyebrows in the pit, but so far nothing that would indicate a stampede."

"How much is still in the account?" Olivia asked.

"Oh, I would have to check on that," Rothstein said. "By the close Friday, we'd bought something like three thousand contracts, I believe it was. I'd guess we still have a bit more than four million, something like that."

Olivia nodded.

"Again, I want to express my sympathies on the death of your father. The funeral will take place in Phoenix, I expect . . ."

"His body has already been cremated," Olivia said.

"Oh, I . . . I see," Rothstein said. "Well, I . . . because Joe and I had planned to fly out, you see . . ."

"There's no need," Olivia said.

"Well," Rothstein said, and nodded.

There was an awkward silence.

He put on his hat and coat.

"Sarge," he said. He took Jessica's hand. "Miss Kidd," he said. "Nice to've met you. Olivia."

He went to the front door. There was silence in the living room until the door closed behind him.

"What are you buying?" Jessica asked. "What's this schedule you were talking about?"

"You'll know Wednesday night," Olivia said, and put on her mink.

"Pop would've told me *now*," Jessica said.

"I sincerely doubt that. In any event, he's dead now, Jessica. And *I'm* in charge. Don't ever forget that." She went to the front door. "I'll see you back at the hotel, Sarge," she said, and went out.

"Bitch," Jessica said.

"Well," Sarge said, "she's got a lot on her mind right now."

"Tell me about it."

"No."

"Would you like a drink? I'm going to have a drink."

"I guess," he said.

"What would you like? Do you know how to mix martinis?"

"I guess."

"Don't *guess* so fucking much, Sarge. You either know how to mix a . . ."

"I know how to mix one."

"Then mix two," Jessica said.

He went to the bar. She watched him as he located the bottle of Beefeater and the vermouth. He reached into the ice bucket, began dumping cubes into the pitcher.

"Make them very dry," she said.

"Okay."

"I know a man who has a secret for dry martinis," she said. "This is a man I met in Acapulco. What he does . . ."

"I don't want to hear about your boyfriends," Sarge said.

"This isn't a boyfriend, he's just a man I met. Why?" she asked suddenly. "Do my boyfriends make you jealous?"

"No, they don't make me jealous."

"They do. I'll bet they do," she said, and grinned. "Anyway, what he does, when he buys his bottle of olives, he pours out all the water, all the salty water in there, you know? And he fills the bottle of olives with vermouth. In place of the water. And he lets the olives sit in the vermouth. Then, when he's mixing a martini, he just uses gin, and instead of the vermouth he drops one of the olives into it. That's soaked with vermouth, you know?"

"Uh-huh."

"Which makes a very dry martini."

"Uh-huh."

"I ought to keep a bottle of olives like that."

"What do you do if you prefer a twist?" Sarge asked.

"Don't ask me hard questions," Jessica said.

He was pouring from the pitcher now. He came to where she was sitting and handed her one of the glasses.

"Thanks," she said. "Here's to the big deal, whatever it is." She sipped at the drink. "Mmm, good," she said, "you really *do* know how to make a martini."

"I told you I did."

"Do you know how to make a fire, too?"

"I have to be leaving soon," he said.

"Nobody asked you to stay, I only asked if you know how to make a fire."

"Of course I know how to make a fire. *Everybody* knows how to make a fire."

"Not me," she said. "Make a fire for me, Sarge."

He sighed and went to the fireplace.

"Poor put-upon bro," she said. "Tell me what we're buying that's so hush-hush."

"No," he said.

"You have to put paper under the logs," she said.

"I know."

"I don't see you using any paper."

"I always put the paper in last."

She watched him as he set the logs in place over his kindling, cross-hatching them.

"So neat," she said.

"If you want a good fire, you have to lay your logs right," he said.

"Oh, my, you're *such* a good log-layer," she said. "When are you going to put the paper in?"

"Now," he said, and began tearing Sunday's *Times* into long strips.

"You're tearing up the story on Pop," she said. "Also you're supposed to crumple the paper, not strip it."

"I prefer stripping it," he said.

He struck a match and held it under the grate.

"I hope you've got a good flue here," he said.

"I haven't had any complaints," she said.

The paper caught.

"Fahrenheit four-fifty-one," he said.

"What?"

"The ignition point of paper. It was also a story by Ray Bradbury."

"Who's Ray Bradbury?"

"Forget it," he said.

"Tell me about the deal," she said.

280

"You'll find out Wednesday."

The kindling caught now.

"You should buy some Georgia fatwood," he said.

"What for?"

"Makes a good fire."

"That's a pretty good one, anyway," she said. "Come sit here beside me, Sarge."

"I have to be going. Olivia's expecting me."

"Fuck Olivia," Jessica said. "Come sit here, warm your toes."

She took off her shoes, stretched her legs toward the fire.

"Mmm," she said.

He sat beside her.

"So tell me," she said.

"I can't. Stop asking me, Jess."

"Why can't you?"

"Because too much is at stake."

"How much? Mmm, that's a good hot fire," she said.

"Billions," he said. "Trillions. After it starts."

"After *what* starts?"

"Well, never mind," he said.

"You make a good fire," she said, and suddenly giggled. "You give great fire, Sarge."

He nodded.

"You didn't get that, did you?" she said.

"Get what?"

"What I just said. About giving great fire."

"No. What do you mean? Get what?"

"Do you know what giving great head is?"

"No."

"What a pity," she said. "Is there any more of this left in the pitcher?"

"Some."

"Pour me another one, will you?"

"And then I have to go," he said, rising.

"Tell me about the deal."

"Can't," he said.

"Secrets, secrets," she said, smiling.

He took her glass and went to the bar. He poured into the glass. The fire crackled. He brought the glass back and handed it to her.

"Thanks," she said, and patted the sofa beside her. "Sit down. Come sit next to your little sister, Sarge. And tell her what the big secret is."

"I can't, Jessie. So please stop asking."

"Sit down," she said, and pulled her legs up under her, sleek knees shining in the light of the fire. He sat beside her.

"Tell me the big secret," she said.

"No," he said, and looked at his watch. "I'd better go."

"Not until you tell me what the big secret is."

"There is no possible way you can convince me to . . ."

"There is a possible way," she said. "Move over," she said, "I want to stretch out."

"You can have the whole sofa," he said, "I'm leaving."

"No, Sarge," she said, "don't go yet."

"Well . . ."

She shifted her weight, stretched her legs out, and put her head in his lap.

"Tell me," she said.

"Olivia would kill me," he said.

"You've been killed before," she said. "For sharing secrets with me."

"What do you mean?"

"That time in the bathroom. Do you remember?"

"I remember."

"Me in the tub, starkers. You sitting on the potty."

"I remember."

"Pop beat the shit out of you," she said.

He nodded.

"Was it worth it?"

"No," he said, and smiled.

"It was worth it, you liar," she said, and

shifted her head in his lap. "Do you remember the other time?"

"What other time?" he said, remembering at once.

"When we were still kids? In the bathroom again? Don't you remember?"

"I have to go," he said.

"When I asked you if they were too small?"

"I guess I remember."

"I'll bet you do," she said. "They were too small, I was only thirteen." She moved her head to look up at him. "You had a hard-on, Sarge."

"I didn't."

"You did. I saw it."

"You're mistaken."

"I saw it."

"No."

"They *were* small," she said again. "But not now," she said, and settled her head in his lap again. "Oh, my," she said.

"What?" he said.

"You know what," she said.

"Jessie . . ."

"Mmm," she said.

"Jessie . . ."

"Be still," she said. "Just sit still, Sarge. Sit still . . . and tell me what the big secret is."

From Joseph Phelps's Sutton Place apartment, you could see the Delacorte fountain in the middle of the East River. Phelps thought the fountain cheapened the neighborhood, goddamn thing shooting up a spray of water into the air every hour, like a fire hydrant turned on in the middle of a Sheepshead Bay street. His wife thought the fountain was "exciting." Kitty found a lot of things exciting that Phelps found either boring or stupid. "Exciting" was his wife's favorite word. She found Dijon mustard "exciting." The only thing Phelps and Kitty agreed on as exciting were her breasts. Kitty had terrific breasts. "Have you ever seen such exciting breasts?" she would ask. He agreed. They *were* exciting. But she was using the word to mean beautiful or extraordinary or compelling, the way she would have said a sunset was exciting or a restaurant was exciting or a Beethoven sonata was exciting or even the goddamn Delacorte fountain was exciting. *He* thought they were exciting because they were exciting. Full and round and firm and pearly white, with large pink nipples. Exciting.

During cocktails that night, Kitty was wearing a low-cut dress that showed her breasts to excellent advantage. They were sitting alone in the living room overlooking the East River where the goddamn Delacorte fountain was shooting up into the air. Cheap goddamn fountain, cost Delacorte millions of dollars probably. Supposed he could afford it, the money they were charging for paperbacks these days. Kitty had black hair cut in a wedge. Kitty had brown eyes. Kitty had exciting breasts and a nose she had picked from Dr. Gerardi's book of possible noses.

"Well, did you pick your nose?" Phelps had asked when she'd got back from the doctor's office that day three years ago.

"Very funny," she'd said. "I'm sorry you don't find this experience as exciting as I do."

The creamy tops of Kitty's breasts were exposed now in the scoop-necked black dress she was wearing. Her right hand, the fingers widespread, rested idly on her left breast. Several travel brochures were spread on the cocktail table.

"I thought three days in Guadeloupe," she said, "that'll make it the fourth, then on to Martinique, which is supposed to be exciting. If we left on New Year's Day . . ."

The telephone rang.

"Shit," Kitty said.

"Excuse me," Phelps said, and rose from the couch.

"Please make it short, Joe," she said. "I really do have to go over this with you."

The phone was still ringing. Phelps went into the study and lifted the receiver.

"Hello?" he said.

"Joe? It's Lowell."

"Yes, Lowell."

"I just got a call from the CFTC," Rothstein said.

"What? Where are you?"

"I'm still at the office."

"What'd they want?"

"They want to see us."

"When?"

"Tomorrow."

"What for?"

"They didn't say."

Phelps was silent for several moments.

"Joe?" Rothstein said.

"They've got our reports," Phelps said. "They'll be asking for disclosure, won't they?"

"Even so, there's nothing to worry about," Rothstein said. "Don't sweat it, we'll see what it's about tomorrow morning, okay?"

"Okay," Phelps said, "thanks for letting me know."

His hand was sweating on the telephone receiver. He replaced the receiver on the cradle, wiped his hand on his trouser leg, and went back into the living room.

"Who was that?" Kitty asked.

"Lowell."

"What'd he want?"

"Nothing that couldn't have waited till morning," Phelps said.

Kitty looked at him. He avoided her glance. Picked up his martini glass. His hand was shaking.

"Joe?" she said.

"Mmm."

"Are you into anything I should know about?"

"No," he said. "Into anything? No. What do you mean?"

"Nothing," she said, but she was still looking at him.

"Tell me about the trip," he said.

A cannel coal fire was going on the grate. The room was candelit, as it had been the first time Reardon was here. They were drinking the white wine he had brought with him. Sandy was wearing what he guessed were called lounging pajamas. He was wearing a sweater over a sports shirt. They both sat on pillows before the fireplace. The wind outside was fierce. Winter had returned with a vengeance.

"I'm an idiot when it comes to money," he said, "so please keep it simple."

"Well, let's see," Sandy said. "You want to know about buying long."

"Yes."

"As opposed to selling short?"

"*Is* there selling short?"

"Oh, sure. But you want it simple, right?"

"Right."

"Well . . ." She sipped at her wine. "Okay. Let's say there's going to be a county fair in May . . ."

"A *what?*"

"A fair. Cows, pigs, chickens, apple pies. You know. A fair. This is a metaphor," she said. "To make it simple."

"Okay, a county fair. Next May."

"Right. This is now December, and I've arranged for a booth at the fair where I'll be selling . . . kisses, let's say. At a dollar a throw."

"Sounds a bit low," Reardon said, and smiled.

"Thank you. But, actually, you're beginning to catch on."

"Am I?"

"Next May, I'll be selling kisses for a dollar apiece. But I look things over, and I see there are going to be three *other* booths selling kisses, and I think maybe I won't *get* any customers at a dollar a throw. Maybe they'll only pay fifty cents, maybe only a quarter . . ."

"Who gave you the dime?" Reardon asked.

"Everybody!" Sandy said. "I *love* that joke. But that's just the point. I decide that by May my kisses may be worth only a dime. But if I contract *now*, to sell them at the *current* price, a *dollar* each kiss, that's what you'll have to pay me for them in May, when I deliver. In other words, I'll have made a ninety-cent profit on each kiss. Got it?"

"No."

"No?" Sandy said, surprised. "Well, okay, let me take another run at it. I am selling *short*—I am taking what's called a *short* position—when I contract *now* to sell something at a price that's higher than I hope it'll be when I deliver. You contract to buy my kisses at a buck a throw in May, do you see? You contract for them *now*. The kisses are worth only a dime in May, but you've got to pay me a buck, 'cause that's what you agreed to. I'm selling short. I'm taking a short position."

"Okay, what's a *long* position?"

"Okay, you're on the other side of the booth. Or you *will* be in May. And because you think I'm so desirable and beautiful and such a good kisser, you decide that the price of my kisses will go *up* by May . . . let's say to *two* dollars each by the time the fair rolls around."

"Inflation," Reardon said.

"Whatever," Sandy said. "The point is, if you contract to buy the kisses *now*, at a *dollar* a throw, you'll be saving a dollar for each kiss you take delivery on in May. That's if the price actually *does* go up." She shrugged and said, "That's a long position. That's buying long."

"In other words, we're both gambling on what the price of those kisses will be in May, five months from now."

"That's why it's called the *futures* market. We're betting on future prices."

"You're betting the price will go *down* . . ."

"So I'm taking insurance, right. Selling *now* at the higher price . . ."

"And I'm betting it'll go up.

291

"Which in real life—never mind kisses —could net you a big bundle of money in five months' time."

Reardon was silent for several moments.

"So if I bought heavily and long . . ." he said.

"You'd be contracting for a *lot* of kisses, and you'd be praying the price went *up*." She grinned suddenly. "And if, by chance, you happened to corner the market . . ."

"What does that mean?"

"Cornering? It means you've bought contracts from *all* the girls who'll be selling kisses. All the contracts, all the kisses—for delivery in May. If any of the guys there at the fair want to buy a kiss or two, they'll have to deal with you."

"Because I own all the contracts."

"All the *kisses*, in effect. And if you own them all, you can charge whatever you want. A dollar, two dollars, five dollars, the sky's the limit." She grinned again. "It's known as having the world by the kisses."

"Has that ever been done?" Reardon asked.

"Not with kisses."

"How about silver?"

"The last time was by the Bank of England . . . in 1717. The Hunts tried it in

. . . 1979? 1980? Whenever. It's pretty much impossible to do nowadays. Too many regulations, too many requirements for reporting and disclosure. It's safer to speculate in kisses. And a lot cheaper."

She lifted her wine glass.

Sipping at the wine, she looked over the rim at him.

"Do you . . . uh . . . think you might be interested?" she asked, and put down the glass. "In . . . uh . . . cornering the market on kisses?" Almost shyly, she said, *My* kisses?"

"Well, I . . . uh . . . ."

"Here's a sample," she said, and leaned in closer to him, and kissed him on the mouth. "What do you think?" she said.

"I think I might be interested," he said.

FROM Nelson Hyde's corner office in the World Trade Center, you could look down onto the construction site of Battery Park City and beyond that to the Hudson River and the Jersey shore. This was Tuesday morning, the twenty-third day of December, two days before Christmas, and the construction workers had erected a Christmas tree on the site below. There was no Christmas tree in Nelson Hyde's office, and the carpeting here at the Commodity Futures Trading Commission was a wear-guaranteed wool-nylon, and the furniture was metal, but the view was splendid. Rothstein and Phelps sat facing the view. Hyde had his back to it. He was a man in his late fifties, graying, soft-spoken. Phelps suspected his mild manner concealed a suspicious nature and a bear-trap mind. He watched as Hyde riffled casually through a sheaf of papers on his desk. Rothstein watched, too.

"How's the traffic out there?" Hyde asked. "Pretty heavy?"

"We walked over," Rothstein said. "We're just around the corner."

"I really appreciate your taking the time to see me," Hyde said, and looked up, and smiled. "So," he said, "how's business?"

"*Comme ci comme ça,*" Phelps said.

"Flurry of activity, this time of year, I expect," Hyde said, still smiling. "All those customers looking for tax losses, eh?"

"Plenty of buying and selling, that's for sure," Rothstein said.

"Reason I asked you to come by . . ." Hyde said, and began looking through the sheaf of papers again. "I got a call from Comex here in New York last week sometime—she never puts anything where I can find it—ah, here. December nineteenth, that would've been last Friday."

A tugboat sounded on the river.

"Yes, last Friday," Hyde said. "It seems you reported quite a bit of silver activity that week." He began riffling through the papers again. "Three separate accounts buying . . . now where the devil . . . yes, here we are. General Business Ventures purchased . . . nine hundred lots, is it? Between Tuesday the sixteenth and Friday the nineteenth.

295

Same time period, we have Quandax Corporation buying nine hundred and forty lots, and Vandam Investment buying nine twenty-five. That comes to . . ." He scribbled some figures on a pad, did his multiplication. "Two thousand, seven hundred and sixty-five lots. At five thousand ounces a lot, comes to . . ." More scribbling. More multiplication. "Thirteen million . . . uh . . . eight hundred and . . . uh . . . twenty-five thousand ounces. That's a lot of silver."

"We're bullish on silver," Rothstein said, smiling.

Mr. Outside, Phelps thought. Smooth as glass.

"Which at current silver prices . . ." Hyde said.

"Well, the prices fluctuate," Phelps said at once.

"Yes, but at the close Friday . . ."

"Mr. Hyde, forgive me," Rothstein said, and leaned forward in his chair, "but surely this isn't an unusually high number of futures contracts for a firm our size. Actually, I imagine our silver purchases will go even higher before the end of the year. For some reason, silver *always* . . ."

"Comex saw fit to call me," Hyde said.

"Meaning what?" Rothstein said. "If

you're suggesting that our firm has done anything illegal . . ."

"Innuendo isn't my style," Hyde said.

"Or even immoral . . ."

"Of course not," Hyde said.

"Then . . . forgive me . . . but what's this all about?"

"It would help if I could know the names of the officers and directors of these three corporations," Hyde said. "I'm sure you have the necessary disclosure forms . . ."

"Yes, of course."

"Do you think someone in your office could fill them in for me? And have them signed by the principals? I would appreciate it."

"We'll put someone on it right away," Phelps said.

"There's no great hurry," Hyde said. "Christmas is almost here, I can imagine how busy you are." He smiled, raised his eyebrows again. "But right after the holidays?"

"Yes, certainly," Rothstein said.

"Well then, fine," Hyde said, and glanced at his watch.

Phelps let out his breath.

On the sidewalk outside, he said, "So now we contact the Kidds."

"No problem," Rothstein said. "We're still under the six-thousand-lot limit for any single principal."

"Yes, but it makes me nervous."

"A routine check," Rothstein said. "Where are you headed now?"

"I've got to meet Kitty. We're seeing a travel agent about that damn Caribbean trip. I should be back in an hour or so."

The trouble with Lowell Rothstein was that he seemed to be lying.

Smooth and slick as ice, a pleasant smile on his handsome face—but nonetheless lying in his teeth.

"You're sure you don't know him, huh?" Reardon said.

"I'm afraid not."

Reardon looked at him long and hard. Sometimes, when they were lying, a long, hard look was enough to turn them around. Not Rothstein. The pleasant smile lingered on his face. His eyes held Reardon's unflinchingly.

"Your partner seems to think he was here last Monday."

"My partner is wrong," Rothstein said.

"A man named Peter Dodge did *not* come here to buy silver contracts?"

"He did not."

"Then where'd your partner get the idea?"

Rothstein shrugged. "We're a big firm with a great many customers," he said, and shrugged again.

"Mr. Rothstein," Reardon said, "I wonder if I could see your appointment calendar for Monday, December fifteenth."

"Why would you want to do that?" Rothstein asked.

"Because your partner seemed certain a Peter Dodge was listed on it."

"My appointment calendar is a personal record, Mr. Reardon. A stock broker's business is as confidential as that of a doctor or a lawyer. If I were a doctor, for example, and you wished to see my appointment calendar in order to ascertain whether a seventeen-year-old girl had been here for an abortion, would you expect me to reveal such information? Of course not. Therefore, to protect the confidentiality between me and my . . ."

"Peter Dodge wasn't here for an abortion," Reardon said. "He was here to . . ."

"He wasn't here at *all*."

"He was here to buy *silver* contracts."

"I'm sorry. I have no such recollection."

"Do you know he's dead?"

299

"Dead?" Rothstein said, looking genuinely surprised. "No. How would I know that?"

Reardon sighed.

"I can get a court order for that calendar," he said. "Would you like me to do that?"

"Do as you see fit, Mr. Reardon," Rothstein said. "I do not know Peter Dodge, and I did not see him on Monday, December fifteenth. You're mistaken. Now, I'm sorry, but . . ."

"Thanks," Reardon said.

He took the elevator down to the ground floor, and was just coming out of the building—starting for the curb, in fact, where Ruiz was waiting behind the wheel of an unmarked sedan—when he saw Phelps coming up the street, a newspaper under his arm, a briefcase in his right hand. He went to him at once.

"Mr. Phelps?" he said.

Phelps was startled for a moment. Then, recognizing Reardon, he said, "Oh, Detective Reardon, how are you? You're back again, I see."

"I just spoke to your partner," Reardon said.

"Ah, good," Phelps said. "Was he able to help you?"

"He doesn't remember seeing Peter Dodge."

"Oh?" Phelps said. The alert look came into his eyes again, the same one that had been there yesterday, when Reardon was asking about silver contracts. "That's strange," he said.

"But you got the information from his secretary, didn't you? That Dodge was here?"

"Well, yes, but . . . we're a big firm, you see . . ."

"With a great many customers, yes."

"Yes. So perhaps . . ."

"And *she* got the information from his appointment calendar, didn't she?"

"Well, I don't really know *where* she . . ."

"You asked Alice, I believe it was, to have Jenny—wasn't that her name?—check Mr. Rothstein's appointment calendar. Do you remember that?"

"Yes, but . . ."

"And you were informed that Peter Dodge had indeed been in to see Mr. Rothstein on Monday afternoon . . . about buying silver."

"I'm sure I wouldn't know *why* he was here, Mr. Reardon. *If* he was here. If Lowell says he wasn't, I'm sure he'd know better than I. Perhaps his secretary misread the appointment calendar, or perhaps Lowell himself . . ."

"Ask him, would you?" Reardon said.

"Ask him what?"

"Whether he was in error about Peter Dodge coming here to buy silver."

"Well, certainly. But if he's already told you . . ."

"Ask him, anyway, would you? And get back to me on it." He fished into his pants pocket, pulled out his wallet, and found a card. "Here's my card," he said.

Phelps looked at it.

"Part of it's in Chinese, huh?" he said, smiling faintly.

"Sometimes *all* of it's in Chinese," Reardon said.

Phelps gave him a puzzled look.

"I'll talk to you," Reardon said, and walked to the waiting car. As he got in beside Ruiz, he could see Phelps going through the revolving doors into the building.

"Where to, your Honor?" Ruiz asked.

"Let's stick around awhile," Reardon said.

He had just worked Phelps the way he would have worked a partner in a holdup or a murder. Separate him from his pal, plant some seeds, wait to see if they take root. Phelps—if indeed the appointment calendar information was correct—now had reason to believe his partner had lied about a man coming here to buy silver. Whether this meant anything at all simply remained to be seen. Sometimes your seeds grew into a forest; sometimes they died on parched earth.

Phelps did not even say "Good morning" to the firm's receptionist. He went immediately past her desk, and opened the door beyond it, and hurried down the hall to Rothstein's office. He did not knock. Rothstein was dictating a letter to his secretary when Phelps barged in.

"Jenny, I'd like to talk to Mr. Rothstein privately," he said.

The secretary looked at Rothstein. Rothstein nodded.

The moment she was gone, Phelps said, "Why are you lying to the police about this Dodge person?"

"What? What Dodge person?"

"Peter Dodge. Why'd you say he wasn't here?"

"Because he wasn't," Rothstein said. "What's the matter with you, Joe?"

"The matter with me . . . Lowell, his name was in your appointment calendar,

Jenny gave me his name. Now why did you tell that detective he . . . ?"

"If he was here," Rothstein said, "I forgot, plain and simple."

"There's not much you forget, Lowell."

"I forgot this."

"A *silver* deal? A man coming here to buy *silver* contracts? *Long?* When we're involved with the Kidds in a big . . ."

"I really don't see the importance of someone calling for an . . ."

"Oh, *did* someone call?"

"If his name was in my appointment calendar, then I'm assuming he called for an appointment."

"Let's look at your appointment calendar, okay, Lowell? Let's see if Peter Dodge's name is in it."

"Assume it's in it," Rothstein said. "Assume he came here, and I *forgot* he was here. What the hell *difference* does it make?"

"Why did you lie to a detective investigating a homicide?"

"I didn't lie to him. I honestly forgot that Dodge was here."

"But now you *remember* he was here, huh?"

"I guess he was here. If you insist he was here, then he was here."

The two men looked at each other. There was a long silence.

"Then why'd you lie to Reardon?" Phelps asked. "If Dodge *did* come here . . ."

"I *didn't* lie. We get a lot of customers in here, I simply forgot . . ."

"No," Phelps said.

"Well, listen," Lowell said, shrugging, "what can I tell you?"

"You can tell me why you lied."

Rothstein said nothing.

"How did Olivia know he'd been here?"

"Reardon? Olivia knows Reardon was . . . ?"

"No, Dodge. Peter Dodge. She mentioned his name. She said he'd taken a position. How'd she know that, Lowell?"

Rothstein said nothing.

"And you can tell me something else, Lowell, while you're at it. Something *else* that's been bothering me." He looked across the desk and nodded, as though silently agreeing with what he was about to say. He nodded again. He kept nodding. "When Olivia was here last week, she mentioned that you'd already seen the purchasing schedule. How come *you* saw it, Lowell, when I didn't?"

"Joe . . ."

"No, don't 'Joe' me. What the hell is

going on? *Did* you see that schedule before I did?"

"No."

"Then why did Olivia *think* you'd seen it?"

"I told you. She has a lot on her mind, she . . ."

"I don't believe you about that, either," Phelps said, and shook his head. "I thought we were partners, I thought . . ."

"We are."

"I'm into this up to my ears . . ."

"So am I."

"The CFTC is asking questions . . ."

"Don't worry about them."

"I worry about my partner *lying* to me!" Phelps said.

"Joe," Rothstein said, "Trust me."

Phelps looked at him, nodding. He kept nodding for a long time. Then he said, "Lowell, whenever anyone says, 'Trust me,' do you know what I do?"

"What do you do, Joe?" Rothstein said, and smiled.

"I hide the family silver," Phelps said.

The two men stared at each other.

Rothstein sighed heavily.

"Okay," he said at last.

"Okay what?"

"This is what happened," Rothstein said.

They'd been waiting outside the building for less than twenty minutes when Phelps came out.

"There he is," Reardon said.

Phelps was carrying a briefcase. He stepped to the curb, and immediately hailed a taxi.

"Stay with him," Reardon said.

The taxi pulled away from the curb. Ruiz pulled the Plymouth sedan out after it.

"Heading uptown," he said.

"Don't lose him, Alex."

The traffic got heavier as they reached the midtown area. This was two days before Christmas and the city was thronged with shoppers. The taxi kept moving slowly and steadily uptown. Santa Clauses rang their bells on street corners. Salvation Army ladies played their trombones and said "God bless you" to anyone who dropped a coin in their kettle. On Fifty-seventh Street, the taxi made a right turn and headed east. The light on the corner turned red just as Ruiz approached it.

"Run it," Reardon said.

Ruiz made the right turn.

307

The traffic cop on the corner yelled at the car.

"Heading for the bridge, you think?" Ruiz asked, ignoring him.

"I don't know," Reardon said.

On Sutton place, the taxi made another right, and then began slowing.

"Back off," Reardon said.

Ruiz slowed the car.

The taxi stopped in front of an apartment building. Phelps got out, nodded to the doorman, and then swiftly entered the building.

"What now?" Ruiz asked.

"We wait," Reardon said.

It was twenty minutes past eleven when Rothstein discovered his partner had left the office. He had called Phelps's secretary to ask if Mr. Phelps was busy for lunch today, figuring he'd take him to a good place, smooth his ruffled feathers. Alice told him there was nothing on Mr. Phelps's appointment calendar, but she couldn't check with him because he was in the vault just now.

"What do you mean?" Rothstein said. "Our vault?"

"Yes, sir. I was carrying some papers to Mr. Donahue's office, and I saw Mr. Phelps going into the vault."

"When was that?" Rothstein asked.

"Oh, about twenty minutes ago."

"And he's still there?"

"Well, I don't know that for sure, sir, but he's not in his office."

"Thank you," Rothstein said, and immediately dialed the vault's extension.

"Hello?" a man's voice said.

"Who's this?" Rothstein asked.

"Donahue."

"Mike, this is Lowell," he said. "Is Joe there in the vault?"

"Nobody here but us chickens," Donahue said.

"You sure he's not in there?"

"Not unless he's hiding in one of the lock boxes," Donahue said.

"Thanks," Rothstein said, and put the receiver back on its cradle. Frowning, he came around his desk, went out of his office, walked past his secretary, went down the hall past Phelps's office, and then turned right at the end of the corridor, heading for the vault. Donahue was just coming out, swinging the heavy steel vault door shut.

"That's okay, leave it," Rothstein said.

Donahue nodded, and went off down the hallway.

The vault was lined with safety deposit

lock boxes in various sizes, each containing securities for the firm's customers. Two keys were necessary to open any box: the customer's individual key and the firm's master key. The customer keys were held by the firm's individual brokers, to facilitate the clipping of coupons on a quarterly basis. Each of the brokers had a master key as well. Except in its design, this was not like a bank vault, where a box holder had to sign in each time he wanted access. The only people using this vault were people employed by Rothstein-Phelps, all of them carefully screened before they were hired, all of them presumably honest.

There was only one lock box that concerned Rothstein at the moment.

If his partner hadn't made that comment about hiding the silver . . .

If his partner hadn't turned absolutely white when Rothstein told him about Dodge's visit . . .

If his partner hadn't seemed on the thin edge of panic when Rothstein told him about the phone call he'd made *after* Dodge's visit . . .

If his partner wasn't running so goddamned scared . . .

Then maybe Rothstein wouldn't have been so concerned about that particular lock box.

That particular box belonged to a widow named Phyllis Katzman.

It contained close to three and a half million dollars in bearer bonds.

Rothstein went directly to that box.

He took his keys from his pocket, searched for the Katzman key and the master key, and unlocked the box.

The box was empty.

Three million four hundred and eighty thousand dollars in U.S. Treasury bonds, payable on demand to the bearer, were gone.

Rothstein broke out in a cold sweat.

He went immediately to the wall phone and dialed the Park Lane Hotel.

In the Plymouth sedan parked outside the apartment building on Sutton place, Ruiz asked, "What do you think?"

"I don't know," Reardon said.

"Does he live here, or is he visiting somebody?"

"Could be either one."

Ruiz looked at his watch.

"I'm getting hungry," he said.

Reardon looked at his watch.

"Yeah," he said.

"Want to check with the doorman, see he's got a Phelps here?"

"He might call upstairs, blow the tail."

"Maybe *we* oughta go upstairs," Ruiz said.

"Without a warrant?"

"What do we want with this guy, anyway?" Ruiz said.

"I'm not sure."

"So we just sit here?"

"See where he's going next," Reardon said.

"Where do you *expect* him to go?"

"I don't know," Reardon said.

"Your Honor," Ruiz said, "I beg your pardon, but I never been on a dumb fuckin' stakeout like this in my life. You don't know what the fuck you *want* with the man, you don't know why we're sitting here . . ."

"He ran in one hell of a hurry, Alex. I tell him his partner's lying, and the next thing you know he's on his bicycle. Don't you think that's interesting, Alex?"

"Yeah, very interesting," Ruiz said drily.

They kept watching the front of the building.

Ruiz looked at his watch again.

"I know a great Italian joint near here," he said.

Reardon said nothing.

People walked past the car.

A lady in a mink coat came out of the building and looked up at the sky.

The doorman looked at his watch.

Ruiz looked at his watch.

"You looking forward to Christmas?" he asked Reardon.

"No," Reardon said.

"Me, neither," Ruiz said. "I *hate* Christmas."

A kid went by on roller skates.

The doorman took off the glove on his right hand and began picking his nose.

"Pick me a winner," Ruiz said.

"Hey!" Reardon said, and sat bolt upright.

Ruiz followed his glance.

"Well, hello," he said.

A brown Mercedes-Benz sedan was pulling up in front of the building.

The door of the Mercedes opened. Three dark-skinned men stepped out of the car and began moving swiftly toward the entrance door. Reardon threw open the door on the curb side of the Plymouth, his gun in his hand. "Police!" he shouted. "Stop or I'll shoot!" Ruiz came around the other side of the car in that instant, running in a low crouch, gun drawn.

The three men stopped dead on the side-

313

walk, not four feet from where the doorman was holding open the door for them. One look was enough to tell Ruiz they weren't Latinos. He didn't know *what* they were, but you could cross off Puerto Rican, Colombian, Cuban, Mexican, whatever. Reardon didn't know what they were, either. But Sadie had labeled them Puerto Ricans, and he was willing to go along with her appraisal, especially since two of them had little flamenco-dancer mustaches. Actually, he didn't *care* what they were. They had arrived in a brown Mercedes-Benz. They had gotten out of the Benz and had started walking toward a building Joseph Phelps had entered not forty minutes ago. Joseph Phelps. Whose firm had sold silver to a man named Peter Dodge. Who'd been killed by three men who'd been seen in a brown Mercedes-Benz. Three men who were here now. That was all that mattered. They were *here*. Except—

They were no longer here.

In the three seconds it took for all those scrambled thoughts to rocket through Reardon's head, the three men were gone. Zip, zap, easy come, easy go, now you see 'em, now you don't.

The two guys with the mustaches had taken a quick look at Reardon's gun and a quicker look at Ruiz's and split for the Fifty-fifth Street corner of Sutton Place. The cleanshaven guy hadn't looked at anything. He'd ducked his head like a bull charging a red flag and began running uptown toward the Queensboro Bridge, arms and legs pumping.

Reardon took off after him.

Ruiz took off after the ones with the mustaches.

This was not a good day for chasing suspects.

Actually, not very many days were good days for chasing suspects because detectives —except in movies—were normally not in very good physical shape, whereas suspects were guys who'd maybe just got out of prison where they'd been lifting weights when they weren't buggering cellmates. Ruiz, being a little younger than Reardon, was in better condition, but First Avenue was packed virtually curb to curb with Christmas shoppers and the two guys with the mustaches had a sizable lead on him. It suddenly occurred to Ruiz that the two guys might be Arabs. This was a brilliant deduction, considering the fact that he was pounding along the pavement and trying to keep sight of them, and deductions do not come too easily in the midst of a movie chase. But the guy on the plane had been an Arab, right? It seemed to make sense.

So he concentrated on not losing them.

On East Fifty-ninth Street, Reardon was concentrating on the same thing, but he was considerably more breathless than Ruiz. Reardon didn't like chasing people. Cop movies were a pain in the ass because they made your average citizen think cops went around chasing people in alleyways and over fences and in subway tunnels and Christ knew where, when what a cop liked to do instead was have a beer and watch some television. Times like this, Reardon wished he could quit smoking. Times like this, Reardon wished he was nineteen again. God, how he could run when he was nineteen! That guy up ahead there, running now in the shadow of the bridge, had to be in his early twenties. Puffing, Reardon pounded along behind him.

On First Avenue, Ruiz got stopped by a traffic light. Or rather, he got stopped by the goddamn crowd standing on the corner waiting for the light to change. The crowd and a Santa Claus.

"Something for the needy, sir?" Santa said.

"Fuck off, Santa!" Ruiz said, and started shoving his way through the crowd. "Police officer!" he shouted. "Move it, move it!"

A truck came around the corner.

Ruiz swore he would never buy Budweiser beer again.

The truck moved.

Across the street, the two Arabs were half-way up the block.

"Shit!" Ruiz said, and sprinted after them.

It's now or never, Reardon thought. Close on him now, tackle him or shoot him, but take him out either way. 'Cause, man, he is running your ass off, and he's gonna get away if you don't make your move.

He made his move.

He came within an ace of throwing up, running as hard as he was, came that close to it, but didn't. He couldn't fire because there were pedestrians on the sidewalk, parting like the Red Sea as he came galloping up with the pistol in his hand, the little cleanshaven, dark-skinned man turning the corner, make your move, he's gonna disappear, make your fuckin' move, and he turned the corner and hurled himself into the air like a tackle for the Jets and whammo, he hit the little fucker in the middle of the back, knocking him flat to the sidewalk, throwing the gun on him as the man rolled over, starting to rise, arms stiff behind him to shove himself off the sidewalk, legs already braced to run again.

"No, don't," Reardon said breathlessly.

The man looked at the gun.

"Really," Reardon said.

The man did not run.

On First Avenue, the Arabs were tangled in a knot of Hare Krishna kids banging their tambourines and singing "Oh My Lord." The Arabs tried to push through, flailing out at bald pates and top knots, saffron robes and sandals, but Ruiz was on them now, and he grabbed the closest one by the lapels of his suit and threw him against the brick wall of a building behind him, and then whirled as the other one rushed him. Ruiz was just turning, his gun hand was blindsided. He drew back his left hand, fingers straight, palm flat, and unleashed a backhanded karate-chop at the Arab's head.

The Arab had a head made of granite.

"Ow!" Ruiz yelled, pulling back his

hand, but the Arab fell like a fucking stone, anyway, and Ruiz turned toward the one he'd thrown against the wall, who was now off the wall and ready to run again.

Ruiz leveled his gun.

"Don't make me shoot you just before Christmas," he said.

The three Arabs—if they were Arabs—spoke in what the detectives guessed was Arabic or something. Ruiz was the one who said Arabs spoke Arabic. *If* they were Arabs. The detectives didn't know *what* they were because none of them would answer any questions, either in English or Arabic, if that was the language they were speaking. It was Lieutenant Farmer who broke the deadlock.

"What are we fuckin' around here for?" he said. "Book 'em for murder."

The three Arabs looked at one another.

"Who'd you send to watch the Phelps building?" Farmer asked Reardon.

"The Pope."

"Alone? He'll be saying his fuckin' beads, 'steada payin' attention."

"Samuels is with him."

"Okay, get these scumbags outa here, take 'em over to Headquarters, make it Murder One." He looked at the three Arabs as if just discovering them in his squadroom. "Unless you feel like tellin' us what you were doin' on Sutton place," he said.

"We have friends in that building there," the cleanshaven one said. He addressed his answer to Reardon, as though Reardon— who had knocked him ass over teacups—was the one he belonged to.

"What friends?" Reardon said.

"*A* friend."

"Named Joseph Phelps?"

"We do not know a Joseph Phelps."

"Do you know a Ralph D'Annunzio?"

No answer.

"Do you know a Peter Dodge?"

No answer.

"We've got a positive make on the car you were driving," Farmer said. "It was spotted outside the Luna Mare last Monday night. What were you doing there?"

"We do not know this restaurant," the Arab said.

"Who said it was a restaurant?" Hoffman said.

"Get on the phone," Farmer said to Ruiz. "I want Sadie picked up and brought here."

"We've got a witness who saw you go in that restaurant with guns," Hoffman said. Ruiz was already dialing. "You want to tell us all about it, or you want to make it tough for us?"

"Sarge," Ruiz said into the phone, "can you get one of the blues to pick up Sadie the bag lady?"

"You make it tough for us," Gianelli said, shrugging philosophically, "we'll make it tough for you."

"We want her up here right away," Ruiz said into the phone. And then, for the benefit of the Arabs, "We've got the three goons who killed D'Annunzio."

He put the phone back on the cradle.

"They'll bring her up here as soon as they find her," he told Farmer.

"So what do you say?" Farmer asked the cleanshaven Arab, and to his great surprise, one of the mustached ones answered.

"It was not *our* idea to . . ." he started to say, but then the second mustached guy yelled something at him in Arabic, if it was Arabic, probably a warning to keep his fucking Arab mouth shut, and the two guys with the mustaches shouted at each other in whatever language it was—it certainly wasn't English—until Reardon yelled for them *both* to shut up. The squadroom went silent again.

"What's your name?" he asked the Arab

who'd been about to say something when the other one shut him up.

"Anwar Biswas," the Arab said.

"What were you about to say before your pal interrupted you, Anwar?"

The other one with the mustache shouted something in the foreign language again, and Anwar shouted "No, Zahir, I will *not* be silent!" and then turned to Reardon. "It was not our idea to do this," he said.

"It was for our country," the cleanshaven one said suddenly.

"What's *your* name?" Reardon asked.

"Fazal Omara."

"And you say you did this for your country?" Farmer said.

"For our leader," Fazal said.

"What leader?" Hoffman said.

"Prince Ahmad Mo . . ."

The third Arab erupted again, verbally and physically. He popped out of his chair spewing a torrent of Arabic or whatever, and simultaneously grabbing for Fazal's throat, his intention undoubtedly being to throttle him, which Hoffman discouraged by kneeing him in the balls.

"Sit down," Hoffman said. "You got anything to say, say it in English. Otherwise shut the fuck up and let your pals here explain the situation. You think you got that? Or would you like another nut-shot?"

"Your heads will be cut off," the Arab said, glaring at his compatriots, his hands clutched between his legs.

"If that's all you got to say, don't say anything at all," Hoffman warned.

"You are both fools," he said to the other two.

"Then *you* remain silent if you wish," Fazal said. "This is the *police* here! *You* are the fool, Zahir."

"Let's hear it," Farmer said.

Another silence.

Reardon thought for a moment they'd lost it.

Then Fazal said, "A messenger from our prince was killed last Sunday."

"Where?" Reardon said at once.

"At the airport," Fazal said. "Coming off the plane from Washington."

"What was his name, this messenger?"

"Amin Abbas."

"Get on the phone," Farmer said to Gianelli. "How do you spell that?" he asked Fazal.

"A-M-I-N," Fazal said. "A-B-B-A-S."

"Have you got that?" Farmer said. "Amin Abbas, run an airlines check."

"Who killed him?" Reardon said.

"Enemies within our government," Anwar said.

"Who?" Reardon said. "Give me names."

"I have no individual names. It was a group called Order of the Holy Crusade."

"What were *you* doing at the airport?" Hoffman asked.

"We were there to meet him," Fazal said.

"We saw him fall . . ." Anwar said.

Zahir was shaking his head. And massaging his groin.

"Detective Gianelli, Fifth Squad," Gianelli said into the phone. "Run this through your computer for me, will you?"

"So many policemen," Fazal said.

"We could not get to him."

"Guy named Amin Abbas," Gianelli said. "Where he was coming from, where he was headed, the complete ticketing. I'll wait."

"We followed the ambulance . . ."

"First to one hospital, then to another . . ."

"And finally took possession of his body."

"Why'd you want his body?" Farmer asked.

"He was carrying the timetable," Fazal said.

"What timetable?" Reardon asked.

"He *should* have had it in his possession.

But it was gone. There was nothing in his pockets."

"What timetable?" Reardon asked again.

Zahir erupted in Arabic again. This time he didn't come up off the bench. He simply said the words softly and menacingly, a short warning meant to silence his pals once and for all. He accompanied this with a stare designed to turn their blood to shit. Neither the words nor the stare worked.

"A timetable that fell into the wrong hands," Fazal said.

"*Whose* hands?" Reardon asked at once.

"A man named Peter Dodge," Fazal said.

"Marvelous, tell them everything," Zahir suddenly said in English.

"Shut up," Hoffman said. "What *about* Dodge?"

"I just told you," Fazal said. "He got possession of the timetable."

"*What* damn timetable?" Reardon said.

"An important timetable," Anwar said.

"For what?" Farmer asked.

"I don't know," Fazal said. "We were only told to get it back."

"From Dodge?"

"Yes," Fazal said.

"Who told you to get it back?"

"He did," Fazal said, and nodded at

Zahir, whose balls were better now, but who still had a scowl on his face.

"You the boss here?" Reardon asked him.

No answer.

Gianelli put down the phone. "Abbas was ticketed Phoenix-Washington-New York, connecting the next day with the Concorde to Rabat."

"Where the fuck is Rabat?" Hoffman said.

"Morocco," Ruiz said.

"What was he doing in Phoenix?" Reardon asked Zahir.

No answer.

"Is that where you guys are from?" Farmer asked. "Morocco?"

No answer. The two friendlies were now having second thoughts, Reardon guessed. In a police station, people always had second thoughts. First they spilled their guts, and then they wondered whether they'd said too much. The bossman's intransigence wasn't helping much, either. Still setting a bad example. Mouth compressed in a tight little line, eyebrows pulled down, all the curses he could think of glowering in his dark eyes.

"Mister, you're the one who's gonna take the fall here, you know that, don't you?" Reardon said.

"Sure, these other jerks are just accomplices," Gianelli said, immediately picking up on Reardon's drift.

"They already said he's the one told them to go get that timetable," Hoffman said. "That makes him . . ."

"I was only following orders," Zahir said.

"What orders?"

"To recover the timetable."

"How'd you get these orders?"

"I received a phone call."

"Who from?" Reardon said.

"I don't know."

"Hold it," Farmer said, "let's take this from the top, okay? What you're saying is that somebody *sent* you to Dodge's apartment to get this timetable—whatever the hell kind of timetable it is—but you don't know who this person is, or was, this person who called you, is that about it?"

"I know the person who *called* me," Zahir said. "But he was only relaying a message from someone else."

"All right, who *called* you, let's start there."

"One of my countrymen."

"A Moroccan?"

"We are *not* Moroccans."

"What*ever* the fuck you are," Hoffman said, "what's this countryman's name?"

"I don't know his name," Zahir said. "Only his voice."

The detectives all looked at each other. Farmer sighed.

"Okay, this man whose voice you know but whose name you don't," he said, "calls you. What did he say?"

"He said that a man named Peter Dodge was in possession of a valuable timetable, and we should recover it from him."

"And that's all he said?"

"That's all he said."

Now it was the turn of the other two Arabs to jump up and start yelling in Arabic. The detectives listened to it, not understanding a word. Ruiz scratched his head. Farmer was wondering if anybody on the uniformed force was of Syrian or perhaps Iraqi extraction. Now and then, a few English words came through.

"Our orders . . ."

More Arabic.

"You know what . . ."

Arabic again.

And finally, from Anwar, in a burst of angry English, his forefinger under Zahir's nose as if he were about to skewer him, "Our orders were to *kill* him!"

Zahir was off the bench again, exploding in Arabic.

Hoffman wondered if he should kick him in the balls again.

Reardon signalled to let them play out the string.

"Or anyone *else* who had seen the timetable!" Fazal shouted.

Silence.

The three Arabs looked at one another.

Gianelli wondered if they were going to kiss and make up.

"You two got the right idea," Reardon said, and wondered how much they knew about American law. "If you were acting on orders, there's no sense you taking the rap."

"But we were!" Anwar said.

"Sure," Reardon said, and turned again to Zahir. "Is that true?" he asked.

Zahir nodded.

"You had *orders* to kill Dodge?"

"To recover the timetable," Zahir said.

"And to *kill* him," Fazal said. "Why are you being such a stubborn fool? Do you *want* to be hanged?"

"Orders to kill him, yes," Zahir said softly, and sighed.

"Because he'd seen this timetable, is that right?"

"He'd seen it, yes."

Marvelous fucking reason to kill a man, Reardon thought, he sees a timetable.

"Let me get this straight," Farmer said. "I'm having trouble keeping this damn thing straight. Your man Abbas . . ."

"Messenger to the Eternal Prince," Zahir said with dignity.

". . . is carrying a timetable with him when he gets off the plane at La Guardia. But he gets shot, and the timetable disappears, and it turns up in Dodge's *apartment?*" He looked at his detectives. "Is that what *you* guys get?" He turned to Zahir again. "How'd this timetable end up in Dodge's hands?"

"A man named Ralph D'Annunzio gave it to him," Zahir said.

"What?" Hoffman said.

Reardon nodded. It was beginning to fall into place.

"He gave it to Dodge at lunch that day," Zahir said. "This is what Dodge told us. He took possession of the timetable in D'Annunzio's restaurant. The Luna Mare."

Silence.

Reardon was putting it all together.

Or at least trying to.

"So you had to kill D'Annunzio, too," Reardon said, nodding.

"Yes," Zahir said.

"Because he'd seen the timetable."

"Yes."

"Important fuckin' timetable," Hoffman said.

"What were you doing on Sutton Place?" Ruiz asked. "Somebody *there* see this timetable?"

"We were sent there," Zahir said.

"Who the fuck keeps *sending* you to these places?" Hoffman said.

"We received a call."

"From your pal again?" Farmer asked. "The one who you know his voice but you don't know his name and you don't know who calls him and tells him to give you these fuckin' mysterious messages, is *that* the one?"

"Yes," Zahir said, exactly as if Farmer had just spoken a simple English sentence.

"And?"

"I was told only that a man named Joseph Phelps had stolen some negotiable securities, and that I was to get to him before the police did."

"What kind of negotiable securities?" Reardon asked.

"I have no idea," Zahir said.

"This guy on the phone just gives you orders, huh?" Farmer said. "And you run out and do whatever the fuck . . ."

"Sounds like the police department," Gianelli said.

"We do it for our country," Zahir said.

Reardon, who'd been quiet for several moments, suddenly said, "You didn't know what was on this timetable, huh?"

Zahir shook his head.

"Then how'd you know what you were looking for?"

Silence.

"You tore up Dodge's apartment, what the hell were you looking for?"

Silence.

Zahir looked at the others.

None of them said a word.

"What's on that timetable?" Reardon said.

Silence.

"Who's gonna tell us what's on that timetable?" Farmer asked.

Stone faces.

End of the road.

"All right, get them out of here," Farmer said.

12

SANDY's office at *Forbes* was about the size of the interrogation room back at the Fifth. She sat behind a desk cluttered with clippings from magazines and newspapers, photocopies of pages from books, a jar of paste, a pair of scissors, a roll of transparent tape, pencils in assorted sizes and colors, and an ashtray brimming with cigarette stubs. The room smelled of stale tobacco smoke. "I quit two weeks ago," she said. "The ashtray is to remind me what a rotten habit it is."

Reardon nodded.

"I know a man, he took fifty or sixty butts, put them in a jar of water, and shook it up like a cocktail," Sandy said. "Whenever he's tempted to have a smoke again, he takes the lid off the jar and sniffs at what's inside. One whiff is enough to make him swear off again."

Reardon wondered if this was the same

man she'd been in bed with last Saturday night.

"I've quit at least three times already," he said.

"Never stuck, huh?"

"The last time was the longest."

"How long?"

"Three years."

"And you went *back?*" Sandy said, astonished.

"Yeah."

"When was this?"

"Last July."

"How come?"

"My wife told me she wanted a divorce."

"Oh," Sandy said.

"Yeah."

"That'll do it every time."

"Yeah."

The room went silent.

"Is it okay if I smoke now?" Reardon asked.

"Sure, go ahead."

"You're sure it won't bother you?"

"It'll kill me, but go ahead."

He reached into his pocket for his cigarettes, looked at her, and changed his mind.

"No, that's okay, really," she said.

"No, no."

"Go ahead, you're making me feel guilty."

"No," he said, "I can wait, really."

"Okay," she said, and smiled.

He really wanted that cigarette. He didn't know what to do with his hands. He scratched his jawline with his right hand.

"The reason I stopped by . . ." he said, and shrugged. "I feel stupid as hell about this, I really do, but you're the only one I could think of."

"Concerning what?"

"This homicide victim."

"The old man you were telling me about? On Mulberry Street?"

"Well, no. Well, yes. Well, they're related, but I can't figure out how. I mean, I *know* how, but I don't know *why*. Or . . . I know *why*, but the why doesn't make any sense. Would you mind terribly if I smoked?" he asked.

"Please do," she said, and shoved the butt-filled ashtray toward him.

"Thank you," he said, and immediately shook a cigarette from the package and lighted it. "I'm sorry," he said, blowing out a stream of smoke.

"No problem," she said.

"You see, this *other* victim, this *related* victim, was a lawyer . . ."

"Uh-huh . . ."

"Who went to see a stockbroker . . ."

"Ah," she said.

"Yeah, which is why I'm here. Or partially why I'm here."

"Why don't you just tell me what you need," Sandy said, and looked at his mouth as he drew in on the cigarette.

"Okay," he said, "this is it. A lawyer named Peter Dodge sees an important timetable . . ."

"What kind of timetable?"

"Well, that's just it. Hold on a minute, okay? He sees this timetable, and he runs right out to buy silver contracts from a firm called Rothstein-Phelps."

"Uh-huh," Sandy said.

"You know them?"

"Biggest commodity dealers in the city."

"Okay. Some Arabs kill Dodge that night and the timetable is taken from him. *Recovered* from him, actually, since it shouldn't have been in his hands to begin with. But a man named Ralph D'Annunzio . . . the one I was telling you about . . . *also* saw the timetable, and he was killed an hour later, more or less."

"Phew," Sandy said. "Important timetable, huh?"

"So it would seem."

"Again . . . what *kind* of timetable?"

"That's what I want to know from you."

"Me? Do I look like a train conductor?" She watched him as he stubbed out the cigarette. Then she said, "You say Dodge bought *silver* after he saw it?"

"Heavily and long," Reardon said, nodding.

"Well, was that accidental? I mean, his rushing out to buy silver? Or was it a direct consequence of his having seen this timetable?"

"I have no idea."

"Mmm," Sandy said.

"What does that mean, mmm?"

"Look, this is just winging it . . ."

"Sure."

"But . . . I mean a timetable is a *schedule*, isn't it? A list of . . . well . . . the *times* at which certain things are supposed to happen, isn't that so? I mean, a train schedule is a timetable, right?"

"Yeah?" Reardon said. He was listening intently. He also wanted another cigarette.

"And this man Dodge saw the schedule and then . . . now this may be entirely unrelated, but nonetheless it's what happened

. . . he ran out to buy silver heavily and long."

"That's right."

"Well . . . suppose this timetable was a schedule for something that would *affect* the price of silver?"

"Affect it?"

"Drive the price up."

"Like what?"

"Well, I don't know."

She was silent for several moments, thinking.

Then she said, "Well, if the price of *oil* goes up, for example, then gold and silver usually follow. You said Arabs are involved, didn't you? Well, suppose OPEC is planning a series of oil-price hikes, and suppose your man Dodge stumbled across a schedule that lists the *dates* and *amounts* of the hikes. If he's wise in the ways of the market, he'd recognize the consequences of these oil hikes and run out to invest heavily in either silver or gold futures. Gold's more expensive, so he might opt for silver—less cash down, you see. Maybe that's what happened."

"A schedule of oil price-hikes, huh?"

"Maybe," she said, and shrugged.

"Which caused him to believe the price of silver would go up, huh?"

"Well, that's the way it usually works, yes."

"So he rushed out to get in on the action, buy his *own* little hoard of silver . . ."

"If that's what you say he did."

"Well, that's what his *partner* says he did. Ran out to Rothstein-Phelps to buy silver heavily and long. Advised her to do the same thing, in fact."

"Let me check on what kind of activity there's been in silver this past week or so, okay?" Sandy said, and looked at her watch. "Can you meet me at the apartment in a few hours? Little after five? I should have something for you by then. We can discuss it over a drink. Okay?"

"I'll be there."

"Wait, you'll need the key," she said, and reached into her handbag. "Oh, shit," she said, "I thought I'd thrown them all out." She handed him an open package of cigarettes. "Here," she said, "smoke your brains out." He took the cigarettes. She was still rummaging for the key. When at last she found it, she handed it across the desk and said, "See you around five."

"Thanks," he said.

"You look troubled," she said.

He shook his head.

"What is it?"

"I'm just wondering. *Could* an OPEC schedule really have caused two murders? Three if we count the one at the airport?"

"You're the cop," she said. "You tell me."

The man sitting in the straight-backed wooden chair was not telling anyone anything.

His name was Joseph Phelps.

Mazzi and Samuels had spotted him coming out of the Sutton place apartment at a little after one o'clock, but before they could even get out of the car, he'd hailed a taxi and was on his way. They arrested him at Kennedy Airport, where he was in the process of buying a one-way ticket to Brazil.

Phelps was carrying in his suitcase close to three and a half million dollars in bearer bonds. Thirty bonds in hundred-thousand-dollar denominations. Five bonds in fifty-thousand-dollar denominations. Eleven bonds in twenty-thousand-dollar denominations. And one ten-thousand-dollar bond. The equivalent of three million four hundred and eighty thousand dollars in cash.

"I thought only Nazis went to Brazil," Gianelli said.

Phelps said nothing.

"That was a good picture," Mazzi said. *"The Boys from Brazil."*

"Who owns these bonds?" Farmer said.

Phelps said nothing.

"What do you know about a timetable Peter Dodge stumbled across?"

Nothing.

"You want a cup of coffee?" Ruiz asked him.

No answer.

Ruiz shrugged.

Reardon was going through Phelps's briefcase. In one of the side zipper pockets he found a folded sheet of paper.

"Well, hello," he said.

He unfolded the paper.

Across the top of the page, he read the words:

KIDD FUTURES SCHEDULE: CMX VIA ROTHSTEIN-PHELPS, NYC

"Here's a schedule," he said, and handed it to Farmer.

Farmer glanced down the rest of the page.

"But is it *the* schedule?" he asked.

"Who—or what—is Kidd?" Reardon asked Phelps.

Phelps said nothing.

"Let me have that phone book," Reardon said.

Hoffman handed the Manhattan directory across the desk, and Reardon began leafing through it.

"Kidd," he said aloud, his finger running down the page, "Kidd, Kidd, Kidd, Kidd . . . there's at least ten of them." He turned the book so that Phelps could see the page. "Know any of these people?" he asked.

Phelps said nothing.

"What do you think, Loot?" Reardon asked.

Farmer thought it over for a moment. Then he said, "Chick, you stay here with me, see if Mr. Phelps wants to tell us anything. You three split those names between you, work 'em solo. Get movin'."

The woman who answered the door was wearing nothing but a peignoir and high-heeled sandals. She was a good five-feet eight-inches tall, Reardon estimated, even without the sandals, which added at least two inches to her height. This was the third Kidd he'd visited in the past hour. He showed her his shield and ID card, told her he was from the Fifth P.D.U. and asked if she was Jessica Kidd.

"I am, yes," she said.

"Would it be all right if I came in for a minute?" he asked.

"Please do," she said, and smiled.

He followed her into the living room. Long black hair trailing down her back, pale blue peignoir over pale pink flesh tones, firm ass jiggling as she walked to the fireplace and stood with the flickering flames behind her, long legs silhouetted.

"Miss Kidd, would you happen to know a man named Joseph Phelps?"

The same question he'd asked all the others.

"Phelps?" she said. "No, who is he?"

"Does this look familiar to you?" he asked, and took from his pocket the sheet of paper he'd taken from Phelps's briefcase.

She looked at it.

"Kidd Futures Schedule," she said.

"Yes, Miss. Do you have any idea what that means?"

"I surely don't," she said.

"Or these column headings under it?" he said, and pointed to the line:

PURCH DATE	ACCT	LOTS	TOTAL OZ	DEL MO

"This would stand for purchase date, wouldn't it?" he said.

"I have no idea."

"And this, of course, is Account . . ."

"Really, Mr. Reardon, I don't . . ."

"And this would be *silver* lots, wouldn't it? And *ounces* of silver. And the delivery month."

"I never studied shorthand," she said.

"Do any of these account names mean anything to you?" he said, and showed her the page again:

PURCH DATE	ACCT	LOTS	TOTAL OZ	DEL MO
12/16/86	GenBus			
	Vent	250	1,000,000	09/87
12/16/86	Quandax	235	1,175,000	08/87
12/16/86	Vandam	230	1,150,000	10/87
12/17/86	GenBus . . .			

"Do I have to read *all* of this?" Jessica said. "Really, Mr. Reardon, I'm far too stupid to understand *anything* about business. My interests lie elsewhere, believe me. Lie?" she said, and wrinkled her nose. "Lay? I always get the two mixed up." She smiled. "Would you care for a drink, Mr. Reardon?"

"No, thanks," he said, and paused. "So you don't know anything about this schedule, huh?"

"Nothing at all."

"And you're sure you don't know anyone named Joseph Phelps."

"Positive. Who is he?"

"A stockbroker. Never handled any accounts for you, huh?"

"Never."

"Or anyone in your family?"

"Not that I know of."

He looked at her.

"Sorry," she said.

"Well . . . thanks, anyway, Miss Kidd," he said, "I appreciate your time." He turned toward the door. "Incidentally," he said, "if anyone *should* ask about Mr. Phelps, he's at the Fifth Precinct. Until we book him, anyway."

"I can't imagine who would ask," she said, and followed him to the door. "Goodbye, Mr. Reardon," she said, and opened the door for him. She locked it behind him the moment he was gone, and then went back into the living room. She turned the knob on the library door, opened it a crack.

"He's gone," she said, and turned on her heel and went to where she'd left the brandy snifter on the coffee table in front of the fire.

Sarge came into the room. He looked enormously troubled.

"He knows," he said, and went immediately to where his coat was hanging in the entry hall.

"Not from anything *I* said."

"No, you were very good. But he knows. Or is damn *close* to knowing." He nodded. "Call Olivia at the Park Lane," he said, buttoning his coat. "Tell her a dumb *cop* is about to blow this thing skyhigh. Would you do that, Jess?"

"Sure," she said. "Where are *you* going?"

"I don't want to lose him," he said.

He kissed her on the cheek.

"I'll be back," he said.

He had told Sandy he'd meet her at a little after five, so he went directly to her apartment from the last Kidd on his list, wondering how Ruiz and Gianelli were making out, wondering if Phelps had finally told Farmer and Hoffman anything. He lighted some candles, draped his jacket and shoulder holster over a wooden ladderback chair in the living room, and then started a cannel-coal fire. He poured himself a scotch, went to his jacket again, took his notebook from the inside pocket, and carried notebook and scotch to the beanbag chair. Sitting, opening the notebook, he sipped at the scotch and tried to make some sense of it.

Approx ten P.M. Sunday night, December fourteenth. Amin Abbas killed getting off the Washington shuttle . . .

Reardon sipped at the scotch again.

Approx eleven P.M. Sunday night, December fourteenth. Associates hijack ambulance, appropriate body, search for timetable, discover it's missing.

He nodded, looked at his notebook again.

Lunch Monday, December fifteenth, say around twelve, twelve-thirty. D'Annunzio shows Dodge the timetable. Or maybe gives Dodge the briefcase Abbas left on the plane. Either way, Dodge is now in possession of the timetable.

Approx six o'clock Monday night. The Arabs kill Peter Dodge and recover the timetable. Seven o'clock, same night. The Arabs kill D'Annunzio because he's *seen* the—

There was a sound at the front door.

"Sandy?" he said, turning. "It's open."

The door was indeed open. As he watched, it opened even wider. The person standing in the doorframe, however, was not Sandy. It was a man who appeared to be six-feet two-inches tall and two hundred and thirty pounds wide, give or take, someone who looked vaguely familiar though Reardon couldn't imagine why. The man came into the room swiftly and deliberately, walking past the ladderback chair over which Reardon's holster and jacket were draped, coming directly to where Reardon was trying to get up as quickly as he could from the low beanbag, reaching Reardon just as he managed a half-crouch, and punching Reardon full in the face with his huge clenched fist.

As Reardon tried to extricate himself from the beanbag yet another time, the man brought his knee up and into his jaw, and then hit him over the bridge of his nose with the clenched fist, wielding it like a hammer, *whap*, blinding little arrows of light splintering up into his head, and *whap* again, he is going to kill me, Reardon thought, before I even get out of this fucking beanbag! The man was bigger than Reardon, and stronger than he was, and he had cold-cocked him in the fucking dumb amoeba-beanbag chair that kept trying to swallow him, and Reardon knew that if he didn't do something fast— why did police work always get down to having to do something fast?—the big guy would stomp him into the floor and throw him into the fire or out the window because this was playing-for-keeps time. This Reardon knew with every gram of intelligence he possessed.

He abandoned trying to stand up, gave up any idea of shoving himself up out of the beanbag, rolled out of it instead, onto the floor and away from a kick the big guy aimed at his head, rolling, rolling, the big guy following him until finally his back hit the wall on the other side of the room, and the big guy reached down for him and grabbed him by the shirt, and yanked him to his feet, and Reardon brought his knee up into his groin, and the big guy yelled and let go of his shirt. Reardon knew he had to get to the gun. This guy would kill him, he was too big and too strong. Reardon desperately needed his pistol. But it was in the holster across the room, and the big guy was between him and the holster, bellowing now in rage because he'd been kneed in the balls, ready to tear Reardon apart in *anger* now.

The anger hadn't been there earlier. Earlier there had been only the methodical pounding and kicking, the certainty that brute strength would prevail, but now there was anger, and Reardon figured the anger would work better for him than it would for the big guy. Anger had a great deal of energy going for it—you didn't start up with a guy who was angry because he could easily kill you with the power of his rage—but that's *all* it had going for it.

Anger made you dumb.

Anger made you reckless.

Anger made you lose.

"Come on, you dumb fuck," Reardon said, playing into the anger, dropping his hands at his sides and sticking his chin out, and then side-stepping to the left, ducking away as the big guy threw another punch at him. "Missed, you asshole," Reardon said, and opened himself up again, balancing himself on the balls of his feet, ready to dart left or right depending on where the next angry punch—there it was, a sharp left jab, he pulled his head to the right, danced away, and grabbed the nearest candlestick by its stem.

The candle fell from the socket, hitting the floor, the wax breaking, the wick holding the pieces like a spinal cord, the flame snuffing out at once. Reardon swung the candlestick toward the big guy's head, the base aimed at his left temple. A big hefty arm came up, diverting the blow, the candlestick base catching him on the left cheek and opening a cut there, nothing serious, nothing to stop him from reacting with a short, sharp, right-handed jab to Reardon's gut.

"Oooof!" Reardon went, and the big guy fell upon him in earnest.

Now I die, he thought, now the son of a bitch kills me. His punches were angry, more powerful because of the anger behind them. He stalked Reardon like a trained killer—Jesus, *is* he a pro?, Reardon wondered—battering him, pounding him, knocking over chairs and tables to get at him, slamming him against the wall and punching him when he bounced off the wall again, anger, anger—and then the mistake that anger caused. Shoved out at him, and closed in on him, both fists bunched for the kill, but shoved him in the direction of the chair with the gun slung over it, momentarily letting his anger get between himself and his own good sense, letting Reardon at the same time get between him and the gun.

A second was all Reardon needed.

He knew this holster, knew this pistol, this holster and pistol were old friends, almost lovers, he knew them intimately. The left hand grabbed for the familiar leather, the right hand closed around the walnut grip, and pulled, and the pistol came up out of the holster and into his hand, and Reardon leveled it immediately at the fucking charging bull who was only three feet away from him now, and he said, "Freeze, shithead!" and the big guy kept coming for a moment, almost as if he hadn't heard Reardon, and Reardon thought *This one goes to the morgue,* but he said, *"Freeze!"* again, louder this time, and the big guy stopped dead in his tracks.

His eyes looked suddenly bewildered.

Anger draining out of them.

Reason returning.

Run.

Get out of here.

Escape.

"No," Reardon said, and waggled the gun at him. "Turn around. *Now! Do it!*"

The big guy turned.

"Hands behind your back," Reardon said. *"Fast!"*

The big guy put his hands behind his back. Reardon cuffed them at once.

"All right, who are you?" he said.

"Am I bleeding?" he asked. "My cheek?"

"I hope you bleed to *death,* you cocksucker," Reardon said. "Who *are* you?"

"Get an ambulance!" the big guy said. "I'm going to sue you, Reardon! I'll sue the city! I'll . . ."

"Oh, you know who *I* am, huh?" Reardon said. "Okay, let's see who *you* are. Sit!" he said, and shoved the big guy into the chair over which his jacket and the empty holster were still draped.

"These handcuffs are too tight," the big guy said.

"Aw, gee," Reardon said, and patted him down till he found the pocket with his wallet. "You know what assaulting a police officer's gonna net you?" he asked. "Attempted murder? Do you know? Huh?" He opened the wallet. "Here we go," he said, and began flipping through the celluloid inserts. "Arizona driver's li . . ." His eyes opened wide in surprise. "Robert Sargent Kidd, well, well!" He lifted Sarge's chin with the barrel of the gun. "Who are you, Mr. Kidd? Her husband? Her brother? Were you there when I dropped in on her?"

"Get me something to put on my cheek," Sarge said. "I'm bleeding, can't you see I'm *bleeding?*"

"Yes, I see that," Reardon said, "what a shame. Why'd you try to kill me?"

353

"I didn't."

"No? You sure coulda fooled me." He lifted his chin again with the gun barrel. "How'd you find me here?"

No answer.

"Did you follow me here?"

No answer.

"From your sister's place? *Is* she your sister?"

"Yes."

"Were you there when we were talking?"

No answer.

"Okay, Mr. Kidd," he said, "I guess I'm going to shoot you."

"No, you're not," Sarge said.

"Yes, I am," Reardon said. "And then I'm going to take those cuffs off you, and I'm going to tell all the friendly cops who come up here that you attacked me and tried to kill me and I had to shoot you in self-defense. Cops don't like people who try to kill other cops. Neither do judges." He smiled pleasantly. "What do you say, Mr. Kidd?"

"Go ahead, shoot me," Sarge said.

"Happy to oblige," Reardon said, and cocked the hammer.

"I'll be better off dead," Sarge said.

"Oh?" Reardon said. "Why? Is some-one apt to be annoyed by your little goof, Mr. Kidd? Assaulting a police officer?" He put the gun under Sarge's nose, just over his upper lip, centered on it. "Who sent you here after me?"

"I came on my own. It was my own idea. Go ahead, shoot me."

"Don't rush me," Reardon said. "Why do you look so familiar?"

Sarge said nothing.

"Robert Sargent Kidd," Reardon said, staring at him. "How do I know that name?" He kept staring at him. "Are you a painter or something? Do you have something to do with painting?" Still staring, puzzled. "No, wait a minute, you *sold* some paintings, I saw you on television. You and your sister. Not Jessica, another one. *What's* her name?"

"Olivia."

"Right, Olivia. And I saw her on tele-vision again Sunday night. Your father just died, didn't he? A stroke. You've been all over *everything* these past few days, haven't you? *Including* me. Why'd you jump me, you son of a bitch? What are you afraid of? Did you hear what I said about Phelps?

Is that what brought you here? The silver schedule?"

Sarge shook his head.

"Okay, pal, so long," Reardon said, and looked down at the gun barrel. "One shot should do it," he said. "Clean and . . ."

"Wait a minute," Sarge said.

"I thought you were in a hurry," Reardon said.

"I had nothing to do with any of it."

"Any of what, Mr. Kidd?"

"Either one of them."

"Are you talking about D'Annunzio?" A nod. "And Dodge?" Another nod. "You had nothing to do with ordering their murders, is that what you're telling me?"

Yet another nod.

Followed by another, this one from Reardon.

"All right," he said. "Who *did?*"

On the street outside, Reardon went into the first phone booth he found and dialed the squadroom. Hoffman picked up.

"Chick," he said, "this is Bry. I've got a guy cuffed to the radiator in an apartment on First Avenue. Here's the address," he said, and read it off. "Have you got that? His

356

name is Robert Sargent Kidd, pick him up, will you?"

"For what?" Hoffman asked.

"Try attempted murder. That may not stick, but he beat the shit out of me and it looked damn close, believe me."

"I'll run right over," Hoffman said.

"Anything from Phelps yet?"

"Diarrhea," Hoffman said. "All we had to do was start hinting at the three counts of homicide, he's ready to trade us his mother. He's been telling us some very interesting things, Bry."

"Like what?" Reardon said. "Let me hear."

He listened.

"Uh-huh," he said.

He kept listening.

"Uh-huh," he said. "Uh-huh. Uh-huh. Very nice. Good work, Chick. Very nice. I've been hearing some interesting things myself, we should have a full house down there in a little while. I'm heading for the Park Lane, I'll be in Olivia Kidd's suite, if you need me. Have you got that? Olivia Kidd. I'm not expecting any trouble, but give me a half-hour, and then send the Marines. Listen, don't forget that guy chained to the radiator, huh? And be careful when you take off the cuffs, he's a fuckin' grizzly bear. See you, Chick."

He hung up, felt in the coin chute for his quarter, shrugged, and then began walking toward where he'd parked his car.

13

WHEN the knock sounded on the door, Olivia said, "There he is."

"Are you *positive* I should be here?" Rothstein asked.

"Why not?" Olivia said. "You're a business associate."

"But he's here about *Joe*. Your sister said . . ."

"All the more reason for your presence. Your partner absconded with three and a half million dollars worth of . . ."

There was another knock at the door.

"Just a moment, please," Olivia called, and then shot Rothstein a warning glance and went into the entrance alcove and opened the door. The man standing there was perhaps thirty-seven, thirty-eight years old, Olivia guessed, with red hair and blue eyes. His complexion looked ruddy from the cold outside. He smiled pleasantly.

"Miss Kidd?" he asked.

"Yes?" she said.

A shield pinned to a leather fob appeared in his right hand.

"Detective Reardon, Fifth P.D.U. All right if I . . . ?"

"Ah, yes," Olivia said. "My sister phoned earlier, said you'd been to see her. How may I help you?"

"May I come in?"

"Certainly. What's the problem, Detective Reardon?"

"No problem. Just a few things I wanted to ask you. I hope I'm not interrupting anything."

"Please," Olivia said.

He followed her through the open arch that led to the living room. Lowell Rothstein was sitting on a sofa near the windows. The drapes were open and the sky over Central Park was littered with stars.

"Hey, hello, Mr. Rothstein," Reardon said pleasantly.

"Hello, how are you?" Rothstein said. "What a surprise."

"Do you know each other?" Olivia asked.

"Only casually," Reardon said. He smiled at Rothstein and said, "I didn't expect to find you here."

"I . . . uh . . . was shopping at F.A.O.'s," Rothstein said.

"Just around the corner," Reardon said, and smiled.

"Lowell and I are old friends," Olivia said.

"Too bad Phelps couldn't join you, huh?" Reardon said, still smiling. "But he's down at the Fifth Precinct. I guess your sister told you, huh?"

"You found him?" Rothstein said. "Good!"

Smooth as glass, Reardon thought. But there was apprehension in his eyes.

"We picked him up at Kennedy, buying a ticket to Rio," he said, and smiled. "Why do they always go to Rio? His briefcase was full of U.S. Treasury bonds. Three million, four hundred and eighty thousand dollars. Lots of money," he said, and whistled softly. "In bearer bonds. That's the same as cash. I guess you know that, Mr. Rothstein, being in the brokerage business and all."

"Yes. The bonds belong to a woman named Phyllis Katzman. I discovered them missing at a little after eleven this morning. I don't know what possessed Joe, I really . . ."

"But you didn't call the police, huh?" Reardon said.

"I beg your pardon?"

361

"When you discovered the theft. You didn't call the police, did you? My partner checked with the First Precinct down there. No record of anyone reporting the theft."

"Well, no, I . . ."

"You went shopping at F.A.O.'s instead."

"Actually, I . . . uh . . . didn't know *what* to do. I was hoping Joe might have had some reason to . . ."

"Like what?"

"I don't know. Instructions from Mrs. Katzman to return the bonds to her? Some reasonable explanation for what he did."

"He had a good reason for *running*, if that's what you mean," Reardon said.

"Well, I guess they *all* have reasons, don't they?" Rothstein said, and smiled. "Thieves, I mean. In any case, thank you for coming here to inform us. And thank you, too, for what I'm sure was splendid police work."

"Only thing our guys did was hang around outside his apartment and follow him to Kennedy," Reardon said, and shrugged.

"What*ever* they did, you've got him," Olivia said. "Forgive me, can I order a drink for you?"

"Well, thank you, but this isn't a social call. I mean, I didn't just stop by to tell

362

you we got Phelps and the bonds." He looked at Rothstein, turned to Olivia again, and then said, "I came here to talk about silver."

"The Lone Ranger's horse?" Olivia said, smiling.

"No, but that's very good, Miss Kidd. I mean *silver* silver."

"And what is that supposed to mean, Mr. Reardon?"

"Well . . . according to what Phelps told my partner, your family's been buying silver contracts, Miss Kidd, lots of silver con . . ."

"There is nothing illegal about buying silver contracts. We've done nothing that wasn't entirely legal and aboveboard."

"How about murder?" Reardon asked. "Is that legal and aboveboard?"

"Oh? Has someone been murdered?"

"*Two* someones. Three if we count the Arab, but you can't be blamed for what some fanatics did, can you?"

"I have *no* idea what you're . . ."

"One of the victims came to see you on the fifteenth, Mr. Rothstein. Remember? I asked you about him this morning, and you said you didn't know him."

"I . . . who do you mean?" Rothstein said.

"A man named Peter Dodge."

"I still don't know him."

"Let me help you," Reardon said. "He bought quite a few silver contracts. Bought them long, in fact. Which is what someone *would* do if he knew the price was going up." He looked at Olivia. "If he'd seen the timetable, right, Miss Kidd?"

"Mr. Reardon, the *legal* buying and selling of silver . . ."

"Oh, sure," Reardon said, and turned to Rothstein again. "Stop me if you've heard this one," he said. "Here's what Phelps says happened. At least, this is what you *told* Phelps happened, after which he ran to clean out Mrs. Katzman's lock box."

"If you're ready to believe a thief . . ."

"Yeah, I'm ready to believe him," Reardon said. "According to Phelps, this is what you told him. Dodge came to you that afternoon and showed you a piece of paper with a lot of dates on it. Dates for buying silver contracts. All spelled out. A textbook for making a fortune. And he *also* showed you . . ."

"No, he didn't show me anything," Rothstein said.

"Ah, you remember him now."

"Vaguely."

"Then why'd you tell me you hadn't seen him?"

"Because . . ."

"Because you knew he'd been killed and you knew *why* he'd been killed!"

"No, I . . ."

"Yes. Which is why Phelps ran, by the way. The minute he knew you were involved in *murder* . . ."

"I had nothing to do with Dodge's murder!"

"But he did come to see you, huh?"

"Yes."

"Lowell," Olivia warned.

"He's accusing me of *murder*, damn it!" He turned to Reardon again. "He came to see me, yes. And, yes, he showed me the purchasing schedule."

"You just told me he didn't show you anything."

"He showed it to me."

"How'd he get it?"

"From a little Italian who owns a restaurant on Mulberry Street."

"Ralph D'Annunzio?"

"Dodge didn't tell me his name."

"It was D'Annunzio. Who'd been sitting next to an Arab named Amin Abbas . . ."

Olivia looked at him sharply.

". . . on the shuttle from Washington, D.C. Go on, Mr. Rothstein."

"Are you charging Lowell with something?" Olivia asked. "Because if you *are*, I feel an attorney . . ."

"Sit tight, Miss Kidd," Reardon said. "You'll have plenty of time for attorneys. Let me hear it, Mr. Rothstein."

"Apparently, they struck up a conversation on the plane. Abbas and the Italian. Abbas left his briefcase behind . . ."

"I know all this," Reardon said, "I have it from D'Annunzio's son. What did Dodge tell you when he came to see you?"

"He said a client of his had come into possession of a briefcase and was afraid to go to the police with it because its owner was the victim of a shooting at La Guardia. That's exactly what he told me."

"And, on the basis of what he found when he *opened* that briefcase, he wanted to buy silver."

"On the basis of the purchasing schedule, yes."

"*And* the timetable."

"I don't know what you mean," Rothstein said. "A timetable? What do you mean? A man came to me to buy silver. I'm a stockbroker, I do a large business in commodities . . ."

"Your partner said Dodge asked for an unlimited line of credit, is that true?"

"Well . . . yes, I suppose . . ."

"Asked you to back him to the hilt in buying silver long, didn't he?"

"Yes, he . . . well, yes, he did."

"And incidentally signed his own death warrant."

"I had nothing to do with Peter Dodge's death," Rothstein said.

"No? You knew he was in possession of the timetable, the one thing that could blow the . . ."

"He's already told you he doesn't know anything about this timetable of yours," Olivia said. "No more answers, Lowell, until we get an attorney up here."

She went directly to the phone on the desk and lifted the receiver.

"By the way," Reardon said, "Abbas was ticketed Phoenix, Washington, New York, and Rabat. In Phoenix he went to see your father. To talk about money."

Olivia looked at him.

"And in Washington," Reardon said, "he went to see Senator Thomas Bailey. To talk about bombers."

She put the receiver back on the cradle.

She turned from the desk.

"You've been busy," she said.

"So have you," Reardon said. "According to your brother . . ."

"My brother? What . . . ?"

"Did I forget to mention him?" He looked at his watch. "He should be down at the precinct by now. He beat me to within an inch of my life, big fella, your brother. But we had a nice little chat afterward. And he told me all about the timetable."

Olivia was watching him intently now. Rothstein was sitting on the edge of his seat, as if he would bolt for the door at any moment.

"Abbas was in Washington to talk to Senator Bailey about getting more planes for his country. Because once the timetable went into effect . . ." He looked at his watch again. "What time do you suppose it is in Saudi Arabia?"

Rothstein looked sharply at Olivia.

"How many hours ahead are they?" Reardon asked. "Eight, nine? Let's say it's three in the morning there, okay? That leaves how much time to six A.M. on Christmas Day?" He paused. "That's when they start bombing the oil fields, isn't it? Six A.M. on Christmas Day?"

Neither of them said anything.

"First wave of planes is supposed to go over the Rub' al Khali at six in the morning, isn't that right?" Reardon said. "According to the timetable?"

Silence.

"Kidd International won't do too bad, will it?" he said. "With a war in Saudi Arabia, and you sitting with oil interests all over the Middle East. Your brother seems to think you'll make trillions of dollars."

"Zillions," Olivia said, and smiled.

He had to hand it to her, that smile.

"But again, Mr. Reardon, we've done nothing illegal," she said. "The silver we're buying . . ."

"How about financing a little war? Your brother says that's why Abbas was in Phoenix, Miss Kidd. To get additional backing from your father. Phoenix to Washington, right? First more cash, then more bombers. Right, Miss Kidd?"

"That may be immoral," she said, smiling again, "but illegal? Really, Mr. Reardon . . ."

"I'm sorry to have to tell you this," he said, "but murder is illegal. According to

369

your brother, the minute Dodge left Rothstein's office . . ."

"I had nothing to do with the murders!" Rothstein said.

"You knew what that timetable meant, didn't you? The minute you laid eyes on it . . ."

"Yes, but . . ."

"The minute you linked it to the silver purchasing schedule . . ."

"Yes, but I'm not the one who . . ."

"Shut up, Lowell!"

"All I did was call Phoenix!"

"Damn you, I . . ."

"*She's* the one who put the Arabs on Dodge! She's the one who ordered them to . . ."

"You are a very stupid man," Olivia said.

Reardon looked at both of them.

"I think you'd better come with me, huh?" he said. "We can talk more about this downtown."

"Why?" Olivia said.

"Miss Kidd, maybe you don't understand the situation here . . ."

"Yes, I quite understand it, Mr. Reardon," she said, and smiled again. "You've stumbled upon what you imagine to be a vast money-making scheme . . ."

"Never mind *imagine*, Miss Kidd."

"All right, you *know*, or at least you *believe* you know because Joseph Phelps has so informed your colleagues—*if* a thief is to be trusted at all—and my brother has seemingly corroborated . . ."

"Your brother isn't a thief."

"No, he's merely a fool. But let us say, Mr. Reardon, that a war *will* in fact begin on Christmas Day, and that there will be fighting around oil fields, and that the Kidd oil interests in the Middle East will benefit from such fighting, and let us also say that greed —there's no other word for it," she said, and smiled, "has led the Kidds to invest heavily in silver, on the premise that the price of silver will rise in tandem with the price of oil, and let us further say that a smart speculator, a man like your Mr. Dodge, for example . . ."

"Who got himself killed . . ."

"Yes, but that was unfortunate. A smart speculator, let's say, who *knew* all about this . . . well, such a speculator could very well get into the market himself, couldn't he?"

Reardon looked at her.

"Buy himself a little silver, Mr. Reardon? Mm?"

371

"If I'm hearing you correctly . . ." Reardon said.

"I believe you're hearing me correctly. Why don't you buy yourself some silver, Mr. Reardon? The price is certain to double, at least, within the next several weeks. You'd be betting on a sure thing, Mr. Reardon. You could make yourself a small fortune."

"Uh-huh," Reardon said.

"How much do you earn, Mr. Reardon? If I may be so bold."

"A Detective/Second makes a bit more than thirty-seven a year."

"Do you know how much you could earn in two *weeks*, Mr. Reardon? If you invested wisely in the silver market at this point in time? If you invested, say, half a million dollars before the close tomorrow? Bought yourself, oh, a hundred and fifty lots, something like that?"

"Half a million, huh?" Reardon said, and shook his head. "Too bad I've only got three thousand and some change in the bank."

"There are people who might be willing to advance you that kind of money . . . perhaps even more . . . huge sums of money, Mr. Reardon, if they knew they were backing a sure winner."

"Olivia's right, you know," Rothstein

372

said. "You could come out of this a very rich man. Not on such a small investment, of course. Not on three thousand dollars."

"What you said was half a million, right?" Reardon said.

"Yes," Olivia said. "Or perhaps more. Depending on what your needs are."

"And you think there are people who'd let me have that kind of money, huh?"

"I'm sure we could find . . . investors for you," Rothstein said, and glanced quickly at Olivia.

"Backers," Olivia said, and smiled.

"You could be a very rich man," Rothstein said again.

"Gee, and here I thought three grand in the bank was rich," Reardon said.

Still smiling, Olivia moved closer to him.

She put her hand on his arm.

In a voice that was almost a whisper, she said, "Move uptown, Mr. Reardon. It's another part of the city up here."

He looked into her eyes.

"You'll like it up here," she said.

He nodded.

"Lowell," she said, "order Mr. Reardon a drink. What would you like to drink, Mr. Rear . . . ?"

"What *I* think," Reardon said, "is we all better move *down*town."

He smiled.

"You'll like it down there," he said.

You wouldn't have known there'd been a pretty interesting fight here just a few hours ago. Everything back in its place, furniture where it belonged, cozy fire going on the grate.

"You shoulda seen the place when I walked in," Sandy said. "I must've had a burglar or something."

"No, you had me," Reardon said.

"Some mess you made."

"You should see the other guy."

"Would you like a drink?"

"I sure could use one."

She poured scotch over ice for him, and they sat by the fire, she curled in the beanbag, he sitting on the floor at her feet, telling her earnestly about the trail that had led to Olivia Kidd.

"The D.A. thinks the case has more holes in it than a sieve," he said. "Actually bawled me out for dragging him over to the precinct too soon. Said we had the Arabs cold—the three Arabs, you know—not because they admitted the murders, but because one of them was carrying a gun we're fairly sure was the murder weapon. An exotic pistol made in Switzerland, Ballistics is running it through now. But he wanted to know how we could prove Olivia *ordered* the hit. I told him we had to work some more on the Arabs, maybe plea-bargain them, find out who their phone connection was, trace that back to Olivia. He told me I shoulda worked on the Arabs *first,* and *then* called him when I knew I had a case that would stick all the way up the line."

Reardon sighed heavily.

"So she walks, right?" he said.

"Maybe not," Sandy said.

"Sure, she'll walk. Her money? Even if we did manage to get her into a courtroom, she'd walk." He shook his head. "This job," he said, and fell silent.

He did not say anything for a long while.

Then he said, "What do I tell the D'Annunzios? They asked me to stop by on Christmas Day. How can I go there, what do I say to Mrs. D'Annunzio? That these three dumb Arab hit men killed her husband, but the one who *ordered* them to do it has a good chance of walking? Two murders to protect a money-making scheme, and she walks? How's that gonna wash? What's *that* gonna tell them about justice?" He shook his head again. "I can't even tell them I'm busy, I'd be lying to them. I mean, my daughter'll be in Jersey with her mother, I've got no real excuse."

"So go," she said. "Tell them the truth."

"Yeah, I guess so," he said, and looked up at her. "Will you come with me?" he asked. "If you're not busy."

"I'm not busy," she said.

"Then . . . would you?"

"If you want me to."

"I want you to," he said. " 'Cause I'll tell you, Sandy, it's not gonna be easy, telling them the truth. I may need some help there. Somebody to hold my hand."

"I'll hold your hand," she said gently.

" 'Cause you see, if she was right, there's no sense being a cop at all."

"Who?" Sandy said, puzzled. "Who do you mean?"

"The Kidd woman. Olivia. I hate to think she might have been right. I'd throw my shield in the East River if I thought she was right."

"I still don't under . . ."

"She said it was another part of the city up there. Well, if it *is* . . . if where the rich people are, the powerful people . . . if that's another part of the city up there . . . then what's the sense, Sandy? There's no sense even *trying*, is there?"

"There's sense," she said.

"I hope so," he said, nodding. "I hope so."

"It's the principle of the thing," she said.

"Yeah, the principle," he said, and sighed heavily. "So, good," he said, "you'll come with me, okay? We'll stay there awhile, and then . . . I don't know . . . we'll find something to do later. Maybe go sing carols or something."

"Or something," Sandy said, and took his hands.

The publishers hope that this
Large Print Book has brought
you pleasurable reading.
Each title is designed to make
the text as easy to see as possible.
G.K. Hall Large Print Books
are available from your library and
your local bookstore. Or, you can
receive information by mail on
upcoming and current Large Print Books
and order directly from the publishers.
Just send your name and address to:

G.K. Hall & Co.
70 Lincoln Street
Boston, Mass. 02111

or call, toll-free:

1-800-343-2806

A note on the text
Large print edition designed by
Kipling West.
Composed in 18 pt Plantin
on a Xyvision 300/Linotron 202N
by Marilyn Ann Richards
of G.K. Hall & Co.

CARMEL CLAY PUBLIC LIBRARY

3 1690 00177 9454

WITHDRAWN FROM
CARMEL CLAY
PUBLIC LIBRARY

CARMEL CLAY PUBLIC LIBRARY

CC08

CARMEL CLAY PUBLIC LIBRARY
515 E. Main St.
Carmel, IN 46032
(317) 844-3361

1. This item is due on the latest date stamped
on the card above.

2. A fine shall be paid on each item which is
not returned according to Library policy. No item
may be borrowed by the person incurring the fine
until it is paid.

3. Any resident of Clay Township, complying
with Library regulations, may borrow materials.

DEMCO